TELLING THE BEES

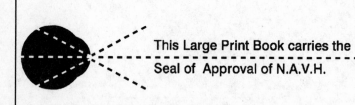

This Large Print Book carries the Seal of Approval of N.A.V.H.

TELLING THE BEES

PEGGY HESKETH

THORNDIKE PRESS
A part of Gale, Cengage Learning

GALE
CENGAGE Learning·

Detroit • New York • San Francisco • New Haven, Conn • Waterville, Maine • London

GALE
CENGAGE Learning®

Thorndike Press® Large Print Basic.
The text of this Large Print edition is unabridged.
Other aspects of the book may vary from the original edition.
Set in 16 pt. Plantin.

LIBRARY OF CONGRESS CATALOGING-IN-PUBLICATION DATA

Hesketh, Peggy.
   Telling the bees / by Peggy Hesketh.
      pages ; cm. — (Thorndike Press large print basic)
   ISBN-13: 978-1-4104-5932-9 (hardcover)
   ISBN-10: 1-4104-5932-2 (hardcover)
   1. Older men—Fiction. 2. Loss (Psychology)—Fiction. 3. Bee culture—Fiction. 4. Large type books. I. Title.
PS3608.E796T45 2013b
813'.6—dc23   2013006609

Published in 2013 by arrangement with G. P. Putnam's Sons, a member of Penguin Group (USA) Inc.

Printed in the United States of America
1 2 3 4 5 6 7 17 16 15 14 13

To Don the Duck, a drunken, pinball-playing, Thanksgiving dinner's last-night stand

To Leroy the Goon, the fearsome bouncer at Dave and Jake's Snake Pit

To George Washington, the motorcycle-riding red-haired madam who was so ugly her face looked like a cow stepped on it and her nose came up through the hoof

And to the gazillion other memorable characters in the heartbreakingly goofy bedtime stories my father used to tell me

TELLING THE BEES
BY JOHN GREENLEAF WHITTIER

Here is the place; right over the hill
Runs the path I took;
You can see the gap in the old wall still,
And the stepping-stones in the shallow
    brook.

There is the house, with the gate
    red-barred,
And the poplars tall;
And the barn's brown length, and the
    cattle-yard,
And the white horns tossing above the
    wall.

There are the beehives ranged in the sun;
And down by the brink
Of the brook are her poor flowers,
    weed-o'errun,
Pansy and daffodil, rose and pink.

A year has gone, as the tortoise goes,
Heavy and slow;
And the same rose blows, and the same
    sun glows,
And the same brook sings of a year ago.

There's the same sweet clover-smell in the
   breeze;
And the June sun warm
Tangles his wings of fire in the trees,
Setting, as then, over Fernside farm.

I mind me how with a lover's care
From my Sunday coat
I brushed off the burrs, and smoothed my
   hair,
And cooled at the brookside my brow and
   throat.

Since we parted, a month had passed, —
To love, a year;
Down through the beeches I looked at last
On the little red gate and the well-sweep
   near.

I can see it all now, — the slantwise rain
Of light through the leaves,
The sundown's blaze on her window-pane,
The bloom of her roses under the eaves.

Just the same as a month before, —
The house and the trees,
The barn's brown gable, the vine by the
   door, —
Nothing changed but the hives of bees.

Before them, under the garden wall,
Forward and back,
Went drearily singing the chore-girl small,
Draping each hive with a shred of black.

Trembling, I listened: the summer sun
Had the chill of snow;
For I knew she was telling the bees of one
Gone on the journey we all must go!

Then I said to myself, "My Mary weeps
For the dead to-day:
Haply her blind old grandsire sleeps
The fret and the pain of his age away."

But her dog whined low; on the doorway
    sill,
With his cane to his chin,
The old man sat; and the chore-girl still
Sung to the bees stealing out and in.

And the song she was singing ever since
In my ear sounds on: —
"Stay at home, pretty bees, fly not hence!
Mistress Mary is dead and gone!"

THE COLONY

ONE

APICULTURE: The art and science of raising honeybees.

The bees travel along the high-tension wires, just as surely as one true sentence follows the next. I am not sure why the bees took to this peculiar mode of travel, but I suspect they have their reasons, and their reasons have everything to do with the Bee Ladies' murder.

There is a family living not far from my home that mistakenly holds the electricity that hums and buzzes over their heads responsible for all the people in our neighborhood who have chanced to die in recent years. It is a complicated theory based on the deleterious effects of electromagnetic fields. I hardly know this family beyond what I have been able to discern from the slogans on the handmade signs they display in their front yard. I know they believe the overhead wires that run above our homes cause all manner of human ailments, and for this reason they have planted a growing field of carefully tended crosses in their lawn, one for each neighbor who has died since they began keeping track of such things shortly after moving into one of the newer housing tracts not far from my home nearly eight years ago.

I only spoke to them once, not long after they'd begun planting crosses in their lawn. It was one of those impossibly warm Southern California days that almost always occurs in early February, the sort of day that sings to those who wish to leave behind the bone-chilling heartbreak of winter and make a new life for themselves in the promise of eternal sunshine.

I probably would not have stopped to talk to this particular family, except that I was driving slowly past their home so that I might get a better look at the crosses and the curious signs on their lawn. Because of the heat, my car windows were open.

"Hey, Grandpa!" I heard a man shout. My initial instinct was to press my acceleration pedal down. But then I heard another voice. A woman's voice. It sounded determined yet vulnerable at the same time.

"You will help us?"

I know it seems foolish. They were strangers. But they were my neighbors as well. I pulled to the curb. The woman smiled and rushed to the edge of her lawn. She was thin and agitated, with dark, lanky hair and an oily copper complexion. She held a clipboard in her hand.

"Can you sign this?" she said, running around to the driver's side of my car. She handed me the clipboard and a pen through my open window.

"*¿Por favor?*"

"May I read it first?"

She glanced back at the man who stood thirty feet away in the gape of the open garage, a beer in one hand and some sort of power tool in the other. She nodded quickly at me.

As I read through the xeroxed copy of the petition which would ban all manner of overhead electrical wires in residential neighborhoods, it seemed prudent to ask the woman who stood so desperately by my car door why she was doing what she was doing, but that wouldn't have been polite.

Instead, I inquired where she was from. That is what new neighbors do. At least, that is what they used to do. This is how I learned she was originally from Texas, somewhere south of Dallas, that she'd moved to California with her father, who was in the military. It is also how I learned that she loved sunshine and open spaces, and that she feared the overhead power lines, which she said reminded her of barbed-wire fences.

When I was finished reading her petition, I told her I was very sorry but I did not wish to sign it. I told her it made no sense to me. She squeezed her eyes shut, and she thanked me just the same, scurrying back to the garage and handing the clipboard to the man I can only assume was her husband. I heard shouting as I pulled away from the curb. It was only later that I realized I'd forgotten to ask her name.

The following December my neighbors took to stringing their crosses with winking colored lights to mark the Christmas season. The spring after that they tied pastel pink and blue and yellow ribbons on the crosses at Eastertide. Independence Day is now demarcated by tiny American flags, and every October they drape their crosses in orange and black crepe paper and set a lighted jack-o'-lantern in their midst. And all the while, their field of crosses continues to grow. I found their agitated theories rather ludicrous, disturbing even. But what disturbed me for far too long is that I did not recognize a single name on any of their crosses.

My neighbors are no longer my neighbors. There is no longer any visceral connection between us other than that they are the strangers who live nearest to me. Day after day all I hear are leaf blowers and cars with pounding speakers that cruise slowly down my street, and night after night sirens wail and helicopters beat the air over my home with a roar that makes my head hurt.

So much noise.

I suspect this is why my bees no longer produce as much honey as they used to, nor does it taste quite as sweet as it once did.

Though I am an old man and my memory has begun to fade, I still recall a quiet time when the road in front of my home was made of dirt and gravel, and my dear mother could rock on our front porch swing and greet each and every one of our neighbors by their given names. But that time is long gone, and with it a definition of home and family that inextricably linked bricks and mortar and genes and bloodlines.

I have tried to adjust as best I can to this modern era, and I have found that thankfully my bees continue to wax and wane with the seasons. They remind me that the hundreds and thousands of births and deaths that occur each honey season are the natural life cycle of the hive, and this in turn has helped to ease my pain at the passing of all of the people I have held dear. Death is a constant in life. I thought I had long since made my peace.

But then, last August, I saw a new cross on my neighbors' front yard. I noticed it because it was different from the rest. Not the cross itself, which was fashioned from the same t-shaped slats of wood, nailed together, scrawled with a name and date of death, and planted in the ground. What *was* different were the flowers and candles and stuffed animals and balloons crowded around its spindly stake. In all the times I had driven past this house on my way to my honey consignments, or the library, the grocery store, the gas station, and whatever other random errand drew me less and less frequently from my home, I had never seen such a singular display on their lawn. Summer was just ending. There was no holiday to commemorate.

Had my neighbors been gathered in their garage workshop with what had become over the years a progressively more menacing group of friends, shouting, listening to loud music, and imbibing liquor, I surely would not have stopped to examine this curious memorial. But on this particular evening their garage door was down, as were my automobile windows, and I thought I caught the faint scent of eucalyptus and orange blossoms in the air. Despite all my better instincts, I pulled to the curb with a firm twist on my unpadded steering wheel, climbed out of my old Ford Fairlane, and approached what was from my rough count the twenty-first cross on the lawn.

There was a flickering phalanx of tall glass candleholders painted with pictures of saints that made the cross appear more like an altar than my neighbors' usual generic protest. Scattered around the candles were prayer cards and hand-scrawled notes. Many were written in Spanish and attached to sprays of carnations and baby's breath wrapped in grocery store cellophane. There were also bunches of roses, geraniums, calla lilies, and hydrangeas that clearly were snipped from backyard gardens, and two or three plush bears and a cheap felt pirate's hat piled among the flowers. Though the memorial was crude, there was no mistaking that the grief expressed was both real and personal.

I bent down to read the hand-painted lettering on the cross: *Christina Perez: 1974–2011.*

19

That I did not recognize the name when I first read it saddened me as none of the other names on the crosses before it had. When the name finally struck a chord, some months later, it shattered what little faith I had left in all I still held dear. And yet, it brought me some small measure of comfort at the same time. The first I'd felt in far too many years.

My neighbors continue to blame the electricity for all that has gone wrong around them because they need something to blame for what they have found lacking in their own lives. They never knew the Bee Ladies, or a time not so long ago when the wires did not whine and sputter over their heads like an angry swarm. They do not recall quiet summer evenings thick with the sweet scent of eucalyptus, jasmine, and orange blossoms as I do. They believe malevolence needs a scientific explanation that can be measured in voltages and magnetic fields.

I do not subscribe to my neighbors' strange theories, or their garish memorial displays, but I am no longer as inclined to judge their scientific folly as harshly as I once did. Perhaps our need to make sense of profound loss is what makes us not so different after all.

TWO

APIS MELLIFERA: A mixed zoological no-
menclature meaning "honey-carrying bee,"
it is used to designate the so-called Western or European honeybee. *Apis* derives
from the Latin word for "bee." *Mellifera*
combines the Greek words for "honey":
melli, and "to carry": *ferre.*

The bees began speaking to me through the
utility wires that crisscross the sky above my
home nearly twenty years ago. It was an
unseasonably warm Sunday morning in
early May — May 10, 1992, to be exact. I
was at the kitchen sink scouring the remains
of my usual breakfast of two poached eggs
and a slice of toast from my plate when I
heard a low-pitched hum that sounded at
first rather like a small group of monks
softly chanting their matins, but before long
there was no mistaking the collective whine
of wings that denotes an angry swarm. The

21

hum seemed to come from nowhere and everywhere at once. Drawn outside, I expected to see a great dark cloud of bees. Instead, my eyes were drawn to the five black utility wires that overhang my house — the wires were alive with the sound of this feverish, disembodied hum. As I walked beneath the wires, the deepening hum grew louder and more insistent as I approached the house next door where the two women I had once called my friends lived.

The Bee Ladies' house was clearly at the epicenter of this strange disturbance, and so I knocked on their front door, and when there was no answer, I knocked again. It was not altogether surprising that they did not answer at once, but given the persistence of my rapping, it concerned me that I heard no response, not even a curt command to go away, and so I went around to the rear of the house and knocked this time on their kitchen door. Again, no answer.

In days gone by, the next place I would have looked for them would have been in the farthest reaches of their almond orchards. Their family had once owned nearly five acres of land, and the Bee Ladies spent hour upon hour deep within the groves tending their hives. But over time, my neighbors had slowly sold off all but a small sliver of their family's former property, holding on to just a small copse of almond trees, their three remaining hives, and the modicum of privacy they craved. While I had been forced to make similar concessions over the years, thanks to my family's thriftiness and the success of our long-standing honey business I'd managed to hold on to more than an acre of our old groves, which were more than enough to sustain the sixteen hives and the simple distribution network of farmers' markets, consignment stores, and mail-order sales that continued to support my modest needs. I do not say this to boast. Business was the last thing on my mind that awful morning. Since I could see that the Bee Ladies weren't in their backyard, I assumed they were most likely in their house.

Putting my ear to the Bee Ladies' door, I heard tinny radio voices projecting from inside, and I thought for a moment that perhaps they had gone off to the market and left the radio playing, as I myself do when I run errands, so as to lend the appearance of occupancy in my absence.

I cast this notion aside, however, as soon as I peeked through the side window of the little garage at the end of their driveway and saw their Rambler station wagon parked inside. I knew that neither of the Bee Ladies cared to stroll the neighborhood for pleasure or need, nor were they likely to travel about in the company of anyone other than themselves. I began to fear something was truly amiss.

I knocked again at their back door, and then I jiggled the doorknob; that was how I discovered the door was unlatched. Opening it slowly, I hesitated on the threshold for a moment, but only for a moment, as I was unable to dismiss the foreboding that urged me past my more cautious self.

I called out their names as I stepped into the service porch just off their kitchen. Still, there was no response, and so I called again, louder, as I proceeded into the kitchen proper.

An iridescent yellow and gold-trimmed china tea service that I keenly recalled having once been served from when I was a boy sat oddly abandoned upon their chrome-edged dinette, leaving the eerie impression that the two women had been enjoying a cup of tea together one minute and had disappeared into a rapture of thin air the next.

A skin had formed on the milky liquid that floated atop the tea. I picked up one of the half-filled china cups. It felt cold, though the liquid in the matching creamer felt warm, which I am sure was more a matter of my own expectations as to what should feel warm or cold than it was an actual temperature differentiation.

Then I noticed the smell. I was not so much struck at that time by the unpleasantness of the sour odor I perceived as I was by its ability to overpower the memory of disinfectant and camphor that had been the dominant aroma in my neighbors' home for as long as I could recall.

Standing in my neighbors' kitchen, I remembered a conversation with my father.

I was six years old. I asked him why we hated the Straussmans. My father was a man of few words. He said that *hate* was a very strong word. He explained simply that there were two kinds of people in the world: those who love bees and those who fear them, and that these two types seldom found common ground. The flowering hedgerow my father planted between our property and our next-door neighbors' was the concrete extension of his philosophy: Out of sight, to him, was out of mind. For the first dozen years of our coexistence, this seemed to accommodate both our families' fairly reclusive natures.

Then one April morning in 1932 we were

rousted from our breakfast table by the sound of a sharp rapping on our front door. When I was sent to answer it, I found our neighbors' two daughters standing uncomfortably on our porch.

The smaller, and the bolder, of the two girls was more than a year older than myself, though she stood a good six inches shorter. Her roan hair was parted in the middle and plaited into two neat braids that hung just below her shoulders. Her sky blue eyes were wide set and frank in their expression. From her pale complexion I surmised that she did not spend nearly as much time out of doors as I did.

"My name is Clarinda Jane Straussman," she said, which of course I knew, having watched her from our back porch since I'd grown tall enough to see over the hedgerow from that vantage. She cleared her throat rather ceremoniously and nodded to my parents. "But you may call me Claire."

The tone of her voice, even then, was more commanding than permissive. She said she needed to speak to my father, and so I bade her and her sister to follow me into the dining room, where I presented them to my family.

"How do you do," my mother replied, a bit more formally than I would have expected until I noticed she wore the same indulgent smile she displayed when sampling one of my sister's more problematic culinary experiments.

"I'm very well, thank you," Claire replied curtly. She turned to the taller, silent girl beside her, whose name should have seemed familiar but did not. With a sweeping gesture that bespoke as much theatricality as maturity she said: "This is my sister, Hilda."

Whereas Claire's features were delicate and finely molded as a porcelain doll's, Hilda's face, and indeed her entire body down to the tips of her limbs, appeared to have been shaped from modeling clay by a child's clumsy fingers. Hilda's short-cropped hair, which sprouted like tufts of dried corn silk from her head, was more lifeless than straight. Even today, I can only guess at the color of her eyes as she so seldom looked directly at anyone.

Hilda curtsied rather stiffly, to my father's seeming bemusement. My mother, who stood by my father's side, gave him a reproving glance.

"How nice to meet you both, at last," she said. "Of course you must already know Albert and Eloise from school."

Strictly speaking, we did not. Both the Straussman sisters were at least several grades ahead of me, and in all the years we had attended the same grammar school we had scarcely spoken to one another, and only in incidental passing. I was only ten years old. I did not understand the reason behind my sister's practiced indifference toward Claire and Hilda any more than I understood the festering power of the insult my mother had been nursing against our neighbors since her initial gift of huckleberry jam had been received indifferently. All I knew is what my father had told me: They weren't bee people. As my father's son, I had been content up until that moment to more or less leave well enough alone.

"Mr. Honig," Claire said, fashioning an expression of impatience at having her clearly rehearsed speech interrupted, "my mother has sent me to ask if you would be so kind as to come with me now to our house. She says there are bees living in our parlor wall and she would like you to remove them at once."

To my young mind, our neighbors' assumptions were manifest: Bees were troublesome creatures to be avoided, the swarm of bees that had taken up residence in their parlor wall must have come from one of our secluded hives and therefore they were our responsibility to remove.

I found such wrongheaded assumptions particularly irksome as the swarming season was nigh upon us and for that very reason my father and I had been particularly watchful that week for signs of restlessness from our hives and we had not yet seen the slightest indication that even one new queen was ready to hatch from any of them. I was prepared to point out to the Straussman sisters that even the most overcrowded hive does not produce a swarm until a new queen is born either to lead the excess bees or, in the case of a weaker regent, to push the old queen and her loyal escort out to search for a suitable new hive.

Perhaps sensing my agitation, my father gently suggested it was much more likely that a wild swarm, freshly emerged from a nearby hollow log or abandoned shed, had chanced upon a tiny crack or some other such entry into the space between the inner and outer walls of the Straussmans' house, which was, unfortunately, where this particular colony had chosen to establish a new hive.

I say "unfortunately" because there is no easy way to remove bees from a wall once they have decided to take up residency inside such awkward quarters. Removal usually requires great skill on the part of the beekeeper, and even more patience on the part of the homeowner, unless of course the homeowner doesn't mind having his wall torn apart and the unwitting home invaders summarily murdered for no good reason other than human convenience.

My father chose not to belabor this point to our young neighbors. Instead, he motioned for me to follow him out to our honey shed where we kept a store of prepared hives ready to receive wild swarms.

I should explain that while beginning beekeepers generally get started by purchasing established hives from a reputable supplier, experienced beekeepers whenever possible prefer to add to their stock by acquiring wild swarms each spring; wild swarms are usually quite robust and free of disease, and they are always without cost. For this reason my father was careful to keep a goodly supply of empty hives ready for new colonies to occupy come the first of April, which is when the Valencia oranges that used to surround our property began to bloom. This way we were ready to act at a moment's notice when the groves reached full blossom and the bees began to swarm.

My father explained as much to Mrs. Straussman when he came to her door with his hiving equipment in hand and me and the Straussman sisters in tow. I was expecting to help my father set up the catcher hive, but Mrs. Straussman had other designs.

A remarkably large woman with gray hair and matching gray eyes the color of winter clouds, Mrs. Straussman came out onto her front porch and leaned heavily on a polished wooden cane as my father told her that it would likely take up to a month to lure the entire colony out of her wall and into the catcher hive. With her permission, he said, he would place the catcher hive just outside the crack in the wall the bees were using as an entryway. The catcher hive was already equipped with two fully drawn brood combs filled with honey and pollen, as well as young brood and larvae and eggs and nurse bees to tend to them all.

My father then showed Mrs. Straussman the ingenious cone he had fashioned from a twelve-by-sixteen-inch piece of window screen that he planned to nail to the opening of the telltale crevice where the brick facing of the chimney met the roof. The wide end of the cone would cover the opening in the wall, he explained. The other end, just about a half inch in diameter, would be wide enough for the bees to exit when they left the hive in search of nectar and pollen.

31

"Reentering the hive will be another matter entirely for our tiny friends," my father said with a knowing wink. He explained how, after crawling around the wall of the house in search of the screened opening, the disoriented worker bees would eventually give up and turn to the primed catcher hive, which would stand invitingly unimpeded beneath the cone. In this way, the great bulk of the hive's inhabitants would gradually transfer themselves to our new hive to combine with the starter brood.

"The new hive is queenless at present," my father said. "But the workers will soon rear a new queen from the brood cells to preside over the bees in the catcher hive and, God willing, the new queen's scent should over time lure the rest of the old colony out from inside your wall."

Mrs. Straussman appeared uninterested in the intricacies of my father's inventive procedure.

"I can hear those bees buzzing inside the wall, right there next to our chimney," she said to my father, pointing peevishly around the side of the porch with her cane. Beckoning to me with her free hand, she said: "Come have a cup of tea with me while your father gets rid of them."

Like the rest of the neighborhood children,

I was more than a little cowed by Mrs. Straussman, who passed many an afternoon hunkered down on the large rattan chair on her front porch, only to rise ponderously and shout invectives at any child who strayed onto her front lawn. I tried to politely decline her invitation, explaining that I did not much care for tea, and that my father would certainly be in need of my assistance, but the woman would have none of my excuses.

"We wouldn't like to see a nice-looking young man like you get all stung up by those nasty bees," she said, beckoning to me with her cane as she turned to go back into the house. When I protested that honeybees were not in the least bit nasty, and that they were, in fact, my dearest friends, my father cut me short with a stern glance. A gentleman to the core, he would brook no disrespect by me toward my elders. And so I was hooked.

Following Mrs. Straussman reluctantly indoors, I was assaulted for the first time by the sharp camphor tang of mothballs as I passed the hall closet. I took a shallow breath and held it in as I trailed her monstrous wake through the hallway. The Straussman sisters followed close upon my heels.

The kitchen was a spotless white room at the back of the house. It was furnished with a pale pine table and four unadorned chairs, an icebox, and a small stove. Glass-faced white wooden cabinets encircled the upper half of the room, and white tile covered the countertops beneath. Not a plate, a dish towel, or even a single bread crumb had been left lying about the Straussmans' perfectly ordered kitchen. Nor were there any lingering odors of bacon or toast or even boiled oatmeal. Certainly nothing of the sweet aroma of my mother's homemade scones and honey. I smelled instead the acrid blending of pine tar and lye soap.

As Mrs. Straussman eased herself into the chair nearest the door, I climbed into the chair across from hers and observed what I could only conclude was a particular Straussman family ritual. Hilda began it by lighting the stove's back right burner with a long kitchen match and setting a hammered-aluminum teakettle to boil while Claire withdrew two fine yellow-and-gold china cups and saucers from a cabinet shelf and set them on the table next to two silver teaspoons. Claire next set out a matching gilded china teapot and creamer between us, scooped several teaspoons of loose tea into the pot, and fetched fresh cream from

the icebox, which she poured into the smaller pitcher beside it. When the water came to a boil, Hilda filled the porcelain teapot with the steaming water from the aluminum pot and waited several more minutes before pouring the steeped tea through a metal strainer into her mother's cup halfway to the brim, and then she did the same into mine.

I had never taken to drinking tea, nor had I been trusted to sip from fine china at home, so I could only follow my hostess's lead as she reached for the china creamer and topped off my cup and then her own.

"It cuts the bitterness," she said, swirling the sweet cream with her silver spoon and urging me with her eyes to do the same. "Take care not to clink the side of the cup with your spoon."

"Why?"

"It's rude, boy," Mrs. Straussman said, setting her spoon gently onto the saucer behind her cup with its handle aligned with the cup's handle. "It's bad luck, besides."

Hilda and Claire were not invited to join us at the table but rather hovered about ever ready to refill our cups with more steaming tea.

"Is this real gold?" I recall asking Mrs. Straussman as I raised the teacup to my lips.

Surprised by my own boldness, I stared into the cup's brilliantly gilded rim.

"Twenty-two carat," she replied. "That's why we only take it out for special company, young man."

I took a certain pride in being deemed "special" by the imperious Mrs. Straussman — more special, if truth be told, than her own two daughters, who seemed to have been relegated to our personal serving staff. As the youngest in my family, I'd never experienced such polite deference before.

Staring once again into those teacups and the dark liquid reservoired within, I found it painful to reconcile the reflection of the gaunt, bespectacled old man I'd become with the innocent boy who'd sipped from that startlingly iridescent tea set for the first time sixty years before.

I don't know how long I would have stood gazing at that abandoned chinaware, dawdling like a schoolboy in my recollections, had not the baleful hum of bees that first drew me to my neighbors' house finally penetrated my reveries. I realized then that the hum seemed to be coming from the front end of the house.

Once again, I called out to my neighbors as I moved cautiously past the kitchen table and on into the narrow dark hallway leading to the parlor. Oddly, the odor of sour milk grew stronger as I moved forward. With rising dread I made my way to the front room, where to my everlasting sorrow I found the Bee Ladies at last.

Lying like rolled rugs on the polished hardwood floor, they stared into each other's faces with blank, unseeing eyes. There was no blood or marks of injury on the women that I could detect from where I stood at the entrance to their parlor.

Nothing appeared to be out of place in the room, nothing at all except of course for the Bee Ladies, who lay face-to-face on their sides with strips of silver duct tape binding their wrists and ankles. It appeared that red bandannas had been stuffed inside both their mouths and fastened in place with more silver tape. My distress continued to mount as I noticed the disquieting gray-green tint to both women's complexions.

It was at least a minute or more before I saw the first bee flitting about the fireplace opening, and perhaps another half minute after that before I spotted three more bees crawling about the framed photographs that were set in a tidy row on the wooden mantelpiece above the hearth.

THREE

HIVE MORALE: When the morale of the honeybee colony is high, its bees are predictable. They make honey, they pollinate flowers, they propagate. When the morale of the hive is adversely affected, the colony reacts in unexpected ways.

The first emergency vehicle arrived no more than ten minutes after I called 911 from the black wall phone set into a tiny vestibule just off the Straussmans' service porch. The coroner followed shortly after several marked and unmarked police cars began rumbling up the Straussmans' graveled driveway.

I noticed somewhat abstractly that everything seemed to be moving slower than normal, yet the lines of the hallway and the grain of the wooden floor seemed preternaturally sharp. I watched with detached curiosity as an official investigator ap-

38

proached me where I stood leaning weakly against the wall. Clad in a square brown suit that seemed cut from an earlier era, he was shorter than me by at least an inch or two but much broader across his shoulders and chest. He nodded to an underling and flipped open his leather billfold containing his badge and photo identification, which he flashed quickly at me. From the easy flick of his wrist, it occurred to me that this was the sort of thing he had been doing for years and that he was loath to acknowledge just how many as his thick sandy hair was now peppered with more gray than what showed in his photograph. Judging from the jowling on his face and the snug fit of his shirt around his middle, he had added another twenty pounds as well since the photo had been taken. I noticed that his leather shoes, like his suit, had clearly been chosen more for utility than style, though they were meticulously enough maintained that I assumed the detective had some military experience in his background. His stylish gray-and-tan diagonally striped tie was the only contradiction of his frank, utilitarian style. Its colors seemed to play nicely off his hazel eyes, which suggested to me that it had been chosen by a more sophisticated sartorial eye than his.

"Detective Grayson," he said. Offering me a printed identification card that he urged me to keep, he slipped his badge back into his jacket pocket and extracted a narrow spiral notebook and pen with his left hand while grabbing my right hand with his, all in an impressively efficient syncopated motion. "And your name is . . . ?"

"Albert. Albert Honig," I said, extricating my hand from his hearty grip. "I live next door."

"That's H—O—N . . ." the detective said, setting his pen to pad and looking up at me expectantly. There was a weariness to his eyes that seemed to absorb rather than reflect the light around him.

"H—O—N—I—G," I said, and the detective dutifully recorded this, followed by my address and telephone number. I remember thinking how absurd it was that the two of us were obliged to dally over such mundane information while my deceased neighbors lay bound and gagged not five feet in front of me. The uncomfortable closeness in the air that I had first noticed upon entering the house had become almost unbearable. Just then the front door creaked open.

"Can you excuse me just a moment?" Detective Grayson said, turning his attention to another team of police investigators who had just arrived.

"Of course," I said.

Detective Grayson nodded and motioned for me to stay where I was. I realized that my hands had begun to shake and I slipped them into my trouser pockets and leaned against the doorframe that separated the hall from the parlor from where I could observe the detective directing one officer to take photographs of the parlor and the kitchen. He then instructed another officer to begin sprinkling the countertops, door-frames, windowsills, and furniture with a fine black dust, after which he turned his team's attention to the Bee Ladies' teacups, teapot, and milk pitcher, which the officers dusted as well, after siphoning samples into individual glass tubes that were then stop-pered and labeled before depositing the emptied tea service into plastic bags, as still more officers busied themselves outside, wrapping yellow tape around the tiny cot-tage and fending off the crowd that had begun to gather in small bunches to whisper and point.

So many people, I remember thinking. *More people than the Bee Ladies had wel-comed into their home in a thousand months of Sundays. What a shame they could not enjoy the company.*

It had been more than a decade since I last had come calling on my neighbors, and nearly as long since I had thought of them as what they once were: my dearest friends. I am sure I was the last person, besides the two women themselves, to call them by their proper Christian names. And regretfully, over time, even I had taken to referring to them by the nickname the neighborhood children had given them after they began selling jars of honey and beeswax candles from a little stand on their front porch.

Of course I had never called them the Bee Ladies to their faces. But in my head, it seemed somehow easier to think of them as something other than what they once were to me, if only to dull the ache of our estrangement.

My melancholic reverie was eventually interrupted by Detective Grayson's return.

"Sorry to keep you waiting," he said, retrieving his notebook from his pocket. "So . . ."

It was just a single word. But he said it softly, as if for all the times he'd had to ask the next question, it was never an easy one: "I understand you found the bodies?"

I closed my eyes, wishing to erase the image from my mind. Reading the gesture as acquiescence, the detective clasped my shoulder as he strode past me into the parlor, where he circled the bodies like a wary beast.

"So," he said again, this time just a bit more firmly, "what can you tell me about all this?"

All this.

I suppose I could have told the detective that long after our stubborn silence had grown into a mighty rift, I had taken to observing Claire and Hilda silently tending their hives from the distance of our two yards. I could have explained that my dear mother, bless her soul, used to say there was no moving me off plumb once I'd dug my heels in, which was true enough, though in my own defense, the same could just as easily have been said about either of the Straussman sisters and that I truly believed that they had found some measure of contentment within the binary solitude of their later years, just as I had taken solace in the companionship of my books and my bees.

The detective, who had bent to examine the body of the larger of the two women, turned his head back to me.

"Her name was Hilda. Hilda Straussman," I said. The name tasted like rust on my tongue.

The detective wrote her name down as he

sidled past Hilda and knelt rather laboriously next to the woman lying frozen at Hilda's side.

"This would be Claire. Claire Straussman," I said. "They were sisters."

I started to walk toward the detective in the parlor, but he held up his hand, which was broad and surprisingly well manicured.

"Please, Mr. Honig. This is a crime scene."

"Of course," I said, chastened.

"I take it this is the younger sister?" Detective Grayson inquired from across the room. I nodded.

Curled into her unnatural repose, Claire seemed so small and withered. That she had taken to wearing her once luxurious curls pulled back into a single silvery braid wrapped around the back of her head in a thick bun reminded me once again of how old we'd both grown. A few strands had sprung loose from the braid and lay in errant wisps across her cheek. Alive, Claire would have suffered not even a single hair out of place, and it seemed to me the detective's thick hand hovered momentarily above her cheek as if to brush the hair from Claire's face as he bent closer to examine her body. Or perhaps I just wished it so.

"Neither one of them ever marry?" the detective wondered aloud. I shook my head

44

no, and his eyes filled with the special pity reserved for elderly spinsters. I thought of my own lifelong bachelorhood and how even after my father's death I had seldom felt the lack of companionship, except perhaps at mealtime when I was forced to cook as well as clean up the detritus of pots and pans and plates I invariably made of even my most meager culinary efforts.

"Any family at all?"

"None to speak of."

We were interrupted, just then, by a string of curses erupting from the back of the house, and I turned to watch two coroner's attendants roll a pair of steel gurneys down the long hallway from the kitchen to the parlor.

"What the Sam Hill?" Detective Grayson fairly barked at the young men.

"*Gosh durned* bees!" the taller of the two attendants exclaimed, pointing to a small cluster of bees in the hallway, except that he didn't say gosh durned, and I felt my cheeks redden at the sound of the Lord's name being taken in vain. Though I no longer attend church as regularly as I did when my dear mother walked this earth, I do believe there is a common decency that should be observed in the avoidance of vulgar epithets.

"There's a *flaming* swarm back there in

the hallway," the first one added, more or less.

Observing my discomfort at what they really said, the good detective intervened.

"Watch your language, son," he said sharply.

"Bees are upset by coarse language," I agreed, and as if to prove my point one of the bees broke away from the cluster to hover skittishly above the nearer of the two attendants. When he tried to swat it away, it drove its stinger defensively into the back of his hand.

"Don't pull it out," I said. I kept my voice low and calm as the young man yelped and flailed about in circles. "Use a knife blade or your fingernail to scrape the stinger off."

Both the attendants and the detective looked at me as if I had grown an extra head.

"Plucking it out only releases more venom into the wound," I tried to explain as the young man continued to worry the offending barb with his forefinger. "Some Mrs. Stewart's Liquid Bluing rubbed on the sting helps to relieve the pain. I'm fairly certain the Straussmans have some on hand — in the pantry, just to the right of the kitchen. Or if not, swabbing on some Clorox helps, or even table salt. I'm also told meat tenderizer contains an enzyme that neutralizes the irritant in the sting, but I have yet to try this remedy myself."

"*Jiminy,* there's more of the little *flamers* on the window over there," the shorter of the two attendants shouted before shrugging apologetically in my direction. "And there, on the mantle!"

"Keep your voice down, and try not to move suddenly," I instructed. "Bees will not sting unless they are frightened or offended. Loud noise and sudden motion both frighten and offend them."

A large drone flew out from the fireplace and lit on Claire Straussman's skirt just then.

"You seem to know a thing or two about bees," the detective said to me. "What do you make of this?"

By this, I assumed he meant the growing number of bees gathering in the Straussmans' parlor, as he did not appear to be well enough schooled in apian habits to find the appearance of a solitary drone outside the hive odd, in and of itself.

"The bees seem to be coming into the house through the chimney," I said as another pair of field bees entered the parlor in just this manner.

"I can see that," the detective replied, a

terseness creeping into his voice that surprised me. "What I'm asking is, why?"

"In my experience," I replied, "I have found that bees are generally forthright, intelligent creatures. It's not in their nature to offer false testament any more than it would be natural for a worker and a drone to mate or a queen to leave the hive to gather pollen. While I might not readily understand their actions or intentions in certain situations, that has always been my shortcoming, not theirs."

Detective Grayson had meanwhile begun to reflexively click his ballpoint pen open and shut in what I could only read as irritation. I wondered what about my measured response had so offended him. As if reading my mind, he repeated his question.

"This time," he added, "in twenty-five words or less."

I told him then as succinctly as I could that I did not know the precise reason for the bees' entry into the Straussmans' house, per se, but it seemed to me the natural rhythm of their precisely ordered world clearly had been disturbed.

Four

DWINDLING: The dying off of old bees in the spring, sometimes called spring dwindling or the disappearing disease.

Though I found myself surprisingly agitated at the thought of abandoning my former friends, I reluctantly allowed myself at this time to be ushered onto the Straussmans' front porch where Detective Grayson solicited additional information from me about the nature of my relationship with the Straussman sisters. I told him that I'd known them all my life, that my parents had moved to this area from Oregon more than seventy years before, and that we — the Straussman sisters, my sister and myself — had all grown up together.

I do not recall the exact progression of our discourse, but I believe it moved at some point from the friendship Claire and I once shared to Aristotle's observations on the general nature of bees and how he was able, through this particular manner of philosophic extrapolation, to glean some further insight into the nature of man.

I, of course, hold no such lofty philosophic conceits. But I did tell the detective that through years of careful observation I have been able to discern quite clearly when my bees are hungry or when they are cold. Through a nuanced pattern of motion and sound, my bees signal just as plainly to me when there's an abundance of honey to be harvested from the hive or when they are set to swarm. Indeed, my bees tell me when a new queen has been born, and though I've gotten more than a few painful stings over the years, I've learned to judge by the tone and pitch of their buzz whether they're glad to see me or if they are on the other hand offended by the smell of a new pair of woolen gloves I am wearing or off-put by the color of my jacket.

"I remember in particular the fuss I stirred up among my hives the time I wore a purple velvet jacket."

I explained to Detective Grayson that I would never have chosen this color or fabric on my own, but one of my honey customers, a young woman with something of an ethereal nature, had presented me with this particular jacket as a thank-you present for helping her to start a bee colony of her own.

"You look like someone who could have worn this in a past life," she'd said. Beaming like a courtesan, she'd reached up to help me into the jacket, and, not wanting to hurt her feelings, I had thanked her heartily and waved good-bye, with her watching all the way as I headed out to my number one hive. This is how I discovered that my bees did not like purple, I told the good detective. "Before I could take the offending jacket off, I received three, perhaps four, bee stings."

"What's your point, Mr. Honig?" Detective Grayson said, flipping his notebook closed and slipping it and his pen back into his jacket pocket.

My point was that bees are extraordinary creatures.

"Did you know that the ancient Egyptians revered honeybees, believing that they were born from the tears of the sun god, Ra?"

"I can't say that I did," Detective Grayson replied, glancing back toward the front door where the attendants stood poised to wheel out the first of the two steel gurneys bearing the Straussman sisters' remains.

Before I had the chance to elaborate on the mythic significance of bees to Egyptian

51

civilization, the detective thanked me rather perfunctorily for what assistance I had been able to provide and called one of his junior officers over to show me to my home just as the Straussmans' front door swung open and the shorter of the two coroner assistants nosed the first gurney out onto the Straussmans' front porch. I assumed it was Claire who was zipped into the black body bag as the straps on the gurney were notched tight with plenty to spare.

Before taking my leave, I asked the detective if I might ask a favor of him. He raised his eyebrows, which, like his hair, were in need of a good trim.

"Would it be possible for you to see to it that they are transported in a single vehicle?" I queried, gesturing to the pair of coroner's vans parked in the driveway. I explained to the detective that in all their years on earth, Hilda and Claire had only rarely found cause to spend time apart.

Detective Grayson took a deep breath and squeezed the raised tendons at the back of his neck.

"As the Lord has seen fit to take them from this life together," I persisted, "it seems so very wrong to send them off to their heavenly repose in separate vehicles."

The detective's eyes flicked from me to

the second gurney that had just begun to nose out the door and back to me again. He shook his big bear head slowly and let out a protracted sigh.

"I'll see what I can do."

I had no choice but to trust his good intentions, and so I let myself be led back across the expanse of the Straussmans' front yard to my own porch, where I bid the young officer a polite farewell at my door-step. I considered for a moment whether I should check on my hives before going inside. Though the sun was still less than midway through its journey across the sky, darkness had already fallen on all I could see, and, in truth, my legs suddenly felt as though weighted with lead. There was a growing constriction in my chest that seemed to ratchet ever tighter with each breath I took. I decided my bees would have to take care of themselves for an afternoon.

Entering my darkened house, I sat for a while in my parlor before slowly climbing the stairs to my bedroom, which by then was bathed in late-afternoon shadows. I switched on the reading light over my mother's old padded rocker. I had moved this chair from my parents' room into mine after my father's death.

Sleep was out of the question, but, for

once, I found no solace in my books. After a time, I switched off the lamp, opened the curtains of my window, and lay down on my bed. I watched the color of the sky shift from gray to mottled black to gray again.

FIVE

QUEEN MANDIBULAR PROTEIN: A pheromone produced by the queen bee that attracts drones for mating, inhibits the production of replacement queens, unites the colony, and stabilizes its temperament by drawing attendants to the queen and stimulating the development of nurse and forager bees to raise its brood and gather honey and pollen to feed it. Without it, robber bees seem to be drawn to the hive.

The next morning, I arose even earlier than was my custom. Finding food as unappealing as sleep, I decided to forgo my usual breakfast routine in favor of a small nibble of dry toast and a teaspoon of jasmine honey. Yet even this slight fare seemed to catch in my throat, and I quickly sought what comfort I could out of doors in the quietude of my own thoughts, where I passed most of the morning tending to my hives, which had been sorely neglected in the distractions of the previous day.

It was close to noon, and I was doing what I could to fend off a small brown ant infestation in my number three hive when I heard my name being shouted from across my backyard. I looked up to see the detective I had met at the Straussman sisters' home the previous day standing at the foot of my back porch.

"Mr. Honig?" he called again to me, this time louder, but with a slight tremor that I naturally ascribed to an apprehension common to those finding themselves in close proximity to so large a number of bees for the first time. I set down my smoker can and the empty container of motor oil I had just finished pouring into the tin pans suspended on the legs of my hive stand. I approached the house, as it was clear by the grip of the detective's hand on the porch railing that he would venture no closer of his own accord. As my mother often said, it is easier to bring Muhammad to the mountain than the mountain to Muhammad.

"Please, call me Albert," I said, extending my hand. I had hoped to put him at ease by dispensing of such formalities as surnames, though, in truth, it was not solely his comfort I sought. For most of my days it had been my father to whom friends and neighbors had referred to as Mr. Honig, while I was known simply as "young Albert." Even though I myself was in my eighth decade, I confess that I was at that moment still loath to accept my natural inheritance.

"Albert?" Detective Grayson said. "Not the Bee Man?"

"No," I said, "just Albert."

"So how come?" the detective prodded, nodding toward the clutch of hives sprinkled throughout my backyard and on into the small orange grove that extended beyond it.

"I beg your pardon?"

"I'm just wondering why you have two little old ladies with a few hives in their backyard and everybody calls them the Bee Ladies, but here you are, right next door, and from what I can see you've got triple, maybe four times as many, hives and you're just plain old Albert. How come?"

"I don't know," I replied. I'd never thought to ask myself this question before. How does one acquire a nickname? Having never been called by anything but my given name, I could only speculate.

"Perhaps because no one knew what else to call them?" I ventured. "They rather liked to keep to themselves."

"Fair enough," the detective said. "So how come you know what to call them?"

"As I said yesterday, we grew up together. We were friends once."

I paused for a moment with my hand on the porch railing as the detective's eyes scanned the sky above him for imagined hordes of murderous bees. I noticed that the veins in my hand seemed quite blue and pronounced beneath my sun-roughened skin. I was struck by how much my hands reminded me of my father's, especially late in life. His fingers had been long and tapered like my own. Musician's hands, my mother used to say, though neither of us could play more than a clumsy note or two on any instrument to speak of. Hopelessly tone-deaf, my mother used to call us.

"Would you care to join me inside for a cool glass of lemonade?" I asked, certain the detective would take me up on my offer of refuge, if not refreshment.

"Don't go to any trouble," Detective Grayson said with a final nervous glance at the nearest stand of hives as he strode past me onto the porch stairs. He made it clear with only the slightest nod of his head that he was used to taking the lead in any given situation and that it was only out of courtesy that he paused at the screen door to allow me to enter first. This I acknowledged with a nod of my own as I passed.

Like the Straussmans' house, my back door opens into a small service porch leading into the kitchen. A stack of unopened mail lay next to the morning paper on my dinette table, and I was most regretfully aware of Detective Grayson's observational eye lingering over the dirty dishes I had left on the counter.

"Forgive the mess," I said, quickly rinsing the dishes and stacking them in the sink as I spoke. "I hurried through my breakfast to get an early start on my daily chores, whereupon I found a band of marauding ants preparing an assault on my number three hive."

The detective turned his attention from the clutter in my sink to me.

"Which means what?" he said. I noticed that in the early-afternoon light his hazel eyes were streaked with silver.

"One of the greatest problems facing beekeepers here in this region are brown ants. They overrun our hives from time to time, yet the poison many beekeepers use to prevent such invasions presents an even greater hazard to the very hives we seek to protect.

"It would be a grave mistake to rid the

premises of ants entirely because during the greater part of the year, these tiny insects perform a useful service keeping our yards and apiary clean. This is especially true during peak honeyflow season, when the hardworking field bees labor so strenuously that they live only a short four to six weeks. If they chance to die in the hive, some hive bees take it upon themselves to carry the deceased worker out into the yard where they drop her to the ground. As soon as she is abandoned, the ants rush in, seemingly from nowhere, to strip the carcass of all edible flesh. This natural arrangement works well, unless a nest of ants grows so greedy as to overstep its bounds and attempt to avail itself of the honey cached within the hives. This is when the prudent beekeeper must intervene."

Detective Grayson, who had meanwhile taken a seat at the kitchen table, began to sweep a clutter of errant toast crumbs into a tiny pile and then off the tabletop into his cupped palm.

"My father first hit upon the idea of making moats out of pie tins to repel the invading forces," I told the detective as I held out my hand. He brushed the crumbs into it, and I rinsed them off into the sink.

"You were saying?" he said.

"The moats are made by sawing off all four hive stands' legs midway up their length and nailing pie tins to the top of the separated leg segments and then reattaching each one to its mated stub with the pie tin between.

"The tins are filled with motor oil. Oil is more difficult for ants to cross than plain water, and if one is careful to keep the pans filled to capacity at all times, and free of leaves and twigs, which ants are clever enough to use as natural bridges, such an arrangement is usually successful in keeping both populations separated."

I explained all this as I collected two clean glasses from the kitchen cabinet and a pitcher of lemonade from my icebox.

"Let's go into the other room, shall we?"

Detective Grayson nodded and stood, wiping his palms on his pant legs, and I led him into the dining room, where he eased his heavy frame into a seat at the polished mahogany table facing the front window.

"Just half a glass, Mr. Honig," he said, running his hand through his robust thatch of curls and unbuttoning his jacket — a rumpled gray one every bit as formless as the brown jacket he'd worn the day before. His crisp, paisley-patterned tie seemed once again almost dapper by contrast. The detec-

61

tive fidgeted in his chair as if to find a spot of comfort that was by nature beyond his reach.

Pouring a half glass for him and a full glass for myself, I waited for Detective Grayson to disclose the reason for his visit, as clearly, by his growing agitation, he had some business to which he wished to attend.

"We got the coroner's preliminary report this morning," he said finally, taking a small sip of lemonade and nodding appreciatively. "It appears your neighbors were dead at least forty-eight hours before you found them. The coroner says they essentially suffocated. Whoever put that tape over their mouths didn't leave much room for them to breathe."

I did not want to know this. I did not want to imagine the rising terror that Claire and Hilda must have felt as they watched each other's chests heave and struggle in vain to fill their lungs with air. I closed my eyes but could not erase the memory of their glassy stares.

"Mr. Honig?"

I opened my eyes to find the detective leaning forward, his narrowed eyes staring directly into mine.

"I know you told me you didn't see anything suspicious yesterday, but I wonder whether you might have noticed anything out of the ordinary on Friday?"

I thought for a moment about what I had been doing just three days earlier.

"Nothing that I can recall," I said after some consideration. I explained to the detective that I had observed a week earlier the telltale signs of several large cells being constructed to prepare for the birth of a new queen bee and so my attention had been thus preoccupied.

"This is all very interesting, Mr. Honig . . ."

"Indeed it is," I agreed. "This wondrous process is begun when a colony's queen grows old and her egg production begins to lag. Did you know, Detective, that queen bees are no different genetically than any other worker bee?"

Taking his silence as tacit acknowledgment of his ignorance in the ways of bees, I proceeded to lay out for him the process of differentiation that occurs in the hive, a process that begins, as any apiarist knows, once the eggs are laid into the queen cells. I explained how, as soon as the eggs hatch, the nurse bees begin to feed the larvae a specially prepared mixture of regurgitated honey and pollen called royal jelly.

"This royal jelly is what causes certain

organs and characteristics to develop in these young bees that transforms each one from an ordinary worker bee into a virgin queen . . ."

"Mr. Honig," the detective interjected. I paused, waiting for him to speak, but after a moment of silence he simply shook his head, and so I continued without offense, explaining that the transformation of a select worker bee into queen has everything to do with the life cycle of the hive.

"Only the first of these proto-queens to emerge from her cell will live. The others are generally dispatched with a lethal sting by the new regent, who then does the same to her weaker queen mother. Of course in the rare instances when the young queen is unable to perform the requisite matricide, or if she herself proves flawed, the hive workers are quick to surround the doomed queen, who surrenders without a fight to suffocation by the rabble.

"It is the law of the hive that only a queen may sting another queen," I explained. "And the queen will sting none but her own."

Having finished the last of his lemonade, the detective began to run his thick forefinger around the rim of his empty glass, producing a high-pitched squeal that was louder, but lower, than that of a newly hatched queen. I pointed out that by whatever means the coup is accomplished, the new virgin queen must next wait for the first sunny day to take wing, where she is quickly followed by a score or so of young drones who pursue her fifty or more feet into the air to mate with her on the fly. The handful of young drones that are successful in their ardor are eviscerated during the mating process. The others are usually cast out of the hive, or killed outright, by the worker bees sometime in early fall, when the drones, having already outlived the only useful purpose for which they were born, are deemed expendable.

"In the beehive, the age-old maxim 'He who does not work does not eat' is strictly adhered to."

"Truly fascinating, Mr. Honig," the detective said somewhat drily to my ear. Pushing his lemonade glass aside, he extracted his notebook from his suit jacket and laid it open in front of him.

"Now, about last Friday . . ."

Six

THE QUEEN BEE: The mother of all bees in the hive, she has two functions: to lay as many eggs as she can and to emit the pheromone that will produce the next queen.

"This is what I've been trying to explain," I said, offering to refill Detective Grayson's lemonade. He cupped his palm over his glass. "I was far too preoccupied requeening my cross-tempered number four hive to have paid any attention to the goings-on at my neighbors' house that unfortunate day."

Beehives, like any human household, have a temperament every bit as distinctive as the dominant personalities that reside within.

"While there are devices we can employ to keep our bees gentle enough to accommodate, and in some cases even relish, our presence, there is only so much a conscientious beekeeper can do before more drastic measures must be taken," I said.

"Just *how* drastic?" Detective Grayson asked. His voice rose to suggest curiosity, but I suspected it was more from investigative reflex than any genuine apian interest.

"Requeening the cross hive," I said. "Requeening is never my first choice. I usually try hanging a wave cloth near the flyway of a particularly testy hive. The constant flapping of the cloth in the breeze helps the bees to become accustomed to motion. This discourages them from rising forth to defend their hive from the occasional passerby. I have also found that several good puffs from a smoker can do much to calm an agitated hive when working in close quarters. But when all else fails, a cantankerous queen must be replaced."

Detective Grayson nodded for me to continue as his eyes flickered about the room before coming to rest on the large picture window that dominated my dining room's west wall.

"You must understand that the queen sets the overall tone of the hive," I said, my eyes instinctively following the detective's. "Just as a gentle queen usually produces a hive of workers and drones as even-tempered as she, a cantankerous queen more often than not holds court over a hive that is easily frightened or offended no matter what care we take to placate it.

"Come the first warm days of spring, it is the cross-tempered hives that are the first to swarm. This is why extra vigilance is required when a new queen is expected to emerge from such a hive," I explained. "The last thing I want is another bad-tempered hive to go with the one I already have."

Detective Grayson continued to stare past me and out the window. I took another sip of lemonade before recounting how, having heard the stirrings of a new brood of queens from my number sixteen hive the night before, my plan was to be up and outside first thing in the morning to watch for a gentle new queen to emerge so that I might use her to requeen my increasingly ill-tempered number four. I was about to explain exactly how such an operation was accomplished when the detective drew a conspicuous breath and refocused his eyes on mine.

"Are you sure you didn't notice anything unusual over at the Straussmans' when you first got up?"

"Nothing that I can recall."

"Think a little harder. How about when you were eating breakfast?" the good detective pressed. "Maybe you noticed something then?"

I told him that I hardly remembered my repast at all, so anxious had I been to get on with my morning's plan. "Why do you ask?"

"We think the old ladies must have died shortly after breakfast, judging from what the coroner found in their stomachs — bits of toast and egg and some undigested chunks of wax," Detective Grayson said, flipping through the pages of the notebook he had withdrawn from his jacket pocket. "What do you make of the wax?"

"That would be their daily dose of honeycomb," I replied. "Claire and Hilda were particularly fond of comb honey. They said the only way to properly enjoy it was to crush it with a knife and spread it on their morning toast — honey, wax, and bread all mashed together. Hilda swore this practice was what helped her ward off colds and all manners of sinus troubles. Myself, I prefer to cut off a bite-size piece of comb honey, chew it awhile, and then discard the wax, though I can't say for sure it does me any more good than Hilda's way during cold and flu season. You know, my grandmother, on the other hand, swore by black walnuts. 'Crack and eat the meat of six walnuts,' she'd say, 'and you will not be sick a day.' "

Detective Grayson chose not to engage in a debate between the merits of honeycomb versus walnuts.

"You wouldn't happen to know what time they normally ate their breakfast?" he prodded.

"Shortly after sunrise, between six and seven, just as I do," I said. "Especially at this time of year. The young queens usually begin to hatch first thing in the morning, so it's best to get an early start on the day's activities. The earlier, the better."

"I take it then that you were up first thing Friday morning, same as the Straussmans were," Detective Grayson said, scribbling a line or two in his notebook and then pausing. "Think now, Mr. Honig. Maybe you heard something odd?"

"Nothing that morning that I can recall," I said. "My number sixteen hive is at the rear of my property, well beyond either eye- or earshot of the Straussmans' house."

"Well, how about the night before? Anything out of the ordinary then?"

"Nothing more or less extraordinary than the squeaks of the unhatched queen eager to break out of her cell," I replied.

Like most people, Detective Grayson knew nothing of the sounds bees make

70

other than the familiar buzz of flight. I enumerated the range of chirps and whines and hums and squeaks emanating from a hive on any given occasion. The prudent beekeeper learns to distinguish which sounds mean what.

"The young queens, for instance, make a high-pitched squeal, not unlike the note of a distant trumpet, shortly before they emerge from their sealed cells," I said. "When I hear this clarion call in the evening, I can predict with a fair degree of certainty that a new queen will be born the following morning."

This is not the only thing I can predict, but I did not say as much as I watched the good detective sketch crude renderings of cartoonish bees wearing crowns upon their heads in his notebook that he'd laid open on the table between us.

So many people have come to me over the years to inquire about the best way to get into beekeeping, and, once in, how to refine their beekeeping techniques, that I find myself automatically evaluating the person-alities of nearly everyone I meet for their suitability to such an endeavor. Observing Detective Grayson's careless doodles, I suspected then that he had neither the patience nor the desire to care for bees. I also suspected that while he strove mightily to appear calm and unruffled, there was an aura of excitability beneath his pragmatic manner that was far too easily aroused. Such passions generally render one incompatible with bees. Claire Straussman had been one of the few exceptions to this rule, for while she had a mercurial personality that could set off more sparks than a Fourth of July celebration, she had an uncanny ability to read the nuances of pitch and tone by which bees communicate to one another and, by extension, to anyone outside the hive who cares to listen. This more than offset her unpredictable nature.

I noticed that Detective Grayson had allowed a small, self-amused smile to creep across his face as he added a trumpet-playing bee to his sketch before setting his pen down and folding his hands atop his notebook. Taking another deliberate breath, he let the corners of his mouth drift back into practiced neutrality.

"Okay, so you heard your bees squeaking last Thursday night?" he said at last.

"Indeed I did. Stronger — and louder, as I recall — than any I had ever heard before."

I recalled — though I kept this to myself — how once upon a time the anticipated birth of a new queen, especially one heralded by such an uncommon racket, would have sent me hurrying next door to share the glorious news with my neighbors. Claire, in particular, took keen delight in observing the inner lives of our hives, and I had been for many years equally fond of imparting to her the finer points of beekeeping that had been passed on to me by my own father and mother. Sadly, however, such conviviality was no longer the norm between us, and so I had waited in solitude the previous Friday morning for the first young queen to break free from her cell. Detective Grayson did not appear to notice my retreat into private reverie as he returned his attention to the large picture window behind me.

"I see you can look right across to the Straussmans' front porch from this window here."

"Indeed I can."

"So, once again, Mr. Honig . . ."

"Albert."

"Mr. Honig," he insisted, perhaps more brusquely than even he had intended, as his shoulders seemed to tighten as if to brace for a blow that didn't come. Slowly, he curled his hand across his mouth and exhaled deeply before speaking again. "I appreciate your hospitality, Mr. Honig, I really do. It's just that I like to keep all my work relationships professional. I'm kind of old school that way."

"I understand, Detective Grayson," I said, though I wondered why such a fine line needed to be drawn between first and last names.

"Just so we're clear on that," the detective said, keeping his eyes to his notebook.

"Of course," I said.

"So let's get back to last Friday," he said, clearing his throat brusquely. "Are you absolutely sure you didn't see anybody hanging round next door while you were eating breakfast?"

"I normally take my breakfast in the kitchen, so I would not have seen anything next door as my kitchen window faces to the rear of my property," I said. I explained once again that I had rushed off directly after breakfast, hoping to observe the birth of my queen and how my hopes had been rewarded when she emerged from the hive with her full retinue of suitors at a little past ten, just as the sun began to take the chill off the morning air. I believe I may have mentioned how sorry I was that Claire had not been there to see the birth of my new queen.

"You know, she was quite a beauty," I said. Detective Grayson, who was scribbling furiously in his notebook, jerked his head up.

"Who? Miss Straussman?"

"What? Oh, goodness no," I replied, equally disconcerted by the detective's interpretive leap, but I smiled in spite of myself. "Of course there was a time when Claire attracted a full complement of eager young beaus."

"I see," he said. His tone remained even, but he shifted slightly forward in his seat. "So how is it she never married?"

"How is it that anyone makes the choices they do?" I replied. Certainly there are those who would say that my life has been diminished by the dearth of human company I have cultivated over my lifetime. I believe that solitude is not the same as loneliness. I recall that I told Detective Grayson something to the effect that I was happily bound to this world by my place in it for good reason. I know I quoted one of my mother's favorite poets who wrote:

"Happy the man, whose wish and care / A few paternal acres bound, / Content to breathe his native air, / In his own ground."

"That's nice," Detective Grayson said. I noticed that the cartoon bees in his notebook had been joined by the phrases *early risers* and *any gentlemen callers???* He had underlined the last phrase twice. As I

75

watched him scribble on the page, my eyes fell upon the simple gold band on the detective's left hand.

"What made you decide to marry?"

Detective Grayson shrugged with much the same motion a bear uses to twitch a gnat off his massive shoulders.

"Seemed like the right thing to do at the time," he said.

"Was it?"

"Was what?"

"Marrying. You seem to question Claire's choice to remain unmarried, and perhaps my own by implication. What makes you so sure your decision was the right one?"

His shoulders twitched again. "We're talking about Miss Straussman, not me," he said, twisting his wedding band around his thick-knuckled finger as he spoke. It was not hard to imagine that the detective had done some boxing in his youth. As quickly as he let his guard down, he brought it right back up again.

"So, how about her sister? Hilda, wasn't it? Did she have a lot of . . . um . . . gentlemen friends, too?"

"No," I said. I would no sooner defame poor Hilda's memory than I would knowingly disparage her to her face.

"No, Hilda wasn't like Claire," I said,

choosing my words delicately. "She was big-boned and not much color to her."

SEVEN

APITHERAPY: The traditional practice of using bee venom and other products from the honeybee, including honey, pollen, royal jelly, and propolis, to treat illnesses and maintain health.

My conversation with Detective Grayson concluded on that most inconclusive note, and so for the next several weeks I arose each morning, hoping against hope that I would hear from the good detective again and that he would somehow help me make sense of this senseless tragedy. But no word came. From time to time I pulled from my billfold the identification card Detective Grayson had given me on the day we met and I thought about calling him. Once I went so far as to dial his office telephone number, but I'm afraid I hung up when a switchboard operator answered and asked me to hold.

"Hold what?" I remember thinking as I stared at the receiver in my hand.

Meanwhile the initial flurry of police activity soon dwindled down to nothing until the only visible reminder that something terrible had taken place next door were the strips of yellow police tape wrapped around the Straussmans' once tidy clapboard house, making it look from the outside like a forlorn birthday gift I had neither the heart to open nor the will to ignore. And all the while, the days grew longer and grayer, and I was left feeling as forgotten as the tattered police tape that finally came unstuck and blew away during an unseasonable rainstorm in early June, nearly a month after the Straussman sisters' murders.

The ground was still wet from the storm the following evening, and I was out of doors, tending to my number one hive, when I heard my name whispered softly above the subtle din of the hive.

"Albert?"

I turned my head toward the direction of the sound. It seemed to come from the shadows beneath the dripping bowers of the orange trees at the edge of my yard. I slipped my glasses off to wipe the mist from the lenses so that I might better peer into the darkness, when I heard my name called out again, only this time from behind me.

"Mr. Honig?"

I spun back around to see Detective Grayson standing at the foot of my back porch. Even without my glasses I could see that in his right hand he carried a large manila envelope. His left hand gripped the damp stair rail that I knew without seeing was sorely in need of a new coat of paint. I motioned for the detective to come join me at the hive. His reluctance resonated in the gathering dusk.

"I only need to talk to you a minute," he said.

"That's quite all right. We can talk out here," I said, raising my voice only slightly so that I wouldn't startle the bees, but that Detective Grayson might yet hear me more clearly from across the short expanse of my backyard. "I assure you, Detective Grayson, there's no need to worry. The field bees have all returned to their hives for the night."

Still, he appeared reluctant to venture any nearer.

"Are you wearing wool?" I inquired.

"How should I know?" he replied, clinging stubbornly to the back stair rail.

"You could check the label on your jacket," I suggested, making no move to return to the house. "It wouldn't be prudent

80

to approach me now if you are wearing wool. Bees don't like wool."

Detective Grayson started to say something, then appeared to think better of it. He opened the front flap of the brown suit jacket, the same one he was wearing when I first met him, and he held it out so that he might read the label sewed into the lining. He shook his head slowly, and once again, by his slow deliberate gestures and carriage, I was taken by how much he resembled a grizzled old bear.

"Polyester blend," he said, bringing his jacket flap back around and buttoning it shut. "Pretty sure the shirt's cotton."

"That's good," I said. "And your tie?"

The detective flattened his lips and drew them back from his teeth, which were surprisingly small and evenly spaced.

"You'd have to ask my wife," he said, confirming my earlier suspicion about his ties. "Probably silk, knowing her."

"Excellent," I said. "What about your socks?"

"Mr. Honig!" he fairly growled at me.

"Never mind," I said, hoping that by this time I'd distracted him just enough to calm his nerves. "Most of my guard bees are already bedded down, and any of the workers who aren't inside producing honey are most likely occupied tending their brood. I doubt there's a single bee still up and about that would pay the least bit of attention to your socks."

I motioned once again for him to approach, and this time he did so very slowly, casting his eyes right and left and right again as he crossed the yard to stand warily by my side. He reached for the clasp on the envelope he carried, but I held up my hand for him to stop.

"Listen," I said, bracing my hand on the hive stand and crouching low. I leaned my head toward the hive's bottom super and paused. "In the summer months, when bees are hardest at work, they beat their wings approximately two hundred fifty times per second. Musicians say that the note the bees' wings produce at this accelerated rate is C-sharp, below middle C, which interestingly enough is the same key in which whales, wolves, and dolphins also communicate. By contrast, the June bug, whose wings beat just forty-six times per second, produces the sound of F-sharp, three octaves below middle C."

"For the love of God, Mr. Honig, I just need to ask you a couple of quick questions," Detective Grayson said, his eyes scanning a tight arc around his head.

"It is for the love of all God's creatures that guides me," I said, and to his credit, the detective appeared at least slightly chastened by my words, and so I continued. "Quick answers are not always the same as the right ones. I find that the truth I seek is most often apparent to me when I take the time to listen."

The detective's ire seemed to deflate, if only a bit, as I spoke. For a long moment, the only sound between us was the dull roar of the hive.

"I wish I had your kind of time," Detective Grayson said at last, ducking suddenly as a moth flitted by his face. "But I've got a murder investigation here, and the longer it stays on the books, the colder the trail gets."

Again I leaned my ear into the hive and motioned for him to do the same.

"Jesus H. . . ." the detective muttered, his hazel eyes widening slightly. Then he shook his woolly head, slipped the manila envelope under his arm, and placed his hands on his knees. Exhaling audibly, he bent his stocky frame and stretched his neck toward the hive, though not quite near enough for his ear to touch the bottom level. We crouched there a moment, face-to-face, his left ear and my right poised mere inches from the hive's lowest level.

"Listen now," I urged. "What do you hear?"

"Please, Mr. Honig . . ." he said. But he did not move away from the hive. Nor did I. After a long pause, he exhaled loudly again. "Okay, it sounds like some kind of an engine, I guess."

"Now bring your head up a few inches," I instructed. "What do you hear?"

I heard the detective's knees creak. And I heard him exhale heavily again, this time through his nose.

"I don't know, Mr. Honig. Sounds pretty much like the same thing to me. Louder, maybe. Maybe a little louder," he conceded, this time moving just a tiny bit closer as he raised his head higher.

"Listen now. Right here. It's almost like a jet engine racing," I said, and then I motioned for him to bring his head even with the top super.

"What do you hear now?"

"It's not as loud," he said with what I perceived to be the first hint of wonder in his voice. "It's more of a whine than a roar. Like the engine's sputtering out or something."

I considered then for the first time that I might have misjudged the good detective. Though his manner could be abrupt, he certainly demonstrated better-than-average powers of observation and a concurrent ability to adjust to the dictates of a given situation. I began to consider the possibility that he might have a natural ear — just as Claire once had — for the delicate voices, slight rustles, and fluttering wings that indicate the many and varied activities that go on inside the hive.

"A week ago, when I listened to this super . . ."

"Super?" the detective interrupted. "What the Sam Hill is that?"

It was a reasonable question, really, for someone who'd never heard the common term for the boxlike hive component that fits on top of the brood chamber that houses the queen and her issue below. But there was something in his voice, an eagerness that floated just beneath the surface of his own awareness, and that's when I suspected he might be prone to bee fever after all. Not that he was bitten yet, but I could see that his eyes were steady now as he squinted into the dying light of the sun.

Patiently, then, I explained how wild bees seek out sheltered places like hollowed trees or crevices in buildings or rocks in which to build a hive.

"Did you know, Detective, that swarming

85

is initiated by a special dance called the *Schwirrlauf?*" I said. "*Schwirrlauf* is German for 'whir dance.' It's quite a choreographed procedure by which the workers move across the comb in a straight line without stopping. And as they move, they vibrate their partially spread wings every few seconds, making occasional contact with other workers, as they sing in a high piping voice. It's really quite lovely to behold."

Despite its aesthetic merits, however, beekeepers do their best to prevent this particular dance as one has little control over where the new colony may choose to settle. To this end we provide honeybees with a ready-made home that consists more or less of a sturdy base upon which we place a wooden box, or hive body, equipped with movable wooden frames with wire-reinforced brood foundations inside. On top of this base we stack, over the course of the honey-producing season, a series of shallower wooden boxes called supers that fit snugly one on top of another like so many stories on an apartment building.

"Inside each super are hung, side by side, ten to twelve wooden frames containing sheets. The uppermost stories are not as deep as the bottom two supers. These are the 'shallows' where our hardworking bees construct additional honeycombs in which they store the excess honey that is not needed to feed their queen and her young below," I explained to Detective Grayson. I pointed to the uppermost story on the hive next to me.

The detective nodded, this time as if he understood more, and not less, than I had told him.

"Only a week ago, even in the middle of the night, the buzz in this shallow was every bit as loud as it was in the levels beneath it," I said, now confident that the detective would make the effort to follow my train of thought. "That's because the bees were laboring round the clock to fill each cell with honey. And now . . . ?"

I paused to allow Detective Grayson time to reason out the answer. I assumed the same curiosity and doggedness that drew him to investigate crimes would spur him to puzzle out the answer to my question. He leaned closer to the hive, allowing his ear to brush against the side.

"By the sound of it, I'd say they're almost done with the job," the detective replied, smiling in spite of himself, as he brought himself back to an upright position with a heavy grunt.

I nodded, inordinately pleased by my

potential convert. "In another day or two, you will barely hear a whisper coming from this super. That's when I'll know it is full and capped and ready to be replaced with a fresh one on the next warm day. With any luck, and the Good Lord willing, I might even find a pot of eucalyptus gold inside."

I explained to the detective that the color and even the consistency of honey are greatly influenced by the nectars from which it is made. Honey from orange blossoms, for example, is milky white and carries a slight citrus tang, and alfalfa honey is amber-hued with a distinctive minty flavor, while the ever-abundant clover flower produces the sweet golden honey most commonly sold on supermarket shelves.

"Infinitely more rare, though sweeter by far than any store-bought honey, is that which is made from the blooms of the eucalyptus tree," I said. Detective Grayson said he had never heard of any such variety, and I told him I was not surprised.

"These magnificent trees will bloom branch by branch from January until July," I told the detective, "and every warm day, for the duration of their flowering season, the most intrepid of my field bees will work with special diligence to harvest the sweet eucalyptus nectar that they will in turn convert into the most savory honey I have ever tasted."

I have only rarely sampled this liquid jewel, however, as my bees seem to favor it above all honeys they produce and so hoard it most exclusively to nurture their brood.

A cool breeze had begun to blow as we spoke, and it set the old eucalyptus trees to creak and rustle almost on cue as I enumerated for Detective Grayson other peculiarities of honey production.

"Did you know, Detective, that honey is classified by the flower from which it is produced. It is further distinguished by color, clarity, and aroma."

"Can't say that I did," he replied.

"I recall a lovely little wildflower that flourished untended in the fields just north of our ranch when I was a boy. It brought forth a strongly flavored honey the color of Chinese jade."

"Green honey?" he said.

"Nearly," I said. Depending on the light, this honey could also resemble pond water reflecting the afternoon sunlight, or passing storm clouds, or, it suddenly occurred to me, Detective Grayson's eyes.

"What kind of flowers were they?"

"Sadly, I didn't think to learn their name," I replied. "I was just a boy, after all, and I assumed they'd always be there for the picking."

I recounted for the detective how after the day's chores were done I used to enjoy evening walks through the old orange and avocado groves that filled in the patchwork of fields and feed stores between the roads and railways that once upon a time surrounded my family's home.

"Summer nights aren't nearly as fragrant now," I said.

"I know what you mean," Detective Grayson said. "Heck, even thirty years ago, when the wife and I bought our first house — it wasn't far from here, by the way — there were still plenty of orange groves, and strawberry fields, and nice big yards and schools and parks and little corner grocery stores where parents didn't have to worry their tails off just to send their kids out to buy a quart of milk."

"Times have certainly changed," I agreed. And indeed I was so engaged in our conversation that I had forgotten all about the manila envelope the detective had been gripping so unobtrusively under his arm until he slipped it out and glanced back toward my unlit house that by this time sat swaddled in evening shadows.

"Kids today have no idea how nice this

neighborhood used to be," he said, running his stout fingers along the edge of the envelope. "Now there's nothing but apartment houses and strip malls and gas stations everywhere you look. It's a damn shame, if you'll pardon my French."

I thought for a moment that I might confess to the good detective that I wasn't altogether sorry that the old stands of avocado trees — which had been nearly as common as the orange groves once were — had likewise disappeared. Honey made from avocado blossoms is a deep dark brown and thick as tar. So dark and thick, in fact, that although the flavor is sweet as any other honey my bees produce, its pitchlike appearance dissuades most people of its palatability. Even I found it nearly impossible to sell.

"Yes, it was lovely here once upon a time," I said. I pulled a red kerchief from my pant pocket and wiped my brow to signal the end of another good day's work. By this time, we had made our way back to the rear of my house and were standing at the foot of the stairs.

"So tell me a little more about the Straussman sisters," the detective said, startling me just a bit by the abrupt change in subject.

"If I recall, they were early risers like your-self."

"I suppose so. At least, in their later years," I said. "Claire wasn't so much an early riser when she was younger, though. In fact, I recall a morning many years ago when I nearly broke her window tapping on it, so eager was I to rouse her with news of a wild swarm my father and I had spotted on our morning rounds."

"I'm not much of an early riser either," the detective said, tucking his shirttail back into his waistband, which was too tight by half an inch, as we trudged up the porch stairs and on into the kitchen. "Good thing the wife is a morning person and that she knows how to make a good strong pot of coffee or I don't think I'd ever get up."

"My mother was an early riser," I said. I crossed to the sink and picked up the bar of Lava soap on the basin's edge and began to scrub off the day's dust and grime as I did every evening before starting my supper preparations. When I turned back around to face Detective Grayson, I saw that he had removed a dozen photographs from the manila envelope he had been carrying and had laid them out on my kitchen table in three neat rows of four each.

"If you don't mind, Mr. Honig, I was hoping you could help me out here," he said. "We've been having a devil of a time locating any next of kin for the Straussman sisters. Or even anyone besides yourself who seems to know much of anything about them."

I finished drying my hands and set the kitchen towel back on the counter as I allowed my eyes to quickly scan the photographs. There was only one I didn't recognize, but just a few over which I wished to linger.

"I've taken the liberty of making copies of the pictures we found on your neighbors' mantelpiece," the detective said. "Do you recognize any of these people here?"

"Of course," I said.

"Excellent," he said, looking up from the photos to stare directly at me. "So what can you tell me about these good people here?"

EIGHT

CASTES: In apiculture, the three types of bees that comprise the colony, or the adult social structure of the hive, are workers, drones, and queen.

Though I had often seen these photographs displayed on the Straussmans' mantelpiece, having so many memories laid out in an evidentiary grid was another matter entirely. In the moment it took to compose myself, I wondered at the extant capacity of light-inflected silver to reach beyond the grave.

"That would be Mrs. Straussman. Mrs. Marvella Straussman," I said, pointing to the top left-hand photograph in the group.

In the photograph, taken more than forty years earlier, Mrs. Straussman was seated in the large wicker chair that had for many years been the sole piece of furniture to grace my neighbors' front porch. In her broad left hand, which had grown gnarled from the ravages of arthritis, she gripped the shaft of her badger-headed cane that leaned like a scepter across her knee and the arm of the chair. Her right elbow was crooked across the other armrest.

"This was Claire and Hilda's mother. She passed on in 1956. Complications of diabetes, I believe."

Mrs. Straussman was a large woman, and in the photograph, as had become her custom in her later years, she wore a dark high-necked dress that billowed down over her ample breasts to the tops of her black ankle-high shoes. Her thin gray hair was pulled tightly in a knot on top of her head, and her wide face was cast almost entirely in shadows, which — and I mean no disrespect — was probably just as well, as her features had grown increasingly bloated and mottled from a combination of sundry ailments.

"That would be Mr. and Mrs. Straussman," I said, moving on to the second photograph in the row, an infinitely more pleasant portrait of a young woman — just a girl, really — still in her teens, with plump rosy cheeks and a soft, wavy haircut. Dressed all in white lace, she held a small rose bouquet in one hand and with the other clutched the arm of a taller, fine-boned young man in his middle twenties who wore a starched white shirt, a diagonally striped tie, and a dark suit with a carnation in his lapel. Both bride and groom wore the unsmiling expressions fashionable with formal portraitures of the time, which would have been right before the start of the First World War.

"They were married in Saint Louis, I believe. Shortly before they moved to California," I added, though I'm not quite sure why I said it, or even why I recalled such a detail at the time.

"So this was the whole family?" Detective Grayson said, picking up the next photo in line and holding it to the light as if to get a better view. Mrs. Straussman was seated this time in the great wing-backed chair that used to dominate the corner next to the fireplace in the family's sitting room. Grown slightly heavier since her wedding photograph, though still not unappealingly so, Mrs. Straussman wore a long-sleeved, straight-waisted dress, most likely made of wool or some other such sturdy fabric. It flared out just below the hips into a loosely pleated skirt trimmed in a curlicued embroidery of sorts. In her arms she cradled a baby, swaddled in a pale hand-crocheted blanket and topped by a tiny lace bonnet.

To one side stood a solemn, plain-featured toddler, wearing a white knee-length sailor dress, white stockings, and white shoes. The older child's stubby fingers were loosely intertwined, allowing her hands to straddle Mrs. Straussman's right knee. Off to the other side, and slightly to the rear, stood Mr. Straussman, clad in a dark suit and fedora. His left hand rested on the back of his wife's chair, his right hand fingered a long, chain-link watch fob.

"Yes," I said. "This is all there was of the family at that time."

"When do you suppose this was?" Detective Grayson said. "I'd make it to be about 1925, maybe '30, by the way they're all dressed."

I shook my head and pointed to the baby in the picture.

"Earlier than that," I said. "Claire can't be more than three or four months old here, and since she was born in 1920 — June twenty-third, to be precise — I would have to say this photograph dates from sometime in the fall of that year."

Detective Grayson nodded and put the photograph back on the table. He picked up the next one in the grid and handed it to me. "So who's this kid?"

I stared at the sepia-toned portrait of the

small, wide-eyed boy with ringlets of light curly hair. He sat perched like one of Botticelli's cherubs on the arm of an overstuffed davenport. No more than two years old, the boy wore the kind of white baby shoes that doting parents used to bronze as keepsakes, white kneesocks, short pants, and a light-colored shirt with large dark buttons. But unlike Botticelli's laughing seraphs', the child's countenance was as somber as his elders, and his pose appeared just as formal, in its own way, with his little-boy legs crossed at the ankles and one chubby arm artificially draped across the back of the sofa.

"This was Claire and Hilda's older brother," I said. Though I never knew him in the flesh, it seems strange the boy's name did not leap readily to my tongue. I stared a moment longer at his preternaturally large, sad eyes. "Henry, I believe his name was. No, that wasn't it," I stammered. "It was Harry. Harry Junior. He died before I was born."

Detective Grayson frowned but did not speak. He had withdrawn his notebook and ballpoint pen from his jacket pocket. He clicked the pen several times.

"What happened to him?" the detective asked. I took a moment to consider how best to answer. Everything I knew about him was only so much hearsay.

"As Claire explained it to me," I said, "Mrs. Straussman was playing with the boy in the front room when she thought she heard someone knock on the kitchen door and she went back to see who it was."

I explained to the detective that since we lived so near the railroad depot, it wasn't at all unusual at that time for the occasional tramp to inquire after odd jobs. But there was no one at the door, at least according to Claire's account, and when her mother returned to the room she found the boy lying unconscious on the floor. After her initial efforts to bring him around failed, she frantically rang up the doctor, and, as the story went, the doctor hurried over to the house, but it was already too late.

"Claire said her mother left Harry Junior alone for only a moment, and just as quick as that he was gone." I put the photograph back down on the table. "He couldn't have been more than two or three years old. Claire often said she didn't think her father ever quite got over young Harry's death. Or her mother either, for that matter."

"How long ago would that have been?" the detective asked.

"Let's see . . . 1915, maybe 1916 at the

latest," I said, and the detective scribbled this information down, too.

"And you say no one ever figured out what killed him?" he said.

"Not to my recollection," I said. "There was some speculation it might have been pneumonia, but no one seemed to recall him being particularly ill at the time. Of course this was all before I was born. Before Hilda and Claire came along, even. And you have to understand that in those days families didn't talk about this sort of thing. What little I know of the poor boy I heard many years later from Claire, who likewise heard the story secondhand, from her father. And this being a particularly painful subject, Claire said her father did not elaborate beyond the bare facts, even when she pressed him as far as she dared."

"So there wasn't any formal inquiry?" he pressed.

"Not that I'm aware of. But again, Detective, back then it wasn't uncommon for a family to lose a child, or even two, before they reached maturity. Tuberculosis was not uncommon. Flus were pandemic. This was before penicillin. Before so many advances in modern medicine. My own dear mother lost a baby at birth. We nearly lost her as well. It's a wonder she even consented to try again. Had she not wanted to give my father a son, I doubt I would even have been born."

The detective seemed to consider how best to respond without making too big a fuss over what he rightly perceived to be a most personal revelation on my part.

"That's a shame," he said at last, though he did not specify the particular shame to which he referred. The detective stared at me a moment more as if he had something else to say, but perhaps I misread his intent as he turned back to his notebook and underlined the last few words he'd written before moving on to the next photograph.

Thankfully, this one brought back much happier memories. Though the face in the snapshot was shrouded by a large beekeeper's hat and veil, the young girl beneath was only too easy to recognize.

"That's Claire, wearing one of my old bee hats," I said, smiling from the memory. "I remember the day I took this picture, with my mother's Brownie camera, out in our backyard."

"And when was that?" Detective Grayson asked.

"The spring of 1932."

"You're sure of that?"

"Absolutely."

I explained that although we had lived next door for many years, Claire and I had not become friendly until after my father was summoned to the Straussmans' home to remove a wild colony of bees that had taken up residency in their parlor wall.

"Claire was frightened of the bees at first, but she was fascinated by them as well," I said. "So much so that shortly after my father had rid her family's home of all its unwanted guests, she began to stop by our house after school to watch us tend our hives. She told me some years later that she had grown so accustomed to the constant hum the bees had produced while they were living in her parlor wall that she began to miss it once they were gone.

"Still, she was hesitant to come close to our bees until my mother presented her with one of our spare beekeeper hats and netting and a pair of white cotton coveralls and a shirt that no longer fit me."

I recounted how my mother had tucked Claire snugly into this borrowed outfit, and my father had taken her by the hand and led her to within a few steps of our gentlest hive. Even after all those years, I could not suppress a smile.

"Unfortunately, a robust party of field bees chose that very moment to return to the hive, and poor Claire went skittering back to the porch like a beetle across a hot stove. She refused to come any closer to the hives again for at least another hour or more."

I chuckled at the memory before remembering that the good detective's initial reaction to my bees that late afternoon had been no less skittish.

"Most people are fearful of bees until they get to know their ways," I said quickly, hoping to defuse any unintended affront. I offered that such trepidation had been growing among the general public ever since reports of great hordes of killer bees advancing northward from Latin America had surfaced.

"While I have yet to see one of these so-called killer bees — or Africanized, as they are more properly called — I am nonetheless certain that their reputed lethal nature is greatly exaggerated."

I set the photograph of young Claire back in its place on the grid.

"Did you know that in Guatemala they now call these fierce creatures *bravo* bees?" The detective did not reply. I sensed a growing restiveness in his demeanor, as he had begun to rub a muscle in his neck just below his left ear with practiced precision. "But I digress, as surely you are more rightfully concerned with the lethal activities of our fellow man."

"I'm afraid so," the detective said, releasing his neck and reaching unexpectedly for a photograph in the bottom row instead of the next one in line. The picture, which appeared to be one of the more recent of any there, was in color, and showed a smiling young serviceman, a Marine, in full uniform, standing next to a large military-style helicopter.

"Tustin, 1975" was inscribed in a photographic studio's gold-stamped imprint in the bottom left corner of the picture.

"Do you know who this is?"

Though the uniform was unfamiliar, there was no mistaking the young man's dark wide-set eyes and the flash of his brilliant white smile, which was made all the more dazzling in contrast to his coppery skin. I shook my head, slowly, sadly, not knowing quite what to say or how to say it.

The detective, whose growing impatience may have affected his perceptiveness, misread my silence for ignorance and replaced the photograph on the table and reached for another. Out of respect for the dead — or at least that is what I told myself then — I decided it best to let sleeping dogs lie.

"That would be Claire and Hilda's cousin, Margaret, from Detroit," I said after a moment that stretched to eternity and back again as I directed my eyes toward the snapshot of a slender middle-aged woman in a bright floral dress that Detective Grayson handed me next. My mind, however, remained riveted on the young soldier in the previous photograph. I had often wondered what had become of David Gilbert. I certainly did not believe Claire's assertion that he had returned to Alabama to live with his grandparents because I believed that there had never been any such Alabama relations. But there had been no opportunity for me to press the issue with her. It had been ten years since I'd last spoken to Claire face-to-face, and our final, long-ago conversation had been disastrous, to say the least.

"Mr. Honig?"

"I'm sorry," I said, shaking my head. I sat down at the table, more to allow myself a moment to clear my head than out of actual fatigue. The detective settled into the seat next to me.

"Do you know how to get in touch with this woman?" he said, tapping the photograph.

"No, I'm afraid not," I said. Margaret had seemed so old when I'd met her in 1963, but decades had passed since then, and what I saw now was a mature woman, to be sure, but one with a youthful, almost defiant tilt to her hip as she posed beneath the shade of the Straussmans' front porch.

"I'm not even sure she's still alive," I said. "It's been so long since I saw her last."

"Do you remember her name then? Or whether she had any children?"

"I'm sorry, Detective Grayson," I said, regretting even as I said it, the number of times I'd already had to apologize for my ignorance in the short span of time I'd known him. "I believe her name was Margaret. I think she was Claire and Hilda's cousin. I only met her once when she came out to California for Mr. Straussman's funeral, and that was . . . oh my goodness . . . thirty years ago at least. I remember her only because she was the sole family member to attend the funeral outside of Claire and Hilda, Mrs. Straussman having passed nearly ten years earlier. Margaret stayed on at the Straussmans' house for a few days after the funeral, but the only time I spoke to her was when my father and I stopped by after the services to pay our respects. We brought a jar of eucalyptus honey from our special cache. I remember that Claire told Margaret that she bet she had never tasted anything this good back in Detroit, and Margaret had agreed. That is how I know where she was from, but that is all I know."

"I see," said the detective, making it plain from the tone of his voice that he did not see at all and was not likely to let the matter of the Straussmans' tangled relations go until he did.

The last of the pictures on the table that Detective Grayson asked me to examine were simple snapshots of Hilda and Claire, posed together at various odd places and stages in their lives.

There was one of Claire and Hilda at the seashore. They weren't much older than toddlers. They were wearing billowy shorts and tiny sun tops, smiling and scooping sand into piles, while ocean waves crashed behind them. Their father must have taken this snapshot. I believe he used to take them to the beach on the Red Car, the electric trolley line that used to run from Anaheim to Huntington Beach. I don't believe Mrs. Straussman ever went in much for beach excursions, even before she lost her health.

There were a few other snapshots that the detective and I examined at some length. I can't say I fully understood his interest in this fishing expedition, as he called it, but mine was surely kindled by the fond memories they recalled. My favorite image of the lot had been taken in one of those old-fashioned amusement park photo booths. In their adolescence, Claire and her sister used to take the Red Car by themselves out to what was known as the Fun Zone, a small seaside attraction near Newport Beach. Claire often urged me to accompany them, but I always found some reason to decline.

"Come on, you silly goose!" Claire would wheedle. "You can see for miles from on top of the Ferris wheel."

Though I have lived my entire life within five miles of the Pacific Ocean, as the crow flies, I have yet to see it firsthand. Looking back now, I think I might have enjoyed the view. That and the pure scent of the sea, which Claire used to say was even saltier up close than what I am able to perceive on the ocean breeze that carries inland most evenings.

Another photograph showed Claire and Hilda well into their middle years, their arms looped at the elbows and standing in front of their father's old humpbacked Buick, which must have been half again as old as they were. I'm guessing they inherited the car from their father when he died, and he'd probably bought it twenty years before that. I think the Rambler station wagon was the only car they bought on their own. The Straussmans were nothing if not frugal.

The most recent of the photographs had to have been taken not more than two or three years before Claire and Hilda died. It pictured them seated on their front porch behind a small table stacked with beeswax candles and jars of honey for sale.

The detective wondered aloud who could have taken it.

"It certainly wasn't me," I assured him. "Perhaps one of their honey customers."

"Anyone in particular come to mind?" the detective prodded.

"Oh, I wouldn't know," I replied. "There were a few who seemed to stop by fairly regularly, but I don't know any of them by name. I couldn't even tell you if they were from round here or just passing through."

While once a quiet country road, the street that fronted our houses at that time had become the main thoroughfare from the city's west end to the freeway, effectively cutting us off from the city's original downtown to the east and with it any real sense of community that once existed here.

Hearkening back in my mind to those earlier days, I lingered a moment longer on the last photograph the detective handed to me. It showed Claire, still in her teens, with her hair swept up in the thick ponytail she took to wearing during that time of her life. She had been in one of her playful moods, sticking her tongue out at the camera bold as you please, while poor Hilda, trying her best to keep her composure, looked as though she had just swallowed a lemon. There was an intimacy in the tilt of Claire's head toward Hilda's I'd not noticed before.

"You know, Mr. Honig, you were right about one thing," Detective Grayson said as he gathered the photographs up and slipped them back into the envelope. "That Claire sure was a looker when she was young."

NINE

DRIFTING OF BEES: The failure of honey-bees to return to their own hive in apiaries comprised of many hives. Young bees tend to drift more than old ones, and bees from dwindling colonies tend to drift to larger ones.

That Claire had been an intriguing child who had grown into a lovely, vibrant young woman was beyond dispute, as far as I was concerned. That she had formed an obvious attachment to her cousin, Margaret, who to my eye came off every bit as drab as Hilda, had always been a mystery in the same way that butterflies and moths are zoologically linked simply because both species share a common, four-winged structure and both undergo a series of transformations, from egg to larva to pupa, emerging re-formed, from a self-constructed chrysalis to an airborne imago.

It was much less difficult for Detective Grayson to establish the comprehensive familial links between Claire and her cousin, whose full married name was Margaret Louise Lennox. Perhaps it was the bulldoggedness of the detective's impersonal curiosity that suited him so well to his vocation, while the personal affinity I feel for my bees fundamentally inclines me to mine.

"She's buried alongside her husband, Ralph, in a family plot in Hillsborough Cemetery, just outside of Detroit," Detective Grayson informed me only three days after our previous conversation. He came by my house at noontime and knocked on my front door just as I was sitting down to a lunch of bread, honey, and sliced oranges that I'd picked only moments before.

"Mind if I come in?" he said.

"Please," I said.

The detective followed me back through the hall that connects my parlor and dining room to the kitchen, and once we were comfortably seated at the dinette he informed me that since we knew that Margaret had been related to the Straussman sisters on their father's side, it had been a fairly simple matter for him to sift through the Wayne County Hall of Records marriage licenses to locate one for a Margaret

Straussman who wed Ralph Lennox in 1949. He told me he found Margaret's and Ralph's respective death certificates, and all their children's birth certificates besides.

"They've got three kids, and eight grandkids so far," Detective Grayson said. "Most of the family's still living in the same neighborhood they grew up in, in case you're wondering."

To be honest, I had not given poor Margaret so much as a passing thought since Detective Grayson slipped her photograph back into the envelope with all the rest, but I certainly did not say so. I invited the detective to join me in my meal, which, to my surprise, he accepted.

"Just a slice of bread, Mr. Honig. And maybe some more of that lemonade, if you have any," he said.

I poured a glass for him and another for myself, and then prepared a slice of bread and honey for him as he withdrew his notebook and pen from his jacket pocket and quickly thumbed to a page midway through the tablet.

"Margaret died about five years ago, from lung cancer," he told me, reading from his notes. "She smoked like a chimney, according to her kids. Three packs a day. Lucky Strikes. I had a real nice chat with her oldest daughter, Susan, on the phone yesterday. She said her mother picked up the habit when she joined the army back during the war — World War Two. Susan said they all tried to get their mother to quit smoking for years, but the old lady was stubborn as a donkey. Told them she'd been smoking since before they were born and that she darn well intended to keep on smoking until the day she died, which is exactly what she did."

It seemed to me I detected a hint of admiration in the detective's voice and I told him so.

"Well, it just sounds like old Margaret was a real character," he said, continuing to scan his notes. "Traveled round a bit after the war, then came back to Detroit and got a job in one of the big auto plants. GM, I think. She worked right on the assembly line with the men and even got herself elected shop steward.

"Margaret was in her early thirties when she met Ralph. Apparently he was some kind of union bigwig. After she got married, Margaret quit her job, and Ralph and her bought a house out in the suburbs and started raising a family. Susan — she's a real nice lady, by the way, you should give her a call sometime."

"Perhaps I will," I said. We both knew I never would, but it seemed the thing to say. The detective stared for a moment longer at his notes, then set the notebook back down on the table, leaned back in his chair, and linked his thick fingers across his expansive belly. I noticed his fingers were freckled. It occurred to me that his hair might have skewed red in his younger years and that he might have made a fine, lusty English lord in another life, though perhaps more reflective, more conflicted, than most. I did not see in him a need for power so much as a sense of duty to move others to do the right thing, whatever he perceived that to be.

"Susan said she never met Claire or Hilda. But her mother used to talk about them from time to time. Claire especially. Seemed like Margaret and Claire were pretty tight when they were younger."

The detective told me that Claire had even moved up to Detroit for a few months, that she'd roomed with Margaret and had held a job selling lingerie in a department store downtown.

"Susan seems to think it was right around the start of the war. Not too long before Margaret enlisted."

I handed the detective his plate of honeyed bread, and orange slices, and sat down in front of the meal I'd already prepared for myself. I took a long sip of lemonade.

"Susan remembers her mother telling her that Claire was sharing an apartment with Margaret, happy as a clam, until Claire's mother showed up one day at their doorstep. The way Susan tells it, old Mrs. Straussman barged right in and told Claire to get herself back home. Something about Claire's sister taking sick."

"Hilda was always a bit fragile," I said, separating the peeled orange half on my plate into seven individual wedges. The detective took a bite of bread.

"Hey, this isn't half bad, Mr. Honig. What kind of honey is this?"

"Just orange blossom," I said. I raised the bread to my lips, and at that moment the sweet aroma of orange blossoms, the same orange blossoms that drew my parents south and infused my childhood with the mild sweet scent of spring, caressed my memory like the transportive aroma of a long-forgotten perfume in a passing crowd.

It was June 24, 1942. I remember the date because it was the evening after Claire's twenty-second birthday. Claire's parents didn't believe in celebrating birthdays, and I had made a point, since we'd first become friends a decade before, to find a way to make her feel as cherished as my own dear parents had made my sister and I feel every year on the anniversaries of our own births. It wasn't as though they spoiled us with extravagance. A simple dinner of our favorite foods, a home-baked cake, a small gift presented at the dinner table, had been enough to make our birthdays feel special. Claire had always seemed so appreciative of our secret celebrations. The evening of her twenty-second birthday had seemed especially sweet.

"This is absolutely delicious," she had cooed as she sucked the honey from the comb she'd lifted dripping from the mason jar I'd wrapped in one of my father's discarded newspapers. She licked the honey from her fingers before she reached for my hand. I don't know why I drew mine back. Only that I did.

"Here," I said. Reaching behind my back, I handed her another, smaller package. It was just another sheet of newsprint folded over a handful of roasted walnuts I'd asked my mother to help me prepare. Claire had opened the packet and this time gripped my hand before I could pull it back. She poured half the nuts into the palm of my hand and the other half into hers and, looking directly into my eyes, she'd urged me to

117

do as she did as she slipped a roasted nut between her lips and began to chew. When the walnuts were gone, we'd sat quietly for a few moments more, simply enjoying the evening breeze. Then Claire reached out and took my hand in hers. There were so many things I wanted to say, but none of the words in my head made any sense. The moon was high in the sky when she rose at last to take her leave.

"Can we meet tomorrow evening?" she asked. An unaccustomed urgency had crept into her voice.

"If you'd like," I said. "I'll be out by our number fourteen hive after dinner. I believe we have a new queen on the way."

"Promise me," she said.

"I promise."

The orange trees were in full bloom the following evening, and I had been so engrossed in the goings-on inside my hive that I had not heard her approach. Unaware of Claire's intentions at the time, I touched my index finger to my lips when she started to speak, and then, stooping down to press my ear to the hive, I had urged her to do the same.

"Can you hear them?"

She stooped down, facing me, and leaned her ear against the hive. I watched her lips part with just the hint of a smile as the moonlight played off her upturned eyes, setting them to glisten like sapphires set in cool alabaster. Had I not known she was made of mortal flesh and blood, I would have sworn at that very moment the mythical goddess Artemis had descended from the night sky to kneel beside me in the dust. I found it hard to breathe. I was twenty years old. At that moment I was convinced we were both immortal.

"Yes!" she said, squeezing my hand and using it at the same time to boost herself upright. "The queen is ready to hatch."

I felt the blood rush through my hand to hers.

"I wish I could be here with you to see your new queen," Claire said. I noticed then that she was dressed in a white linen skirt and matching jacket that I had never seen her wear before. I saw also that she was clutching a pair of white gloves in one hand, and a small, battered suitcase was leaning against a tree a few yards away.

"Claire?" I said, releasing her hand.

"I have a train to catch tonight," she replied, bending slightly at the waist to brush the dust from her knees and smooth her skirt. "I only just came here to say good-bye."

"Where are you going?" I said.

"That's for me to know and you to find out," she said, laughing coquettishly.

I repeated my question, and Claire's face lost its playful edge. She squeezed her eyes shut and ran her fingers through her hair.

"I can't tell you that," she said. When I asked her why, she sighed, and then she told me she didn't want anyone to know her plans and that telling me was the surest way to broadcast them all over the neighborhood. When I assured her that I could keep her secret, she shook her head. Her dark curls rippled down her shoulders like a waterfall.

"I know you think you could," she said. "But the problem with you is, you think of truth as an absolute."

"Truth does not blush," I said.

"That's exactly what I'm talking about, Albert. There are no shades of gray in your perfectly ordered world. If somebody happened to ask you where I'd gone, you'd tell them."

"And why shouldn't I?"

"What would life be without secrets?" she said.

"I don't understand. I thought I was your friend."

"You are, silly. Just not the kind to tell

secrets to."

"But why?"

"Because you'd never lie for me. It's just not in your nature."

"I swear to you, Claire," I started to plead. She stopped me at once.

"Don't, Albert. Don't make a promise both of us know you can't keep," she said. "You're just going to have to trust me when I say I have my reasons."

"How can I trust you when you won't trust me in return?"

"I trust your heart, Albert. It's that darn head of yours," she said softly, tapping my temple with her slender white finger. "You think too much. And you think you always have to tell the truth, the whole truth, and nothing but the truth, so help you God."

"But Claire . . ."

She held up that impossibly perfect finger again and pressed it this time to my lips. "You know it's true, Albert. You couldn't tell a little white lie for me and say I'd gone off to New York or Paris or even Kathmandu even if I asked you pretty please with sugar on top. And God forbid I should ask you to simply say nothing. No, you couldn't do that either. What's that you call it? Sins of omission."

Well, of course I had to ask her what was

so wrong with telling the truth. But as soon as I'd uttered the words, I wished that I could call them back. Claire turned away from me to face the darkness beyond the grove, and I watched her shoulders droop ever so slightly as I listened to the slow exhale of her breath.

"Perhaps no one will even ask me where you've gone," I said hopefully, but Claire only laughed one last time, softer and without mirth.

"Oh, Albert, you know they will," she said. "Between you and me, let's just say I'm going somewhere far, far away. And that I may never come back."

"But why, Claire?" I said, trying as best I could to match the soft intonation of her voice if only to calm the flutter of panic beating in my chest. If I were as divorced from my feelings as Claire claimed, why could I not conjure up a single logical reason to convince her to stay? Why did I feel as if there wasn't enough oxygen in all the world to fill my lungs?

Chewing her bottom lip, Claire picked at the lace cuff of one of her gloves for a moment or two. Then she extended her arms and began to hum a soft, piping melody. Shuffling delicately to a three-step cadence that seemed to stir her soul beneath the moonlight, she came to a stop in front of me.

"Albert," she said at last, grasping my hand in hers, "haven't you ever wondered what it would be like to go anywhere you liked, whenever and with whomever you wished, with no one to answer to but your-self?"

I shook my head and wondered instead how to explain to Claire that I did not feel in the least constrained by the boundaries of my life.

"My home, my family, and of course my bees, provide me with all I could want in the way of company and creature comforts," I replied in all sincerity. "Honestly, Claire, I see no need to look beyond my own back-yard to find whatever my heart might de-sire."

"That's nice enough for you and Dorothy Gale. But maybe my backyard isn't all that swell," Claire said, turning her face skyward. Her eyes glistened in the moonlight, which continued to work radiant magic on her finely chiseled features. I imagined a bow slung over her shoulder, a stag at her feet. "Haven't you ever wanted to see the world, Albert?"

"All that I care about in the world is right here with me," I said softly — so softly, in fact, that I am not altogether certain even today that Claire heard me.

"That's the beauty of it, Albert. Don't you see?"

When I shook my head, she placed her lips close to my ear, barely whispering, "I'm the ship. You're the mooring. There's something to be said for knowing our places in the world."

I believe she must have read something in my eyes of the confusion I felt when I turned to face her because she gripped my hand tightly and gave me a quick kiss on the cheek. Then she turned, picked up her valise, and ran swiftly into the night.

I had taken some bittersweet pleasure over the years wondering at the sights she'd seen, the people she'd met, the unimaginable things she'd done to calm her restless spirit. I had imagined Claire going off to find all manner of high adventure: riding the trolleys in New York, dining at a sidewalk cafe in Paris, booking passage on the famous *Orient Express*. When she returned home less than six months after she'd gone, she never spoke a word to me about where she'd been. She made it clear I was never to ask. This is why I had believed many wild and improbable things about Claire, but never in all the intervening years between her absence and

Detective Grayson's unexpected revelation had I imagined she'd run away from home to become a department store clerk in Detroit.

"Mr. Honig?" The detective's voice seemed to float like a feather just beyond my reach. "Mr. Honig? Are you okay?"

"I'm sorry," I said, placing my honeyed bread back on my plate uneaten. The sweet orange tang seemed suddenly less appealing than it had only moments before. "You're telling me that Claire went to Detroit?"

"Apparently so," he said. "Funny how Margaret was the only one of her bunch that ever traveled much beyond Detroit."

"I suppose so," I said, though *funny* is not the word I would have chosen. Detective Grayson folded the remainder of his bread in half and swallowed it all in one large bite.

"Would you like another piece?" I said, sliding my plate across the table. "I'm not as hungry as I thought."

"If you're sure you're not going to eat it," Detective Grayson replied after only the slightest hesitation. "I'm going to have to tell my wife about this. She's always bugging me to eat something besides junk food for lunch. This stuff's good for you, right?"

"As my father used to say, 'A little sweet

honey is good for whatever ails you,' " I told him.

"I don't doubt it," the detective said, downing the last of his lemonade. "Say, I almost forgot. Margaret's daughter didn't know too much more about Claire or Hilda other than what I've already told you, but she said she thought they had some relatives living down South, in Mississippi or Alabama, maybe. You wouldn't have any idea who that might be or how we could get hold of them now?"

I reflected on the nature of lies and the sins of omission.

"No," I said, finding the weight of my silence more bearable than Claire had once predicted I would. "No, I'm sorry, Detective, I don't."

TEN

CELTIC LORE: Bees are the purveyors of wisdom from the otherworld; when a bee flies into a house, a stranger is coming.

Though my bees kept me busy during the bright daylight hours following Claire's and Hilda's untimely deaths, the gray light of dawn and gathering dusk provoked me to inward reflection, and at these times I found myself most unable to quell the sense growing within me that even though I had washed my hands of the Straussman family years before, they had not relinquished their hold on me.

As was quickly becoming the pattern, it was several more weeks before I heard from Detective Grayson again, and in the intervening time I found myself rising even earlier than had been my custom, to pace my bedroom lost in old memories and forgotten plans, and then again at night lingering in my parlor chair long past my bedtime, rereading passages from familiar philosophical treatises. Other times I perused our family Bible, or leafed through the scrapbooks of newspaper articles and photographs of historic events, noteworthy exploits of hometown acquaintances, and quoted words of wisdom from famous men that it had been my dear mother's habit to collect in chronological volumes until her death.

"An idle mind is the devil's playground," she used to say any time she saw me lolling about with nothing to do. It was my mother who taught me my letters before I'd turned three. By the time I was five, she was helping me sound out words in the books she had cherished when she was just a child. *Little Lord Fauntleroy* was our very favorite, so much so that I took to rolling my britches up to my knees in imitation of the young lord's fashion of the day.

"Little Lord Albert," my mother used to call me once upon a time. There was a poem by Henry Wadsworth Longfellow that my mother insisted I learn just to teach me elocution.

"Repeat after me, my little lord," she'd say, patting my knee as we sat side by side on the davenport after dinner.

There was a little girl, / Who had a little curl, / Right in the middle of her forehead. / When she was good, / She was very good indeed, / But when she was bad she was horrid.

It took me some time to reconcile the letters and sounds to fashion a rhyme between *forehead* and *horrid,* but my mother said this would serve me well someday. Truth be told, I had by that time begun to prefer young Jim Hawkins's adventures to the subtleties of Henry Wadsworth Longfellow's rhyme schemes. But of course I soon put such childish fancies aside as I began to explore more serious literary pursuits. I have my mother to thank for that as well, as she was the one who first took me by the hand and walked me the mile from our house to the public library.

"Anything you want to know, my little lord, you will find here," my mother said, introducing me to Mrs. Bass, the head librarian. Mrs. Bass was reluctant to allow me to explore the library on my own, at least at first. She taught Sunday school along with my mother, and I believe she thought I might be drawn like many boys my age to some of the racier books on the shelves. I assured her I had no such interests.

I asked her to show me to the poetry section on my first visit, which she did with a prim nod to my mother, who kissed me lightly on my cheek and thereafter left me alone to build upon the literary foundation she had laid.

As I reflect now upon those dark weeks that followed Claire's and Hilda's murders, I find myself returning to a quotation from Henry Wadsworth Longfellow that my mother had pasted in one of her scrapbooks: "The cruelest lies are often told in silence."

And kept in darkness, I should like to add. Though we had not spoken for more than a decade before their deaths, I found myself struck at last, that melancholy autumn, by the finality of our estrangement. Late into the chill of a particular evening, six months and twelve days after they had died, as I sat on my front porch stitching a patch onto the knee of my worn dungarees, I found myself staring into the dying light for impossible signs of activity from within my neighbors' sealed house when I caught a glimpse of a dark figure standing in the window of the parlor. It was just for an instant, but it was enough to cause me to grip the arms of my chair until I felt the rough wood bite into my palms. I confess I had been having trouble sleeping through the night and so it is possible that I may have dozed off for a moment or two. But whether I did or not is beside the point. I reacted with the same instinctive gasp of horror and pity I invariably feel, if only for a second, when I mistake a shard of blown tire from a distance for the body of a cat that has been thrown to the side of the road by a speeding car. In those unguarded moments of distant perception, what we think we see, real or not, causes us to feel what we do. And once we've felt whatever we've felt, we can't take it back.

Claire tried to tell me that more than once. To my regret, I dismissed her emotions as vehemently as she dismissed my empiricism. Perhaps we should have listened to each other more.

I do believe now that I may have been the only one who might have lifted the shroud of pain that cloaked the dark interior of the Straussman house while anyone worth caring about still lived within, but for any number of reasons I did not.

In my own defense, I can only say that Saint Thomas Aquinas once wrote that there are three things necessary for the salvation of man: to know what he ought to believe, to know what he ought to desire, and to know what he ought to do. Until recently, I thought I knew my mind in this regard, but when I take into account my lifelong connection to the Straussman family I find my personal salvation wanting on all three counts.

ELEVEN

SWARM: A natural method of honeybee propagation when a collection of bees that includes a healthy queen breaks off from the mother colony to establish a new, independent hive.

"Bee fever" is what those of my generation used to call it when a man fell in love with honeybees and got himself his first hive. Strictly speaking, I never had to take the plunge myself, as there have been beehives in our family for at least three generations. I suppose you could say I was born with the fever already aboil in my blood, passed down from father to son, and to son again, and I never had to do any more to stoke the fire of this singular passion than to step outside my back door and observe our bees busying themselves around and about any of the dozens of hives we'd always kept.

Happily, my mother was readily persuaded

133

to share my father's dispositional affinity for bees. They were wed in June of 1915, directly after my mother graduated from high school and my father was nigh on his twenty-first year. Though bee fever isn't as common in a woman as a man, neither is it rare enough to seem particularly odd that hardly had their wedding vows been spoken that my mother took to hurrying through her household chores — cooking and cleaning, bustling beyond the norm even among the hardworking farmwives of her day — in order to join my father out at the hives by midafternoon. Together they would fuss and fret over a listless queen one day or fight off an invasion of small brown ants the next.

It seems somehow stranger to me, coming from the bloodlines we did, that my elder sister grew up unaffected by our family's affection for bees. While she would cheerily confess to a fondness for the fruits of our tireless labor, she found little pain in leaving the hives behind when she chose to marry and move back up the Pacific Coast to where her husband found permanent employment in the shipyards of Washington State.

I suppose my sister was not so much rejecting our parents' way of life as she was following in my mother's reverse footsteps by abandoning her childhood home to follow her husband's penchant. Convinced by my father of the advantages of a warm, dry climate over their native Oregon's cold, wet coast in terms of optimum honey production, my mother had wholeheartedly endorsed his decision to migrate southward in the second year of their long and happy marriage. In her own cheerful manner, she helped my father scour the sprawling bean fields and orchards that blanketed the coastal plain south of Los Angeles for the ideal location to establish strong hives and a good home for the family they hoped to raise together. After a considerable search, my parents chose a ten-acre parcel of land with a small orange grove to the rear of the property in the county named after those selfsame groves that to their delight were situated directly beneath a well-traveled flyway of wild bees from two different directions. The east side of the property abutted a Santa Fe Railway depot and switching yard, and the west bordered the Straussmans' farm, which abounded with walnut and almond orchards fronted by an imposing clutch of peppertrees that shaded their single-story wood-frame bungalow.

Although there already was a small cottage, not unlike the Straussmans', on our property when acquired, it had suffered noticeable flood damage the previous winter. Unfortunate as the flooding from the Santa Ana River had been to the community, however, it allowed my parents to purchase the property and existing building at a discount.

My father used the money he'd saved on the property to order a new Sears Roebuck and Co. two-story, six-room bungalow, known familiarly as "The Sherbourne." Like all catalog homes of its ilk, the materials and plans — including all lumber, millwork, laths, shingles, pipes, gutters, sash weights, hardware, and paint — were shipped, as advertised, directly to the nearby freight depot in two boxcars. My parents lived in the original cottage, which was eventually converted into a honey shed, during the two years it took to build our new home. My father took pride in its sturdy design after the fashion of the day, with its gabled roof, wide clapboard siding, and large front porch. He found it pleasing to sit on the porch swing he built after the house was finally done and relish the evening breeze that blew in from the ocean after a hard day's work.

"This is built to last," he would often say, smacking his hand on the beam that supported the porch roof.

I am sure that when the Straussmans moved into their home only a few years before my parents built theirs, they were just as convinced of its enduring legacy.

My mother died more than forty years ago, on by far the hottest day of what had been an uncommonly hot summer. My father followed her to the grave thirteen long years later on a cold winter's day, leaving me alone to honor their memory in the house they built.

When I think of my dear mother, which is often even after all these years, I think of her standing by the stove, an apron tied around her midriff, a tea towel draped over her shoulder, and a light dusting of flour covering her hands, as she watches over a batch of chicken frying in the cast-iron skillet her mother gave her as a wedding present.

"Go set the table," she would call out to my sister and me as the chicken browned. "Hurry up, now."

She rarely had to call us twice. My father was another matter. It wasn't that he consciously ignored her, but I think he found it most difficult to relinquish those quiet moments at the end of the day when he used to sit by himself on the front porch swing gathering his thoughts.

My father once told me, in a rare conversation we shared on that very swing, that he knew he would marry my mother the very moment she offered to help him change a super. He told me that he had first spoken to her only the day before when by chance they sat next to each other at church and after the service she invited him to join her at her Bible study class the following evening. He had at first politely declined, explaining that one of his hives was full to the brim with honey ready to harvest. He told her he didn't think he could manage to tend to his beekeeping chores that afternoon and still find time to accompany her to her evening class as well.

That was when my mother offered to help my father with his chores, though she didn't have the faintest notion of what a super was or what it entailed to lift a full one off a buzzing, teaming hive of one hundred thousand or so riled honeybees and replace it with a fresh one primed with empty foundation frames.

My father didn't know my mother well enough at the time to know that once she set her mind to something, she seldom saw fit to change it, or that she clearly had seen something in his shy but steady ways that appealed to her.

I didn't mind my father's silence. I will admit the sound of another voice might have been a comfort in the long, hard days we spent together changing supers and harvesting our honey, especially after my mother died. But I believe this may be the reason why I'm not particularly lonely these days, not missing a voice I never grew accustomed to hearing.

I do not wish to imply by this that my father was a distant man, nor was he a mean or vindictive man like some I have seen who use stony silence as a weapon, every bit as withering to a child's spirit as a harsh word or a hand raised in anger. I believe my father could be quite instructive when the need or the want for speech arose. He just chose not to waste words on idle chatter.

My mother was hardly a chatterbox, but she seemed to crave human conversation, and she demonstrated right from the start an uncanny facility for deciphering the language of bees. As did Claire.

And my mother, bless her soul, possessed an uncanny talent for sizing up people and situations in order to take whatever action she deemed fitting for the circumstances at hand. I believe that is why she and Claire got on so well.

Upon learning of my invitation into the Straussmans' house for tea on the day my father and I had been summoned to take care of the "bee problem," my mother decided that common courtesy dictated a reciprocal invitation to the Straussman sisters. While my sister Eloise was closest in age to the offspring and so should have been the natural bearer of this neighborly gesture, she rather indignantly pointed out that since I had been the beneficiary of our neighbors' hospitality I should shoulder the unenviable task of inviting them over to our house on Friday afternoon for some of my mother's honeyed scones and lemonade.

I was surprised when my mother agreed. Knowing that I had inherited my father's tendency toward reticence, she took the precaution of writing out a formal invitation to our young neighbors, in what seemed to me an unusually flowery script, before sending me off to deliver it directly after supper.

It was Hilda who answered the door when I knocked the second time, the first and somewhat softer knock having brought no response whatsoever.

"This is for you. And your sister," I believe I stammered, and then I thrust the note my mother had written in her hand.

140

Wordlessly, Hilda unfolded the scented paper. And, after reading the invitation, she just as wordlessly turned and closed the front door behind her, leaving me standing dumbfounded on the unlit porch.

Given Hilda's less-than-forthcoming response, I was surprised to see my mother bustling about our kitchen Friday morning preparing for the afternoon get-together with the Straussman sisters that my sister and I were convinced would never take place.

When we returned home from school that same day, we found a plate of my mother's fresh scones laid out on the dining room table along with two small serving bowls filled with orange blossom honey and home-made currant jam.

My sister shook her head as if to say "She's gone mad as a hatter" when my mother entered the room carrying an iced pitcher of lemonade and four crystal tumblers on her best silver tray.

"Mother, what makes you think they'll come?" Eloise said. "We haven't heard a word from them all week. They're really a couple of odd ducks, the way they keep to themselves. Even when they're at school, they never talk to anyone besides each other. I don't think they have any friends at all."

"All the more reason to open our doors and our hearts to them," my mother had replied, setting down the tray and arranging the tumblers in a semicircle around the pitcher that she had placed in the middle of the table. "Poor dears . . ."

My sister and I had been right, of course. The Straussman sisters never arrived that Friday, or the next Friday, and still my mother was prepared, I think, to send off yet another invitation to our neighbors' house had not my father issued a rare opinion as to what he termed to be my mother's "strange fixation with the Straussman sisters."

"You've got two growing children of your own to fret over," he said. "And those girls have a perfectly fine family of their own to take care of them."

"How would you know, Walter?" my mother responded. "They've got a father who's hardly ever home, and that mother of theirs . . . well, you know how I feel about her. Sitting on that front porch in her fancy chair all day long like the Queen of Sheba — and those girls waiting on her hand and foot. It's bad enough she and her husband don't attend church, but to deny those poor girls the Lord's teachings just because of what a few old busybodies had to say after the boy . . ."

"You don't know that's the reason," my father interrupted just as my mother appeared to be working herself into what my father used to call one of her moods. "Just let it go."

But as was her nature, my mother seldom let anything go once she'd gotten hold of it in the first place.

"Hello, Claire," my mother called out cheerily when she observed Claire lingering beyond our hedgerow on her way home from school the following Monday. Hilda, who stood silent watch from the roadway, started like a filly at the sound of my mother's voice and dashed clumsily down the road to her house with Claire trailing somewhat more slowly behind her.

Yet my mother swore Claire smiled back when she greeted her. And within another week, Claire accepted my mother's entreaty to join her on the front porch for a nice cool glass of lemonade. Eloise stayed upstairs in her room the whole afternoon. I know because I saw her watching from her window.

I believe Hilda kept a silent vigil by the roadside the entire time Claire sat with my mother, but I can't say for sure as the passage of the years has only served to accentuate Hilda's considerable insubstantiality in my recall.

"She seems such an old soul for such a young girl," my mother remarked after spending a half hour on the porch with Claire that first afternoon. They chatted, I suppose, about the sort of things the fairer sex find interesting and I myself can only imagine. My mother declined to reveal the details, but the next afternoon Claire came directly around the side of our house bold as you please to join my mother on the back porch, where together they sat quietly watching my father and me add a new super to our number two hive as they sipped from dewy glasses of lemonade.

I still can picture how cool and refreshing those lemonade glasses looked from afar as my father and I labored under the hot sun that day. And the next day and the next.

"It's a slow process, gaining that girl's confidence," my mother confided to my father one evening after supper when she thought I'd gone off to bed. I had slipped out onto the back porch to watch the stars, however, which I do on occasion even now when I have trouble sleeping.

"Do you know what that dear girl said to

me this afternoon, Walter?" my mother said, and without waiting for my father to reply she lowered her voice so that I had to strain to hear her. "She said she sorely misses the sound of the bees in her parlor wall. She said she found something comforting in the hum of activity that she heard as she went about her daily chores. You know, Walter, I do believe she's bitten by the fever, but she just doesn't know it yet."

I could not hear my father's response, but I did hear my mother's musical laughter burst from the parlor like wind chimes on a summer breeze, fading down the hall and up the stairs, as the lights in our house blinked out one by one.

Two days later, my mother convinced Claire to venture off the back porch and take a few tentative steps toward the hive we were fretting over that particular afternoon, but, try as my mother might, she could urge her no farther. They reached the same impasse every day for the next week or so until my mother remarked loud enough for both my father and me to hear that it looked like a rainstorm was brewing and, despite his protest that the skies looked clear to him, she dashed indoors.

"Try these on for size," my mother said when she emerged from the house, a dusty cobweb or two clinging to her strawberry blond hair, and my old coveralls, a spare beekeeper's hat and veil, and a worn pair of gloves bundled in her sun-freckled arms. "They were Albert's. I've been saving them for a rainy day."

Patiently, she showed our young neighbor how to tuck the legs of the coveralls into her stockings and the long sleeves into the cuffs of the canvas gloves she slipped over her slender fingers. Though Claire was nearly two years older than myself, at ten years old I was already being described as a "strapping" lad while Claire, as I have said before, was of a more delicate stature — so much so, in fact, that my coveralls, which I had outgrown by half a foot by then, were rather comically outsized on her.

Thus clothed, Claire was gently convinced by my mother that with such proper precautions, a contented hive of industrious honeybees was no more dangerous than a mewling basket of newborn kittens.

"Just remember to walk slowly and deliberately when you approach the hives, and don't make any sudden noise or movements," my mother admonished as Claire allowed the comforting drone of our precious honeybees to envelop her at last.

TWELVE

STING: A barbed, modified ovipositor, it is used by worker bees primarily in defense of the hive. Drones do not have stings. The queen bee's sting is smooth and is not used for defense of the hive but to vanquish her rivals.

Whereas I am content to assist in the day-to-day survival of the hive in return for a small measure of the excess honey its inhabitants are able to share with me, from the very beginning Claire craved a more intimate interaction with the bees. She seemed to draw surprising strength and inner resolve from what she liked to call the spirit of the hive, the wondrous and constant striving of each and every worker, drone, forager, guard, nurse, and even its exalted queen toward the collective future of the colony, a spirit that supersedes the will and well-being of each individual hive inhabitant for the good of the whole.

The honey Claire harvested, after all was said and done, seemed somehow incidental to her ardent application on the hive's behalf — so much so, in fact, as to give the impression that she considered herself not so much a benevolent keeper of bees as she did their oddly configured sibling.

There was no mistaking that Claire was hard bitten by the fever that long-ago spring. Her weekday visits to our backyard enterprise soon became regular as clockwork. Arriving shortly after school let out, she would dive into whatever task my father and I were doing with unmitigated vigor and enthusiasm until four o'clock on the dot when Hilda came and stood at the entrance of our side yard and silently telegraphed their departure time.

I soon learned that there had been a terrible row between the two sisters over Claire's first halting steps toward her apicultural avocation.

"Hilda doesn't like me coming over here," Claire confided to me one day out of the blue as we walked together through the orchard, stopping to check the oil pans on our hive bases and refilling any that had grown perilously low as we went. Taken aback by her candor, I was hard-pressed to respond, though I needn't have worried as she, like my mother, possessed the verbal facility for carrying on a conversation when, technically speaking, none yet existed.

"She thinks Mother will be angry at her if she finds out where I'm spending my afternoons."

Not knowing what to say, I headed for the next hive on our circuit through the orange grove.

"I told Hilda, 'Don't be silly, the only way she'll find out is if you tell her.' But Hilda doesn't like it. I think she's jealous, if you ask me, because I have a friend now and she doesn't have any."

I was uncomfortably aware at that moment that Claire had stooped to the ground and grabbed her slender ankles with her hands in a maneuver that brought her eyes level with mine as I bent down to get a better look at the two pans fastened to the back side of the hive with considerably more concentration than such a task usually requires.

There was a warm, unnaturally dry breeze blowing through the trees that particular spring day, rustling the supple young leaves and pale blossoms above our head and leaving my mouth thick and parched at the same time.

"You mean your parents don't know you're here?" I stammered, setting down the container of oil with a thump that sent a puff of dust spurting up from the dry ground.

"Well, not exactly," Claire replied. "Mother isn't well. She has the sugar, you know. Last month, the doctor ordered her to bed. She's not supposed to, but sometimes when she's feeling up to it she still likes to come out of her room and join us for dinner, but hardly ever, and even when she does she never gets up before five. So you see, I'm doing Mother a favor, really, coming over here in the afternoon so she is able to nap. I make quite enough ruckus for two without hardly trying, or so Hilda tells me."

"What about your father. Doesn't he wonder where you are?"

"My father works for the railroad. He's a conductor on the Southern Pacific's Los Angeles–to–Portland run," she replied with an odd lilt to her voice that I took to mean she was either exceedingly proud or, conversely, distressed by his chosen occupation. "Father comes home only on weekends."

I sat down on the bare ground and began drawing concentric circles in the dust next to my oilcan. I could no more imagine going off somewhere — even next door — without first informing my parents of my intentions than I could conceive of lying to them about my whereabouts after the fact. Claire, I believe, read something of my thoughts in my eyes. She sat down on the ground next to me and wiped my slate of circles clean.

"I don't see the harm in coming over here for a bit while Mother rests as long as I'm home in time to help prepare supper," she said with the same disarming lilt in her voice as before. "And Hilda makes quite certain that I am."

Which had been true enough until the day some weeks hence that my father came upon a wild swarm affixed to a crook in a gnarled old walnut tree limb on the far side of our family's orchards.

"Albert! Claire! Come with me to the honey shed. I need your help with a catcher hive," my father called out when he spied us silently observing a squadron of pollen-laden field bees alighting with great excitement on the landing board of our number fifteen hive.

"There it is," my father whispered, halting some twenty feet from where the swarm hung in a low-slung branch that seemed to droop like the flesh of an old woman's arm.

"Would you like to feel it?" my father asked Claire as he nodded at the swarm and back to Claire again.

"You mean touch the swarm?" Claire stared wide-eyed at my father. He nodded. Even from our distant vantage, we could hear the swarm's rapturous hymn of emancipation.

"Don't worry," I assured Claire, seeing the fear in her eyes. "Bees are gentle as lambs when they swarm. They won't hurt you."

I don't believe it was my persuasive skills that convinced Claire to set aside her misgivings, however. I think it was the swarm itself that called to her in its collective song of ecstasy, for such is the state of a colony of bees that chooses to forsake the comfort and wealth of the hive to follow its deposed regent in search of a new home.

I told Claire what I knew: that even the most disgruntled faction of bees will not abandon its hive in times of need or scarcity of resources. Only in the full ripeness of spring, when the hive is teeming with healthy worker bees and brood and its combs are stocked to the brim with honey, does the colony think to raise up a new virgin queen to displace the old. Such is the democratic nature of their magnificently ordered society that any one of a hundred thousand anonymous handmaidens, soldiers, nurses, or workers may be snatched from a life of unyielding toil to be transformed while still in the cradle into the sole reigning matriarch of the hive.

Though there may be a battle for supremacy once the new regent, having reached maturity, returns from her marriage flight, newly widowed yet fully impregnated with the seed of a million future lives, to take up her rightful place as revered queen mother of the hive, usually there is not. Occasionally, however, an aging regent, sensing some greater imperative, will grow increasingly agitated as the birth of an heiress to her throne approaches until she incites as many as half the hive's inhabitants to join in her quest for a new realm. Bursting forth from the hive into the sunshine she has not felt on her wings since her own nuptial flight, she takes to the sky with a legion of loyal daughters trailing in her wake.

They seldom travel far, for, in truth, the queen's wings will have atrophied almost to the point of dysfunction over the dark months of her royal confinement, and so it is that she generally alights upon the first inviting branch or fence post that she encounters. No doubt exhausted by her bold adventure, she is surrounded at once by her band of mutineers, who now huddle close to warm and comfort their exiled queen while a party of scouts sets off to find suitable new quarters for them all.

It was just such an assemblage of queen and courtiers that Claire so tremulously approached that long-ago afternoon, her palm held upward as if reaching for a gift from God. And I suppose this description is as close as anything to what she did in fact receive, for I have never witnessed a look at once so full of fear and bliss as that I saw come over Claire's countenance when she stepped up onto the cement block my father and I had placed beneath the limb and she inserted her hand directly into the core of the swarm. Like the enraptured Saint Teresa, only the slightest gasp of surprise escaped her lips before they parted in a smile.

Honeybees are at their most docile state when they swarm. So docile, in fact, that their normally exposed stingers lie sheathed within the hilt of their downy bodies so that their aggregate mass is not at all prickly to the touch as one might anticipate, but rather the feel is infinitely more forgiving, like

154

velvet-covered pebbles slipping through one's outstretched fingers in an ebb and flow of motion as gentle as a lover's caress.

Later, Claire would say, "It was so soft. So warm. So accepting. It moved all over and around and through my open fingers as if it was of a single living, breathing mind that wished to know everything about me in an instant and for all of eternity, and I don't quite know how but I felt I was becoming a part of it. The longer I held my hand inside the swarm, the less it felt like my own flesh and blood and bone and the more I thought I would never, ever let go."

I sometimes think she never would have either had my father not finally taken her free hand, which by this time was clenched tight around a fistful of her cotton skirt, and pulled her slowly but insistently off her concrete perch. Even as she allowed herself to be led away from the swarm, her head was turned and her eyes remained riveted on the pulsing mass, as my father whispered softly, "Come now, Claire. There's work to be done."

My father set the open-topped catcher hive he had fetched from the honey shed on the concrete block beneath the swarm. Meanwhile, I drew a pail of cold water from a nearby irrigation line and into this my father plunged his arms up to his elbows, and I quickly followed his lead.

"This old branch is too thick to shake," my father said as he reached up and wrapped one of his hands around its un-yielding base. Still holding on to the limb, he called out to Claire, who stood off a ways stroking her hand.

"See those two wooden ladles by the bucket? Bring them here, girl."

Roused perhaps by the firmness of his voice, Claire dashed over to the pail and retrieved the ladles. My father took one and handed the other to me.

"Now, go stand back there and watch."

Reaching into the center of the mass, my father ladled out a living spoonful of bees and deposited it in the new hive. I quickly plunged my ladle into another section of the swarm and did the same. Moving in a slow, syncopated rhythm, my father and I ladled most of the swarm into the awaiting hive like creamed corn into a cooking pot. Indeed, there was liquidity to the swarm that soon caused great dripping gobs to fall off the tree limb into the hive below. Most, but not all, of the bees were transferred to the hive in this manner, while a few strays flitted harmlessly about our hands and faces, filling the air with their joyous aria.

Just as Claire had no need to fear their touch en masse, these happy stragglers were no less peaceable.

The entire operation took less than two hours from start to finish, but we were so engrossed that neither my father, Claire, nor myself took note of the dwindling light that played out as we at last capped the hive. Still feeling the exhilaration of a job well done, we made the leisurely stroll from the far end of our property back to the honey shed to return our tools to their proper shelves.

"A place for everything and everything in its place," my father intoned from habit.

Emerging from the shed into the dusky shadows of the oncoming evening, Claire uttered a tiny gasp not unlike the one that had issued from her lips earlier that day.

"What time is it?" she asked.

"Half past six or thereabouts," my father replied after a quick glance at the sky above.

"Are you hungry? I am sure Mrs. Honig would love for you to join us for supper," my father uttered in a practically unheard-of glut of verbiage.

"Oh no. I have to go," she said, but she made no move to leave at first. Claire looked to me and then to my father as if to speak, but no words came. Instead, she stared a moment or two longer at the setting sun and then turned and made a mad dash for home.

THIRTEEN

BEE SPACE: Measuring between one-quarter to three-eighths of an inch, it is the space around which modern, movable-frame hives are designed as it is large enough to permit comfortable passage by worker bees but too small to encourage comb building and too large to induce pro-polizing activities.

Claire stopped coming around our house the very next day. Though I thought to ask her when I ran into her at school from time to time over the next few days, she seemed reluctant to stop and talk whenever I approached.

Which was just as well, I suppose, as I learned later that my mother had gone next door one morning shortly after Claire's daily visits had ceased to inquire after her health only to be told in no uncertain terms by Mrs. Straussman that Claire was just fine, thank you, and furthermore that she would not be coming around to dally with our bees or any other such nonsense in the future.

I learned of my mother's visit to the Straussmans' house when I overheard her telling my father what had occurred that same evening as I sat on the front porch swing after dinner silently observing the constellations overhead.

Eloise had already retired to her bedroom to work on her homework, and my mother and father sat in our parlor — he in his overstuffed chair and she in her wooden rocker — discussing the day's events, as was their after-dinner habit.

"I realize a family has a right to conduct their own business as they see fit," my mother said, a trace of indignation tainting her usually sunny voice. "But there is just no call for that sort of rudeness between neighbors. The very idea, calling me 'meddlesome,' Walter. I was simply worried about the girl. I thought she might have taken ill, after all."

I heard the rustle of paper, and even as I stared at the handle of the Big Dipper, counting and recounting the number of stars from tip to tip, I could visualize the deliberate way my father had of opening the

160

newspaper wide and giving it a shake before turning the page, shaking it once more, and folding it back to readable proportions.

"I worry about her, Walter," my mother said, and then she lowered her voice so that I could barely hear her whisper. "We still don't know what happened to that boy."

"That's right. You don't know what happened," my father said. "And no good can come of stirring that hornet's nest up again, Elizabeth. There's already been enough ill will to last a lifetime."

I heard the newspaper rustle again and then my mother's voice. It was louder, more insistent, than before.

"Now, you know I believe what the Good Book says about judging not lest ye be judged, but, Walter, I swear to you, there's something not right about that family. You've seen that poor girl's mother as I have, sitting on her front porch, shaking her cane at everyone who passes by like they've no right at all to stroll along a perfectly lovely public street. I've seen her frighten the living daylights out of innocent school-children who've done no more harm than to step an inch or two onto her precious front lawn. Why she holds it so dear, dry and neglected as it is, I'll never know. Even you must admit I've always held my tongue when it has come to that woman until this very moment. But really, Walter, there's just no call for it. No call for it at all."

It was true that most of the neighborhood children, myself included, were loath to walk past the Straussman house for fear of incurring Mrs. Straussman's considerable wrath. It was also true that as time wore on and her tetchy reputation seemed to grow right along with her girth, quite a few of these same children took to spreading tales, especially around Halloween, about seeing Mrs. Straussman — dressed all in black, as was her habit — hunkered over an enormous iron cauldron when the moon was full. It was said that she could be seen stirring all manner of ghoulish ingredients. Some even said they'd seen little children tossed, kicking and screaming, into the pot as she chanted mysterious incantations that made one's hair curl. I'd even heard some of the older children say that they'd heard from their own parents that the Straussman family had stolen a baby years ago to replace the one they'd lost, while others insisted they'd used it for far darker purposes.

I myself refrained from such fanciful slander, but I cannot say I spoke out on her behalf either. Perhaps it was because I, through my family home's proximity to hers, had been one of the more frequent recipients of her increasingly vitriolic confrontations.

This is what had made the experience of sipping tea from golden cups with Mrs. Straussman all the more disquieting. It had somehow singled me out from the rest of my schoolmates, at least in my own mind.

Though I had told none of them of my experience, I had begun to nurture an unaccustomed sense of superiority over them, as though I alone had entered the belly of the beast and, having returned unscathed, I alone need not fear the specter of their childish fantasies.

I was still basking in my clandestine glory on a blustery morning nearly six weeks after "my little tea party," which is how I'd come to think of my semiprivate audience with Mrs. Straussman. I had just come out of my house to join a group of my classmates who were walking to school together when a sudden gust of wind whipped some homework papers right out of Mary McMasters's hands. The next thing we all knew, Mary was gasping in horror, and her homework was skittering across the lawn and up onto the Straussmans' front porch. Though Mrs. Straussman's porch seat was vacant, even the possibility that she might open the door at any moment was enough to prevent any of the other assembled children from venturing onto the forbidden lawn to retrieve Mary's errant papers.

"Cowards die many times before their deaths; / The valiant never taste of death but once," I solemnly intoned as if I'd coined the words myself, confident none of my school chums had read William Shakespeare, another of the cherished poets whose verses my mother had helped me memorize. Then with what I fancied a gallant nod to Mary McMasters, I dashed across the lawn and up the porch steps after the fluttering papers, which by this time were plastered against the Straussmans' front door. With a triumphant flourish, I snatched the papers up and returned slowly — more slowly, in fact, than I knew even the bravest among the gathering before me would have dared.

"Here you are," I said simply, straightening the papers and handing them to Mary, who stood dumbstruck by the side of the road.

"Thank you, Albert," she said, making the statement sound more like a question than a declaration.

"You're welcome," I said with only the

slightest hint of a bow before I turned and began walking to school with an unfamiliar spring in my step.

I did not tell Mary McMasters, or any in the cluster of awestruck children around her, that only the afternoon before Claire had mentioned to me that their family doctor had prescribed twenty-four hours' bed rest for her mother after a flare-up of gout and high blood pressure and so I was fairly certain she would not interrupt my heroics with a sudden looming appearance at her front door.

Seldom recognized outside my home for anything other than my taller-than-average frame and disproportionate shyness, I did not consider beforehand how my simple rescue of a classmate's homework assignment would become the talk of the school that day or how many times Claire or Hilda Straussman would overhear the tale. Nor did I anticipate that the story would grow ever more exaggerated with each retelling until, by day's end, I was said to have stood bold as you please on the Straussmans' front porch, thumbs cocked to my ears as I waggled my hands up and down and dared the old witch — for sadly that is what my classmates said I had called Mrs. Straussman, though I swear I said no such thing —

to come out and get me.

"I dare you! I dare you, you old hag!" I was said to have shouted one last time before turning on my heels and strutting down her porch stairs and all the way to school, my newfound admirers trailing behind me.

And so it went all day long. After school, I was stopped on the dirt road in front of the schoolhouse by yet another group of classmates, who were clapping me on the back and urging me to tell the tale again, when I spied Claire and Hilda cutting across the school lawn so as to avoid having to pass by us. Breaking away from my admirers with hurried apologies, I walked slowly around the corner after them before sprinting to Claire's and Hilda's sides. Wordlessly, the sisters quickened their pace.

"Wait up, Claire," I beseeched. "Let me explain."

"What's to explain?" Claire replied without turning her head.

"I just retrieved Mary McMasters's homework," I said. "It blew out of her hands and got stuck up against your front door. I just ran and got it back."

Claire said nothing, but she stopped, as did Hilda. Slowly they turned around, and then Claire lifted her eyes to mine and held them there. Hilda, silent as always, seemed to fade like watercolors into the background.

"I didn't do what they said I did. I wouldn't do that."

"Then why did you let them say you did?" Claire asked at last.

I shrugged. I did not want to admit it to Claire, but it had felt good — if only for a moment — to feel like a hero. And it had all seemed harmless enough.

"I thought you were my friend," Claire said as if everything that has a beginning must also have an end. "You're the one who's always preaching to me about the truth."

"I didn't lie. I didn't start the stories. That was Robert Hooker and his brother Ellis. But once all the stories got started, I didn't know how to stop them," I said, knowing even as I uttered the words how full of smoke and mirrors they were. Claire continued to hold her eyes on mine. Another of my mother's scrapbook quotes came to mind, this one from Mark Twain: "When in doubt, tell the truth."

It was as simple and as complicated as that, and it was, I knew, exactly what I should have done all along.

"I am truly sorry, Claire," I said, and I

truly meant what I said. But for Claire, it was never enough.

"You know, Albert, for all your fancy words, you're not always so good at living up to them," Claire said.

I started to protest, but just then a group of schoolmates rounded the bend and shouted their greetings to me. I turned my head to wave, and when I turned back around Claire and Hilda had resumed their brisk walk home.

Claire continued to avoid me for the rest of the week after the homework incident. The week after that, school let out for the summer, and I did not speak to her again until after Labor Day. I wish that I had.

I watched her from my backyard gathering walnuts that long-ago summer. I even waved to her once or twice as I made my rounds between our front hives, but she turned her head without acknowledging me and walked quickly back into her house. It's hard to say whether she stayed away because of her mother's or her own accord or some combination of the two. I only know it was a long, lonely summer, and my bees and my books were my only small comfort.

When we first met again at school the following September, Claire made a good show of ignoring me when I first attempted to greet her on the steps of the building.

"My mother was worried when you stopped coming round," I said after I pursued her down the hallway, hardly able to contain my sincere expression of joy at being able to speak to her after so long an absence. Indeed, I surprised myself with my exuberance. "Have you been well? My mother inquired after your health, you know."

I could see by the softening of the set of her jaw that Claire had been unaware of any such efforts on her behalf. So I told her that my mother had gone not once but twice to her house to inquire after her despite my father's admonition to leave well enough alone. It had been Hilda who met my mother at the door the second time and it was she who had quietly but assuredly discouraged her from any further intervention on Claire's account.

"I missed you," I said. Or at least that is what I intended to say, but the bell rang just after Claire whispered that she had missed me and she had already run off to class.

I saw Claire later that morning, and despite the teasing I feared I would face when I returned to my desk after lunch I invited her to sit with me and eat. It wasn't exactly like old times, as we'd hardly had time the preceding spring to sow anything but the most tenuous friendship, but I attempted to reseed the garden by turning the conversation back to our shared love of bees.

"Remember the swarm you helped us capture?" I said in a voice barely above a whisper, and I was instantly rewarded with the ignition of a flinty spark in her sky blue eyes. I had forgotten how intensely that spark could shine. "Honestly, Claire, you should see how strong the hive has grown."

FOURTEEN

KISSED BY BEES: When Plato was still a child in the cradle, bees were said to have settled on his mouth, which was taken as a sign, as Pliny wrote, "announcing the sweetness of his enchanting soul." Similar stories were told of Socrates, Pindar, Saint Ambrose, and others. To be touched on the lips by bees, the ancients believed, was to be touched by the gift of eloquence.

In her younger years, there was something about Claire that drew people to her. My mother clearly adored her, and while my father's words toward her could appear abrupt or even harsh to those unfamiliar with his somewhat taciturn demeanor, I believe he held a grudging fondness for Claire that at times surpassed even that which he felt for his own daughter. Of course I do not mean to imply that my father did not love my sister, for indeed he did. But here is the difference: My sister had giggled uncontrollably the one time he had led her to a wild swarm and had asked her to repeat what for him was a sacred charm passed on from his father's father to him.

To her credit, Eloise had tried to hold a straight face as she'd knelt on the ground next to our new hive with my father and, following his lead, had scooped up a handful of dirt and flung it into the air. Unfortunately, she'd flung hers straight upward, covering both her hair and my father's in a shower of soil and leaves that left them both sputtering and shaking their heads.

"It's all right," my father said. "Just say the words."

"Oh, Papa," Eloise replied, wiping the dirt and tears of laughter from her eyes, "I feel so silly."

"Against a swarm of bees, take earth, stumble with thy right hand under right foot," my father had instructed Claire to say as they knelt beside the next wild swarm we'd captured. Unlike Eloise, Claire had not laughed when she'd been asked to scoop up a handful of dirt.

"Now say," my father solemnly said, and Claire had echoed his words, "I catch underfoot. Earth avails against all creatures whatever, and against envy, and against forgetfulness, and against the great tongue of man."

And with that, my father had tossed his handful of dirt on the stragglers from the swarm that crawled among the blades of grass where he and she had knelt as I watched.

"There's just something so spirited about her," my mother so often said that my sister Eloise began to refer to her as "ghost girl" to everyone save my parents. Claire was thirteen years old then, and unlike her older sister, who even as a child foreshadowed her mother's looming hulk that presumed to dwarf the sun itself, Claire was as light as a moonbeam.

"I can't imagine where she gets her spark. Certainly not from that woman," I overheard my mother whisper one evening after dinner as she and my father sat together in the parlor discussing the day's events. Earlier that afternoon Claire had popped up from behind the honeysuckle hedgerow separating our two families' properties shouting an Indian war whoop that had nearly startled my father out of his bee suit. While my father had rightfully scolded her for making such a loud and sudden racket so near to the bees, even he had had to concede that most of the field workers had been away from the hive collecting honey at the time and so no real harm was done.

"And forgive me for saying so, Walter, but I believe she frightened you more than she did the bees," my mother gently chided, and when my father protested she laughed. "Why, you'd think you'd just been ambushed by Sitting Bull himself instead of that little slip of a girl."

"It just seems as if she's always underfoot these days," my father had replied. The uncharacteristic harshness of his words surprised me, for at the time I had begun to think he preferred her company not only over my sister but me.

"Can't you see that poor girl's starved for attention?" my mother said, but she said nothing more, at least that I could hear above the steady *click-click-click* of her knitting needles.

"She's starved for something," my father said, and then he shook his newspaper open to signal the conversation had concluded as far as he was concerned. I could not help but be struck by the contrasting images of an undernourished young girl and her hulking mother that my father's remark produced in my own mind as I opened the door to the back porch and slipped into the silent

174

embrace of the evening sky.

It certainly was true that sparks seemed to fly whenever Claire was around. And sometimes even when she wasn't. I sensed that more was said between my parents that night regarding Claire's antics, as the air seemed thicker than the temperature warranted when I sat down to breakfast the next morning. I had little chance to contemplate the atmospheric anomaly, however, as I was compelled to hurry off directly after breakfast to practice for our school's upcoming fall recital.

I had only recently taken up playing the tuba, in the main to please my mother who said she always wanted a little "German band" in the house, and though my lack of musical aptitude was soon evident I felt obliged to attempt to fulfill her modest desire, as did Eloise, who, contrary to my parents' wishes, took up the clarinet instead of the accordion. I showed not the least inkling of musical talent and so within another year or so I was thankfully allowed to discontinue my hapless efforts. My sister showed no more musical aptitude than me, though she did develop a lifelong affinity for big band music and jazz. But in the meantime, while my mother still held out hope for us both, we'd been hooked into performing in our school's annual fall concert. For me, at least, this meant early-morning and after-school practice sessions every weekday without fail. The point of which is that I was sorely disappointed to learn that Claire was already in the honey shed helping my father load some foundation frames into the extractor when I arrived home from school one day in late September after an extended musical practice. I say disappointed, not so much because Claire was there but because I feared I might have missed what was for me my most cherished aspect of beekeeping: the long-awaited harvesting of the excess honey from the hive.

This is not a complicated procedure, but it is best accomplished when working in tandem — one lifting and uncapping the foundation frames brimming with honey while the other fastens them into the frame holders inside the drum of the extracting machine. A machine of true beauty, the extractor resembles in size and shape an old-fashioned mechanical clothes washer in which one lifts, one by one, the still-dripping articles of clothing from the washer's drum and passes them through a metal hand-cranked platen, except that there is no platen, and the extractor drum is made of sparkling stainless steel instead of the infinitely less glamorous white enamel. I believe some of the glamour of the extractor lies in its function. Instead of cranking loads of wet clothing by hand through a pair of rollers to wring the moisture from workaday garments, as my mother and sister did each Monday without fail, the foundation frames are attached like spokes to a central hub and, when cranked at the proper speed, extrude glorious golden honey from the combs by centrifugal force. Though it seems a simple enough motion, there is a knack to turning the crank, slowly at first, then building to a moderate easy-to-turn pace so as not to risk breaking the combs out of the frame. When extracting is done properly, the honey soon begins to collect on the walls of the extractor and drains out into a gallon-sized collector can that we place beneath the spigot.

As a boy, it generally was my job to fasten the frames to the anchor chains of the extractor and, when everything was secured, to turn the crank and watch to see that the honey did not overflow, while my father's job was to slice away the protective wax topping the bees make over each of the comb chambers of the foundation frame after it has been filled with honey. Working as a team, with my father preparing the frames and me cranking the extractor, we could harvest a full super in an hour or less, which was a demanding but necessary pace to maintain during the height of the honey-flow season when our industrious bees worked night and day to keep up with the wildflower bloom.

On this particular occasion, my father and I had for several days previous been keeping an eye on our number thirteen hive, which appeared to be nearing time for harvest, and hoping for a warm day so as to cause the least discomfort to our bees when we opened the hive to remove the full supers and replace them with newly prepared frames to fill with more golden honey. On the afternoon of the first temperate day in nearly a week, I found myself fidgeting through a particularly frustrating bass line of a John Philip Sousa composition. When at last our ragtag school band was dismissed for the afternoon, I ran all the way home only to be informed by my mother, who greeted me as she always did when I arrived home from school, that the supers on our number thirteen had already been replaced.

"Calm yourself," my mother said, tousling my hair when she beheld my obvious dejection. "There's no use crying over spilt milk."

She urged me to take a seat at the kitchen table and had soon laid out for me a consoling plate of leftover breakfast scones and a glass of cool lemonade. As I ate, she explained that my father had been anxious to take advantage of the afternoon's warmth. When Claire arrived directly after school, he enlisted her aid in removing the full supers and carrying them to the honey shed.

"All right, young lord," my mother said with an approving smile once I'd finished my snack and appeared adequately calmed to her eye, "run along now. I'll bet they can still use some help."

Of course my mother's instincts had been correct. Even before I entered the shed, I could hear the agitation in Claire's voice as she insisted that she knew exactly what she was doing over my father's equally emphatic insistence that surely she did not.

When I opened the door to the shed, I found my father hunkered awkwardly over her tiny shoulders trying, it seemed to me, to wrestle the uncapping knife from her grasp as she struggled to balance a foundation frame on the pivot bar that steadied it during the uncapping process. The sudden shaft of sunlight that flooded the room from the open door seemed to startle them both, and the frame and knife clattered to the wooden floor of the shed as Claire darted from beneath my father's arms to stand and fiddle with the crank of the extractor. As I believe I've mentioned many times, Claire was slightly built, but never in life did she seem so frail as she did at that moment, frozen in a hailstorm of dust motes that swirled in the stark sunlight surrounding her.

She began to cry then, not loudly, but as though a soft stream of air was seeping from a punctured bicycle tire. She stood there like that, even after my father called for me to come quickly to help him retrieve the fallen frame.

"We'll take it from here, Claire," my father said gruffly as my chest swelled with self-importance. Luckily the frame had not yet been uncapped and so no honey was spilt in the mishap. Still, Claire seemed so distraught by her clumsiness that after a moment of indecision she excused herself and hurried into the house, where she spent the rest of the afternoon helping my mother clean out the icebox. Neither my father nor I mentioned the incident in the honey shed that evening at dinner, or ever. Nor did Claire say anything about it to my father, as far as I know. She did, however, seem less inclined to spend time out of doors with either my father or myself for quite some time after that. I can't be certain, as nothing was ever certain in my mind when it came to Claire, but I believe this unfortunate incident was one of the few times in her life when Claire clearly regretted biting off more than she could chew.

■ ■ ■ ■

THE HARVEST

■ ■ ■ ■

FIFTEEN

THE DRONE'S EYE: Larger than either the worker's or the queen's, it can contain as many as eight thousand lenses. Able to perceive a full 360-degree range of vision, it is designed for optimal mating pursuit of the queen on the fly.

I am an old man now, an old man whose memories pulse more strongly than the blood in my veins. Marcel Proust described these remnants of the past as "souls bearing resiliently, on tiny and almost impalpable drops of their essence." I am no French philosopher, but I think I understand what he meant. If the breeze is just right, I can catch a whiff of eucalyptus, pungent as camphor and lye, and my thoughts turn, almost against my will, to the place where Claire lived and died.

Of course I know that the eucalyptus windbreak that ran alongside the north border of the Straussmans' property is long gone. But somewhere deep inside the cluster of asphalt and stucco and artificial wood trim that engulfs me on all sides now, something of Claire remains in the ephemeral perfume of these old trees, especially on warm summer evenings when the fragrance is so strong that I wonder if I am the only one left who desires nothing more than to savor this heady aroma like an elixir that used to infuse the thick air with such possibilities.

On such nights, I close my eyes and I am drawn once again to the siren song of the Harmony Park Ballroom where dances were held once upon a time every Saturday night.

For nearly three-quarters of a century, the Harmony Park Ballroom hunkered like the hull of a giant overturned boat run aground in a dusty clearing overhung with peppertrees and backed by another tall windbreak of eucalyptus that abutted the railway switchyard. On balmy nights when I was still a teen, I used to sit out on our back porch immersed in the redolent jumble of car doors slamming and whiskey glasses and beer bottles clinking amid bursts of smoky laughter while an armada of guitars strummed hot-blooded song after song, the music seeming to float through the thickly scented air, while truckloads of soldiers and farm workers, reeking of Fels-Naptha soap and cheap whiskey, swaggered across the graveled parking lot and on through the Harmony's big double doors to celebrate the end of another backbreaking week while the music played into the dawn of another Sabbath.

Even as a young man, I was struck by the contrast between my parents' shy first rendezvous at their long-ago church social, and the raucous goings-on down the road, and I found myself more often than not wondering what it would be like to stand in the shadows of the dance floor for an hour or so and to judge for myself if the men were as dangerous and the women as wanton as I imagined they must be to drink and dance until the wee hours of the night in the cavernous darkness of the Harmony Park Ballroom.

I can recall as if it were yesterday how after a particularly boisterous night of revelry at the Harmony, I confessed these guilty thoughts to Claire.

I was thirteen and a half years old. Claire had just turned fifteen the month before. We had spent most of the evening collecting fallen walnuts from her family's grove. When the basket was full, I asked her if she minded coming with me to my family's number twelve hive.

"I forgot my smoker can," I stammered.

"Silly goose," she said, laughing, reaching for my hand. "Let's go. The night is still young."

And I would have taken her hand, too, had I not been carrying the bushel basketful of walnuts we'd just gathered. I did manage to keep up with her as she skipped and danced beneath the bowers all the way to our number twelve hive, which was near enough to the Harmony Ballroom that we could hear the music, which in the viscous night air seemed sung by mermaids. I had never heard a song so beautiful. But then, my family frowned upon secular music.

"I like this," I said, staring into her eyes.

"You too?" Claire finally whispered, and then it was my turn to stare. Something in her eyes told me it wasn't the music she was referring to. I felt my cheeks flush with the realization that such forbidden urges were harbored by this delicate girl who had grown into my most cherished — and, in fact, my only — friend if one didn't count my bees.

That our friendship had survived during our early adolescence, despite the restrictions placed upon Claire's activities by her mother, I once believed we owed to the relative freedom I enjoyed within my own family.

Looking back now, I realize I may have exaggerated Claire's deceptive talent, as between her father's extended absences, her sister's obsessive reclusiveness, and her mother's lack of mobility — old Mrs. Straussman's left leg having been amputated due to the complications from diabetes — it may not have been as difficult as I once imagined for Claire to invent the litany of plausibilities that enabled her and I to retrieve a bushel of almonds from her family's orchard or fetch a quart of milk and a pound of butter from the neighborhood grocer. Nor did it take much effort on my part to sit on my back porch and watch for her to stand on her own back porch, hands on hips, breathing in the summer fragrances, before trotting off to fetch a bushel basket or grocery sack or whatever else she needed to signal wordlessly from across the distance of our two yards where to find her later if I had a mind to follow.

And of course I always did.

SIXTEEN

ARTEMIS: The Greek goddess of the hunt, forests, and childbirth, she was often portrayed as the virgin protectress of young girls, who ritualistically sacrificed their tunics, toys, dolls, and all youthful belongings to her as a farewell to their youth on the night before their marriage. Her priests were generally eunuchs, and her priestesses were virgins called the *Melissae*, meaning honeybees.

In the dark months following Claire's death, my thoughts drifted like desert sand around the regret of hours that had transformed fleeting days into long weeks and months, and on into irretrievable years of stubborn silence.

It all seems so foolish now, but throughout the drift of those wasted years I peevishly clung to the belief that as long as the silence could be broken, should either of us choose to do so, then the silence was somehow less complete.

But we did not speak, choosing instead to cultivate in the hothouses of our solitude all the real and imagined slights like so many rare and exotic orchids, and then all at once, in no more time than it took to stuff a dirty red bandanna inside a human mouth and fasten a careless strip of silver tape across it, the choice was rendered moot and the silence eternal.

And so I am left with nothing but memories.

When I was still in my teens, I used to sit out on our back porch late into the evening watching for signs that Claire was out and about, and I often overheard my mother lament to my father that she was afraid for "that poor dear girl." I knew without her saying so that she meant Claire.

"You have a daughter, Elizabeth," I heard my father say more than once.

"But she's not like me," my mother always replied.

I am not exactly like my father either. I wonder sometimes if this is the dichotomy of hope that all parents face. The wish, on the one hand, that their child, will carry their own dreams forward while at the same time hoping they will do so somehow better, yet, on the other hand, not so much better as to lose sight of who they are and where they came from.

My father's consternation that night, however, was more straightforward. He worried about what he considered to be an unseemly meddling into other people's affairs.

My mother had other concerns. While hesitant to defy my father's wishes outright, she often wondered aloud whether it might not be best to at least question the girl after she noticed, just as I had, what looked to be bruises on Claire's delicate wrists and forearms and another on her jawbone.

"She's fifteen. Surely she's too old to be getting those kinds of marks from innocent roughhousing," my mother had pointed out rather indignantly to my father as they sat together in the parlor one evening after dinner. "As God as my witness, they look to be deliberately made."

"Spare the rod, spoil the child," I heard my father firmly reply after a long moment's consideration. His voice seemed to punctuate the rhythmic squeak of my mother's wooden rocker.

"That's what the Good Book says, Elizabeth."

"But does not the Bible also say, 'As ye

sow, so shall ye reap'?" my mother had said in rejoinder. Regrettably, I could not hear my father's response to this as Eloise, who was old enough to know better, chose that most inopportune moment to intrude upon my solitary stargazing with a shouted invitation to join her in the dining room for a game of checkers, which I declined despite her loud and repeated entreaties.

My parents' conversation had long since concluded by the time I finally was able to quiet my sister by promising to play one game with her later that evening, so I can only assume my mother eventually deferred to my father's entreaty, at least for the time being, as I did not hear them discuss the matter again for the rest of that summer.

As had become the cycle, Claire's mother had ordered her once again to stop coming around to our house to "dally," as she put it, in our family's apiary shortly after my parents' initial conversation. But the ban was only haphazardly enforced after a time, and by the following winter Claire had more or less resumed her daily routine.

"That poor girl didn't seem to be herself last week. She seemed so pale and distracted," my mother said to no one in particular as she passed a bowl of mashed potatoes to my father when the subject of

Claire's sudden absence came up once again the following spring. "Did either of you see Claire at school at all last week?"

Eloise never warmed to Claire the way my parents and I did. And Claire had likewise avoided any significant conversation with Eloise, having confided in me that she had been angered many years earlier when she chanced to overhear my sister and some of her schoolmates mocking Hilda's rather awkward attempt to join in one of the girls' schoolyard games.

"Just because your mother teaches Sunday school doesn't give that snooty sister of yours the right to act all holier than thou," Claire had fumed.

Of course I agreed with Claire that my sister had acted insensitively, but in her defense I also ventured that Hilda had hardly given Eloise, or anyone else for that matter, much in the way of neighborly encouragement.

"She may not say much, but that doesn't mean she can't hear what people say about her," Claire had snapped back. But then, just as abruptly, her demeanor softened and her eyes took on that distant cast they often did when she spoke of her family. "You know, Hilda wasn't always this way. When she was small, my father used to call her his little chatterbox."

I tried to picture the eerily silent young woman I knew as a loquacious child, but the image would not form in my mind. Claire, I believe, must have read something of the skepticism in my face.

"Well, it's the truth, Albert," Claire said defiantly. "You could hardly get a word in edgewise with her when she was little."

"I believe you," I said, not wishing to rile her further, as Claire could work up quite a lather when she believed her family, especially her older sister, was under attack.

But even if what Claire had said was true, what was there to do about it? Claire stared into my eyes as if searching for the answer to my own question, and when I faltered under her gaze, I could not help feeling that I had somehow come up short.

This is why I felt it was my duty, though I hadn't been asked directly, to inform my mother on that particular occasion that I had not seen Claire since the previous Thursday.

"Now, Elizabeth, don't go getting yourself all worked up over nothing again," my father said. "She's probably just come down with a cold."

"Fiddlesticks!"

"I said leave it be, Elizabeth," my father

insisted in a tone at once so cold and firm that even my sister looked up from her dinner plate.

"But Walter . . ." my mother started to object.

"I tell you that girl can take care of herself," my father insisted. My mother's mouth snapped shut and remained uncharacteristically so until the conclusion of the meal. She remained noticeably taciturn for another day or two, her sunny disposition returning only after Claire reappeared on our doorstep the following week. My mother welcomed her back with a flurry of hugs and warm words of affection that seemed excessive even for her normally demonstrative self. My father, however, maintained his usual dignified demeanor. And Claire, for her part, seemed unmoved by either response and volunteered no more concrete explanation for her extended absence than to say she hadn't been feeling well, which I suspect both my mother and father interpreted according to their own inclinations.

We probably wouldn't have noticed the new set of bruises on her at all, since Claire tended at that time to favor long sleeves and high necklines, had she not chanced that day to snag the back of her sweater on an overhanging bramble as she was carrying a load of new foundation frames from the honey shed to our number sixteen hive.

Claire was wearing a peach-colored pull-over sweater and she had gotten entangled in a particularly awkward spot right between her shoulder blades. Not wanting to drop the frames to extricate herself, she had called out for help. My mother and I had come running at the sound of her voice in distress.

Quickly assessing the situation, my mother ordered me to relieve Claire of her burden. I am sure my mother saw the discoloration at the base of Claire's throat at the same moment I did because I heard her gasp just as I did when she tugged at the stubborn snag at the neckline of Claire's sweater and a mass of angry purple-and-yellow splotches just above her collarbone was revealed.

Of course having witnessed Mrs. Straussman's dauntingly mercurial verbal assaults on numerous prior occasions, I am sure my mother naturally presumed, as I did, a propensity for physical violence as well. I assume as much as neither of us spoke directly to Claire or to each other about what we saw or suspected. Which is not to say we weren't concerned about Claire's welfare, but there was only so much we could do under the circumstances. My father was quite firm in his directive that we should refrain from meddling in the Straussmans' affairs.

Times were very different back then. My father was not alone in his sincere belief that what went on between family members was nobody's business but their own, nor was he swimming against the tide of common wisdom when he exhorted my mother not to go stirring up a hornet's nest in her own backyard.

"You'll just get yourself stung like before," my father had said. "And the rest of us right along with you."

"But you can't expect me to stand by and do nothing."

"That's exactly what I expect you to do, Elizabeth. You have no more proof now than you did with that boy of theirs. What makes you think it would be any different this time?"

This time.

I could not know what my mother could have done about the tragic circumstances of Harry Junior's death. But I could imagine myself Claire's heroic rescuer — her knight in shining armor who stood up for her when no one else would. But what I allowed myself to imagine, and what I could realistically be expected to act upon, were two entirely different matters.

"You're awfully quiet," Claire said as we strolled together through her family's walnut grove, stopping to pick up the ripened nuts that had fallen to the ground and deposit them in the customary bushel basket she'd brought along as a ruse should her parents inquire where she'd gotten off to. The last of the sun's rays were glinting through the tops of the trees. It could not have been more than a week after my mother and I had discovered the unsettling bruises on her neck.

"I could say the same of you," I replied.

"I haven't been sleeping well," she said. Dark circles ringed her eyes, and her hair seemed to hang rather more limply than usual across her forehead and pale cheeks.

"Perhaps if you drank a glass of warm milk at bedtime," I ventured, "that might help you sleep."

"I don't want to sleep," she said.

And then she said nothing more for several minutes until we found ourselves standing in a small clearing to the rear of her family's property.

"I used to hate when Father went away for work, but I loved it when he came back home," Claire said. She set her basket on the ground. "Hilda too. She used to look forward to his presents."

When it appeared that Claire might never speak again, I cleared my throat, and then she told me that the previous March her father had brought Hilda home a beautiful china doll with long red curls and a green satin dress. Claire said that instead of reacting with her customary delight to her father's latest gift, Hilda had taken one look at the doll and thrown it right back at him. Claire said it hit the wall behind her father's head and its face shattered into what had seemed like a thousand pieces.

"Father never said a word," Claire said. "He just turned round and went straight to the dining room and poured himself a glass of whiskey from the bottle he keeps on the top shelf of the hutch. I think he thinks he's hiding it from us up there. He forgets that Hilda and I do all the dusting since Mother's taken ill.

"Mother made me pick up the broken doll because Hilda refused to come out of her room until she heard Father leave the house," Claire continued. "I didn't know what to do with it, so I brought it out here."

I nodded, more out of sympathy than understanding, as I could no more imagine what had possessed her to dispose of a lifeless object in so eccentric a manner as I could see myself asking her why she had chosen to share the details of Hilda's tantrum with me. Clearly her mother wasn't the only Straussman prone to violent fits of temper. Having been the recipient of my own sister's not-inconsiderable wrath on occasion, it made me reconsider whether the sister, and not the mother, might not be the actual source of Claire's torment.

"Father gave me a present on his next trip home," Claire said, and again I nodded, if for no other reason than I imagined the gesture was just enough to signify interest in her disclosure without implying outright understanding. "It was a china doll almost just like Hilda's. I used to keep it on top of my bureau, but it seemed to upset Hilda so much that I finally put it in my underwear drawer."

Claire reached into the basket and withdrew a bundle from beneath the walnuts she had gathered. Slowly she unwrapped the cloth to reveal a china doll with long golden locks and a blue satin dress. Then she reached back into the basket and took out a gardener's trowel.

"When I finally fell asleep last night, I had a dream," Claire said. "I dreamed there was a herd of horses grazing in the orchard behind our house. White horses with flames for manes. They were frightening to look at, but somehow I wasn't afraid. I ran straight to the biggest one of all and I reached up and grabbed the flaming strands of his mane and I pulled myself onto his bare back. I could feel the flames crackling all around my fingers, but I didn't care. I knew the pain would not begin until I let go, so I held on for all I was worth, and the horse took off running through the trees."

"I didn't know you liked horses," I said.

"I don't," she said. "I don't like them at all."

After a moment or two, she began to dig a hole, clearly not the first she'd dug at this spot. I saw a small cross, roughly fashioned from twigs tied together with long grass, that appeared to have fallen over beside a dry mound of dirt.

"The horse was galloping so fast," Claire whispered, "I was afraid I might be knocked off by a tree branch and so I leaned down as far as I could until my face was buried in the flames on his neck and I closed my eyes, and that's when I knew what it felt like to die."

"Claire," I said as gently as I could. The sound of my voice seemed to rouse her from the memory of her nightmare. "Why are you telling me this?"

Claire did not look up, but she nodded her head and began to scrabble the ground with the trowel even more furiously. "Because you're the only one I can tell," she said.

"But I don't understand," I protested.

"You don't have to," she said, picking up the fallen cross and working it back into the ground.

"But Claire," I persisted.

"Let's just say I'm too old to play with dolls and let it go at that."

Seventeen

THE DRONE: Distinguished by his large size, rectangular abdomen, and additional eye facets, he neither gathers honey nor guards the hive. His sole purpose is to mate with a newly emerged queen. Once that function has been fulfilled, the surviving drones are generally driven from the hive when winter comes.

How does one measure time? Physicists now believe Albert Einstein may have been wrong, that subatomic particles may be able to move faster than the speed of light. From what I've read, this may ultimately alter the way we perceive the universe.

I find the implications of such calculations fascinating in the abstract sense, yet I am a simple beekeeper. Like my bees, I was raised to perceive time by the passing of seasons. It is, I admit, a less precise measurement, but it has for most of my life allowed me the comfort of predictability. Spring is the season of new life. Summer marks its fullness. Fall, the decline. And winter heralds both death and with the first blades of spring, the ultimate hope of renewal.

And then time fell apart.

It fell apart for me on that awful spring morning when I discovered Claire and Hilda Straussman's lifeless bodies lying bound and gagged on their parlor floor. The memory of Claire's eyes, fixed and milky with dead fright, plagued the certainty of my days and the silence of my nights.

Not that I am unfamiliar with acts of violence within the rhythm of the natural world, for even within the circumscription of my daily orbit I have witnessed my own honeybees driven to such hard-hearted acts against members of their own species that I shudder to recollect them. I have had, more times than I care to recount, the distinct misfortune of coming upon a horde of robber bees in the midst of a murderous raid on one of my hives and I have wept with grief seeing these hapless creatures pulling at one another and tumbling about the entrance to the hive in a brutal fight to the death. And if truth be told, though I am ashamed to admit it, on such occasions I have been tempted to curse the Good Lord for the hardness of His grand design even as I hasten to swat and kill these rogue maidens engaged against their own in mortal combat.

But while it pains my heart beyond measure to see this cruel perversion of a honeybee's communal spirit, I have accepted the necessity of this harsh struggle. I understand the rhythm of the hive dictates that when honey is scarce or flaunted unnecessarily by a careless keeper, the inhabitants of a rival hive or a feral swarm are naturally driven to set upon their neighbors to steal their precious store of food. In such cases, I can only hope I am lucky enough to come upon these warring factions while there is yet time to stay the carnage. That this can be accomplished I know because I have gained a regrettable expertise in fitting the entrance of the besieged hive with small wooden cleats made to narrow the opening until no more than a single invader or two may enter at a time, thus improving the defensive odds in favor of the hive's guard bees stationed on the inside of the landing board to repel such attacks.

If only the Straussman sisters had had such vigilance discharged on their behalf. At one time, I would like to think it would have been me. It should have been me.

Certainly Hilda could not defend herself nor, I fear, would not. Slowed as she was by age and a corpulent infirmity that resembled more each year the funereal fabric that had likewise shrouded her mother's bleak spirit, I believe there was a large part of Hilda that would have welcomed the inevitability, if not the exact manner, of her demise. Which left only Claire — poor, proud Claire — whose delicate spine, though it seemed no thicker than a bird's leg, refused to stoop even under the burden of all the years it carried. But for all her exalted pride, what defense could she hope to mount for herself and her sister, all alone and unprotected, against the senseless depravity of her fellow man or woman?

Such had been the connective thread of my tortured thoughts in the six long months that had passed since I'd last heard from Detective Grayson. I'd just come upon my number seven hive to find scores of dead bees, some with their attackers' lethal stingers still embedded in their bodies, littering the landing board, and nothing but more dead bodies inside piled in heaps on the bottom cover.

Consumed as I was, working with feverish speed to nail the last cleat down to the landing board before all was lost to marauding interlopers, I make no excuses for my startled reaction to Detective Grayson's sudden looming appearance on the doorstep of my honey shed, where I had gone to put away my smoker and bee brush.

"Sorry, Mr. Honig, I didn't mean to scare you like that," Detective Grayson demurred, extending one of his great bear paws and clapping me on the back in greeting as I bent over to pick up the tin smoker can and brush I'd just dropped.

"No need to apologize," I assured the detective, who I noted had added a disturbing ring of shadows beneath his hazel eyes since our last conversation regarding Claire's enigmatic excursion to Detroit. "You gave me quite a start, that's all."

"Sorry anyway," he insisted. "So how you been doing?"

"I've kept myself busy," I replied.

"That's good to hear. I've been keeping pretty busy myself," he said, and in the unnatural pause between his sentences I intuited his amiable grin was somewhat forced. "Maybe a little busier than I'd like."

He pulled a color photograph from his jacket pocket and handed it to me. I recognized it at once.

"Can I ask you again what you might be able to tell me about this young fellow here?" he said. I noticed another slight hitch in his voice, this time between *young* and *fellow* that confirmed my suspicion.

"What can you tell me about him?" he pressed.

Only everything and nothing at all, I thought, but I did not say as much. Yet I could not repress a small sigh as I stared once again at the smiling face of the young Marine in the photograph that had mingled for so long among the other faded snapshots perched upon the Straussmans' polished mantle. I handed the photograph back to the detective and turned to my workbench to put away the smoker and brush I'd retrieved.

"What is it you want to know?" I said. Having held my silence for so long, how much I should reveal at that particular moment was still a matter of debate in my mind.

"Well, Mr. Honig, I'd like to know why you didn't tell me you knew who this was the first time I showed you his picture or how come you didn't say anything about him when I asked you if the Straussman sisters had any next of kin?"

Why indeed?

When I thought for a moment of all the things I should have said or done in my life, all the real and imagined crimes of commission and omission, and all the reasons and regrets I had accumulated in the face of everything that had gone before, I could not help feeling this one small silence was the very least of my transgressions.

"My mother always told me to let sleeping dogs lie," I said, though, in truth, it was not my mother who had made for me the most adamant argument for such discretion.

"Well, my mother had a saying of her own," Detective Grayson said after a moment's consideration. "She used to say that he is not an honest man who has burned his tongue and does not tell the company the soup is hot."

"I don't understand."

"I think you do, Mr. Honig." He narrowed his eyes and caught mine in his. "No more bee stories. No more BS."

For once, I did not blink.

"His name is David Gilbert," I said. I couldn't swear that I felt better, but for the first time in what seemed like forever I didn't feel worse.

Detective Grayson smiled. His eyes held mine, but it seemed to me the tension in his shoulders had eased a bit. He pulled his ubiquitous notebook and pen from his jacket pocket. "So, Mr. Honig, can you tell me how the heck to find this guy?"

I was sure at that moment that I was the only one who had known where David Gilbert had come from and, besides Claire herself, why he had left, but to my shame and sorrow I never cared to find out what had become of him since. In this deliberate dearth of concern, I had always been my father's son.

"I'm sorry, Detective," I replied with sincere remorse, though I believe the good detective had begun to find my abjurations ever less compelling than I intended, "I have no idea where he is or how to find him. I truly don't."

The detective, who had flipped open his notebook and clicked his pen at the ready, took a great measured breath.

"Well then, Mr. Honig, perhaps you can tell me this: When was the last time you saw our mysterious Mr. David Gilbert?"

Eighteen

ROYAL JELLY: A protein-rich secretion that comes from the hypopharyngeal glands of mature workers, it is fed to all worker bees for the first three days of their larval stage, but only to potential queens for the rest of their lives thereafter. It is the steady diet of this substance that turns the ordinary worker bee into a queen.

Detective Grayson held the photograph up to my face again as if to prod my memory further, though I needed no such prompt. I could have told him without the slightest hesitation that it had been exactly eleven years four months three weeks and four days since I'd last set eyes on David Gilbert.

"Why don't we go back to the house?" I said at last, removing my gloves and laying them on the workbench next to my smoker can and brush. "It's more comfortable inside. I'll make us a pot of tea and we can talk."

"We can do that, Mr. Honig," Detective Grayson said. "Just promise me you'll play straight with me this time."

"I have never tried to deceive you, Detective."

"I didn't say you did."

"Then what are you saying?"

Detective Grayson let out another long sigh that reminded me of the temperamental radiator in our family's old Buick.

"Did you know I've been with the police department for almost thirty years?"

I admitted that I had not been aware of this fact.

"Well, I have," he said. "And I'm planning on retiring at the end of this year."

I was not sure whether to offer congratulations or condolences, but the detective gave me no time to decide. Instead, by way of impressing upon me a certain self-imposed deadline to his investigations, he proceeded to digress into a brief account of his plans to sell his house, buy several reasonably priced acres of land in Idaho, and perhaps take up fishing as a hobby.

"If you're looking for a retirement avocation, perhaps you should consider beekeeping. As Saint Ambrose discovered, beekeep-

213

ing is an excellent way to develop the virtue of patience," I said with no irony intended. I further told the detective that much like Saint Ambrose, he clearly possessed a keen sense of observation, which had served them both well in their chosen vocations.

"Okay, Mr. Honig, you win." The detective uttered a soft laugh — more of a grunt, really. He tapped the photograph one more time. "What do you say we just cut the chitchat and you tell me all about the last time you saw this guy?"

In the dim light of the honey shed, David Gilbert's scimitar grin flashed like a glint of steel across the dark contours of his face.

"October 15, 1981," I said at last. The detective slipped the photograph back into his jacket pocket and nodded, waiting for me to proceed, and so I did. I told him how I'd stopped by the Straussmans' house that day to bring them a jar of freshly harvested honey and to tell Claire about a new brand of foundation frames I'd just read about in one of the mail-order catalogs I subscribed to.

"I don't believe the company that makes them is still in business, but I couldn't say for sure as I haven't had the need to order any new foundation frames in quite some time. Not since I made the acquaintance of young Mr. Sweeny," I explained. "He lives about three or maybe four blocks from here, just past the railroad tracks. He's really quite a fine carpenter, especially for this day and age. He builds custom cabinets for a living, I believe, but he has the wherewithal to construct foundation frames for me, and at a fair market price."

"Mr. Honig, if you don't mind, we were talking about the last time you saw David Gilbert."

"Of course," I said, removing a clean rag from a drawer in my workbench. I began to wipe down my smoker can, as was my habit before placing it on a shelf in my tool cabinet next to several cans of motor oil I always kept on hand for emergencies. A place for everything and everything in its place.

"I was more than a bit surprised to see David Gilbert that day as he hadn't been to the house for quite some time. Not since he graduated from high school."

The detective began to scribble in his notebook as he stood beside me.

"To be quite honest, Detective, I'd always assumed David Gilbert would go away to college," I said. "Of course in my day a high school diploma was considered a luxury."

"When was that, Mr. Honig?"

"That would have been the Great Depression, Detective," I said, "well before your time. Or David Gilbert's, for that matter. Most of us did whatever we could to help support our families back then. Besides, there was a perfectly fine public library less than a mile down the road, my father used to say, so what did I need with school?"

"But what about David Gilbert?"

"Well, after the war it seemed like all the young boys couldn't wait to leave the family farms and businesses to go off to college. And David Gilbert was such a bright boy, I naturally assumed that's where he'd end up. But the fool went off half-cocked and joined the Marines just as soon as he turned eighteen."

"When was that?"

"Oh, heavens, that would have been almost thirty years ago at least. Nineteen sixty-three at the latest?"

"What happened to him then?" the detective prodded.

"I believe he was stationed out of state for a spell. Texas, or Arizona, perhaps. Somewhere in the Southwest. If I recall correctly, he got married to a Mexican girl not too long after he reenlisted. Carmella or Carmelina, I believe her name was. Something like that. She wasn't especially fluent in

English, but she was quite a lovely girl. I only met her the one time, but I remember she had a sweet smile and a spark in her eyes such as I hadn't seen since Claire was a young girl."

"Do you remember anything else about her or her family?"

"Not really. But as I said, I hadn't seen or heard anything about David Gilbert for quite some time, so I was a bit taken aback to find him and his family, sitting bold as you please, right there in the parlor with Claire and Hilda that day. He and Carmen — yes, I believe it was Carmen — they had a little girl with them. Tina or Tini, I think they called her. Just a slip of a thing, really. Straight dark hair like her mother's and his, but fair-skinned and delicate. She was a pretty little thing. Quiet, but sharp. You know how you can just tell with some children, even if they don't say anything, that they're taking it all in.

"As far as I could tell, they were all getting along just fine at first. Claire and Hilda had brought out the company tea set, and they were sitting around the parlor chatting about David Gilbert's travels, and Carmen's family, and then all at once Claire and him got into a horrible argument. The little girl had gone off with Hilda somewhere else in

217

the house by the time David Gilbert and Claire started shouting back and forth at each other, until Carmen began to cry, and then he went looking for the little girl and as soon as he found her he gathered up their belongings and stormed out of the house with his wife and daughter and that's the last I ever saw of him or his family. It was the last Claire or Hilda ever saw any of them either, as far as I know."

"As far as you know?" the detective repeated.

"I can't be certain," I said, closing the door on my tool cabinet and turning back around to face the detective. "I never spoke another word to Claire or Hilda after that day."

I stepped past Detective Grayson and out into the sunlight again. I waited for him to follow, and then, locking the door of the honey shed behind me — a regrettable habit I'd acquired in recent years as the face of the neighborhood had begun to change — I ushered the detective across the yard.

"So what was this fight all about?" the detective persisted.

I considered how best to put my answer. I did not wish to air Claire's dirty laundry in public if I did not have to.

"They disagreed over the proper way to

raise a child," I said, which was true enough, and enough said as far as I was concerned.

"Doesn't seem like much to start a family feud over."

"I suppose not," I said. "But Claire had a way of letting her emotions run away with her."

"So what about you?" the detective said.

"I beg your pardon?"

"You say you never spoke to Claire after that day," the detective pressed. "How come?"

Again, I weighed my words as best I could. "Well, Detective Grayson," I said, "let's just say that I allowed myself to be dragged into the fray against my better judgment."

"Sort of stuck your nose in where it didn't belong, eh?"

"I suppose you could say that," I replied. "Though, to be quite honest, I did so most unwillingly."

"Well, meaning no disrespect, Mr. Honig, but in my line of work I've found that despite what anybody says, people seldom do anything they don't want to do."

"You may be right," I acknowledged. "At least, in the general sense. But I can assure you I had no desire to meddle in the Straussman family's affairs."

"I believe you, Mr. Honig," Detective

Grayson said. "I just have to wonder why you didn't see fit to tell me about all this earlier?"

"I was raised to believe that what went on between families in private should stay that way."

"Are you sure that's the only reason?"

What I was sure of was that Detective Grayson was sincere in his desire to solve this one last troubling case, that it would somehow be a satisfying coda to his long career. I could only hope he might allow me my own motivations.

"If I thought for a moment that this long-ago spat had been germane to Claire's murder, I assure you I would have been more forthcoming," I said.

"Well, how about from now on you just answer my questions and let me be the judge of what's relevant?"

It was a fair request. While I had not deliberately set out to mislead him, I had most certainly allowed him to proceed under some faulty assumptions through my guilty silence.

I nodded my assent.

"Okay, then," the detective said, "what can you tell me about David Gilbert?"

I took a deep breath.

"I believe he was stationed at the Tustin

Marine Base the last time I saw him, if that will help."

"I believe it will," Detective Grayson said, his voice softening just a bit.

"Please, let's go inside where it's warm," I said. "I promise I'll do my best to answer any more questions you have."

"Sounds good."

Taking the detective's elbow in my hand, I turned him gently toward the house. As I mentioned before, I never did acquire any real fondness for tea, but the detective's stomach seemed to be bothering him a bit, judging from the way he grimaced and grabbed at his belt from time to time as we walked. Though having no love of tea for tea's sake alone, I suggested that a soothing pot of chamomile might do us both a world of good.

"I should warn you now," I said as we reached the foot of the porch stairs, "I really don't know much more about David Gilbert than what I've already told you."

"We'll see," he said as he followed me up onto the porch and through my back door. Once inside the kitchen, the good detective at first declined my offer of toast and honey. But I insisted.

"It's eucalyptus," I said, setting the jar down on the kitchen table next to the plate of buttered toast I had prepared while the water was boiling. "Do you take cream?"

"No thanks," he said. "I don't care for it."

"Nor do I," I said. "I prefer a spot of honey to sweeten my cup. Would you care for some?"

The detective shrugged. I took his indifference as acquiescence.

"David Gilbert loved honey on toast," I said. "I believe that's why Claire took up beekeeping herself. And by that I mean not just helping us out, which she had been doing on and off since we were adolescents, but taking on hives of her own. That came many years later. She must have been in her mid-twenties by then. Both her parents were still alive, as I recall, but they didn't get around as well as they used to. Not that they ever spent too much time out in the orchard even when they were able. Mr. and Mrs. Straussman weren't what you would call out-of-doors types. But then again, neither was Claire, except when it came to bees. My father and I helped Claire set up her first hive, way out there beyond the almond trees," I said, pointing to the north end of the Straussmans' orchard, where patches of weeds, nut hulls, and rotted fruit littered the ground.

The detective's eyes followed the direc-

222

tion of my gesture. Then he pulled his battered notebook back out of his jacket pocket, where I assume he had replaced it during our walk from the honey shed to the house, and he set it down next to his teacup.

"It was the eucalyptus honey that did it," I said, placing a chamomile tea bag in his cup and mine.

"Did what?"

"Why, it's what got everything started," I replied. "Claire decided she wanted a hive of her own right after David Gilbert's first taste of eucalyptus honey. It was from a jar I'd given her on her previous birthday — shortly after the war, I believe. No, on second thought, it would have had to have been a bit later than that because David Gilbert wasn't born until the war was almost over and Claire didn't start keeping her own hives until he was at least five years old."

The detective opened his notebook, and I poured hot water into his teacup and mine. We sat for a moment, allowing the fragrant steam to rise from our cups. I dipped my teaspoon into the jar of eucalyptus honey I'd set on the table and stirred a dollop into the detective's cup and then another into my own. The aroma was intoxicating. I let my mind wander.

"I want to surprise him," Claire had confided. My parents had gone off to church, while I stayed home to clean up the breakfast dishes. Claire had come knocking on our back door just as I was wiping the last plate dry. She seemed surprised when I opened our back door.

"Is your father home?" she'd stammered. "Or your mother?"

"No. It's Sunday," I said.

"Of course." Her shoulders drooped just a bit as she turned to go.

"Is there something I can help you with?" I said. Holding the door open with my shoulder, I wiped my hands dry with the dish towel.

"No. No, thank you, Albert." She started down the porch steps, but then stopped and turned.

"Do you know how much your father would charge me for one of his beehives?"

"Goodness, Claire, we couldn't take your money," I said, regretting my words as soon as I saw Claire's jaw begin to set.

"I don't need your charity."

"Of course not, Claire," I said. I stepped out onto the porch, letting the door swing softly closed behind me. "It's just that my family has always believed that bees should never be bought or sold for money. Bees *may* be acquired through trade, however, and I am sure that providing you with a starter hive and the basic equipment you'll need would constitute more than fair trade for the all the labor you've freely given on our bees' behalf over the years."

This last pronouncement seemed to sufficiently mollify Claire.

"There's a nice clearing, out beyond our almond grove," she said, the barest hint of a smile beginning to play at the edges of her lips. "This is where I want the hive to go."

What she didn't say was that this particular clearing was as far away from her family's house as physically possible and still be located within the Straussmans' property lines. Since this was hardly the most convenient placement, I'd naturally assumed it had been chosen to preempt any objections from her parents.

"We'll bring everything over this evening after dinner," I said, feeling rather pleased with myself.

"I'll meet you in the grove at seven," Claire said.

Though I was the junior partner in our family's beekeeping enterprise, my father heartily endorsed the independent arrangement I'd just made when he returned home from church later that afternoon.

I had assumed that Claire would bring David Gilbert with her since he had been the inspiration for her sudden decision to acquire her own hive. Yet when my father and I arrived at the clearing at the appointed time, we found Hilda standing silently by Claire's side instead. I noticed that when she saw that my father had come with me, Claire's demeanor visibly softened. It was a funny thing. Though Claire was by this time a grown woman who usually projected a hardened air of self-sufficiency, whenever my father was present she tended to remind me of the wonder-struck girl who'd just touched her first swarm.

"Hilda's offered to help me tend our hive," Claire said in that way she had of closing off all further discussion with a simple declarative sentence. Hilda smiled rather nervously, but she nodded her assent, more to her sister than either my father or myself. I was about to wonder aloud whether Hilda's offer had been as voluntary as Claire made it out to be when I caught a sharp look from my father that stayed any further comment. Perhaps such filial deference from a grown man such as myself might seem strange today, but in my day respect for one's elders did not come with an expiration date. Nor did common courtesy.

My father told Hilda he was glad that she'd decided to join in Claire's enterprise, and with that we began unfastening the ropes we'd used to secure the hive and equipment to the old wooden pushcart we generally used to haul loads of full supers from our outlying hives to our honey shed. My father explained that he was confident we would be able to acquire a replacement swarm over the coming season and so he'd decided to give Claire one of our established hives rather than a small nucleus brood and queen as I'd assumed he would.

"This is a gentle queenright colony. It should give you a strong start in your move up from assistant to full-fledged beekeeper," he'd said, and then, turning to Hilda, he graciously added, "Especially now that Claire has you to help."

"It'll be fun, you'll see," Claire said to Hilda, who nodded back at Claire though her accompanying smile seemed tentative at best.

While Claire was familiar enough with all the hive components and tools my father and I had brought, Hilda was not, and so I took it upon myself to name each piece of equipment and its use as I unloaded it from the cart.

"This is the hive stand," I said, placing the four-legged wooden support platform on a patch of level ground while my father unfastened the mooring ropes that had held the hive body securely on the cart during its transport. "The stand keeps the hive up and away from predators and preserves the bottom board by keeping it off the damp ground."

I gathered into my arms an old smoker can, bellows, and a can of smoker fuel and was about to set them all on the ground next to the hive stand when my father handed Claire my old bee veil, the same one my mother had loaned her when she first started working in my family's apiary.

"You might as well keep this over here now," my father said. There was a slight hitch in his voice, which surprised me as my father wasn't normally given to sentimentality toward such utilitarian objects. "I think we have another one we can spare for Hilda. Albert will bring it round tomorrow."

"Thank you, Mr. Honig," Claire said. She smiled at Hilda.

"Well," I said, "you use this smoker here to keep your bees gentle during hive inspections and honey harvesting."

I explained to Hilda how smoke kindled

the bees' natural instinct to gorge themselves on honey in preparation for fleeing a burning hive. And once so subdued, a beekeeper may move and manipulate his or her bees without undue fear of defensive stings.

"What about this?" Hilda said, pointing a doughy finger at the flat metal device lying on the cart next to the hive body.

"It's called a hive tool," Claire said.

"Yes," I confirmed after a moment's pause. I honestly couldn't remember the last time Hilda had spoken directly to me. Her voice was raspier than I'd remembered, as if her words had to claw their way out into the open air.

"The curved end is for scraping the foundation frames," Claire explained as she picked the tool up and turned it around for Hilda to see. "You use this flat side here to pry the hive open."

"And then you take this brush," I said, picking up the bee brush to demonstrate how it was used to gently whisk bees from the hive's foundation frames when my father called for me to give him a hand in removing the staples from the hive components, which we had secured in preparation for the move. As we slid off the C-shaped staples, I told Hilda that the bottom part of the hive was called the brood chamber and that it contained developing eggs, larvae, young nurse bees and attendants, and a queen bee.

"These lower supers are where the worker bees store the honey the colony needs to survive. We harvest only the excess honey that they store in these shallow top supers."

"Are there bees in the hive now?" Hilda inquired, a hint of alarm creeping into her odd scratchy voice.

"Of course," I replied. I hoped to allay her fears by explaining that we had waited until the colony was bedded down for the night before moving the hive.

"Don't worry, Hilda," Claire added, "you can tell they're asleep. Listen."

Nodding to my father, Claire explained to her sister that the low, steady hum we could all clearly hear coming from the hive signified the bees inside were safely at rest. Nevertheless, Hilda took a few steps back when my father and I gripped the body of the hive and heaved it off the cart and onto its stand in one quick move. Then, after we had situated the hive squarely onto its platform, my father took a weathered hammer from the cart and abruptly began to give the brood chamber a series of sharp raps all around.

"Don't make them mad!" Hilda exclaimed as she quickly skittered a dozen yards back as the distinctive whine of rapidly beating wings began to emanate from within the awakening hive.

"Keep your voice down and they won't bother you," my father said in a slow, even tone, further reassuring Hilda by explaining that bees seldom leave their hive after sundown. "We're just letting them know that a change in their circumstances has occurred."

The moon was just tipping the tops of the almond trees by the time the din inside the hive finally subsided, and in the meantime my father and I tried to allay any lingering doubts and questions the two sisters might yet harbor.

"All quiet again," my father said at last. He then instructed Claire and Hilda to gather a few handfuls of dried grass and make a barrier of it all around the entrance to the hive. "When your field bees come out of the hive in the morning, this will remind them that a change has indeed been made."

Claire had been around my father long enough to know that when he spoke, he had something important to say, and so she appeared prepared to do whatever he told her to do in order to ensure the well-being of her newly acquired charges. Hilda, on the other hand, remained skeptical, judging from the halfhearted way she had begun to pluck at a few blades of grass near her feet.

I decided to appeal to what I assumed was an inherently more rational nature than that of Claire's. I explained to Hilda that bees use the sun's position to orient themselves in their foraging flights to and from the hive. Without some radical reminders that their hive location has changed in relation to the sun's position, bees often revert to their familiar orientation point and return to the former site of their hive.

"The grass at the entrance disrupts their normal routine and this prompts many of them to fly round in circles to get their bearings. This reorients them and seems to help them remember where to return after they've collected their fill of nectar and pollen," I said, adding that in the morning we would also place a shoe box on the old hive stand so that if any stragglers mistakenly return to their former home, they could be brought back to their new hive that evening. "We'll cut a hole into one end of the box so that they will have shelter in the meantime."

"You'll see," Claire said to Hilda, taking the grass from her sister's hands and adding it to the pile she'd already arranged on the landing board of the hive.

"One more thing," my father said, turning back to Claire, who was whispering something I could not hear to Hilda. "First thing tomorrow morning, be sure to tell your bees that you are their new mistress."

My father assured them both that this was a very simple ritual but that it must be observed when a change in ownership takes place.

"Otherwise your bees may never settle into their new home," I chimed in. "This could severely disrupt your hive's honey-flow or, worse, the colony might decide to swarm or your queen could stop laying altogether."

Claire placed a hand on her sister's shoulder as if to silence any objections, spoken or otherwise.

"Albert can come back over in the morning to show you what you must do," my father said. "Tonight, though, you're going to want to find a safe, dry place to store your equipment."

"I know, Mr. Honig, a place for everything and everything in its place," Claire said with a wry smile as she began gathering up the beekeeping gear we'd brought. "We have a little shed behind the house where we keep our gardening tools and baskets. We can store all this there."

And then, to my father's surprise, Claire took his right hand in hers and shook it heartily. "Thank you, Mr. Honig."

"You're welcome, Claire," my father said, withdrawing his hand and slipping it quickly into his pocket as he gripped one of the cart handles with his left hand and instructed me to grab the other.

"You too, Albert," Claire called out to me as she and Hilda, their arms laden with gear, headed back through the grove toward their house.

"Mr. Honig?" There was an urgency to Detective Grayson's tone. "Are you all right?"

"I'm fine," I assured him as I unclenched my hand from the arm of my chair. The detective nodded and picked up his notebook.

"I kinda lost you there for a minute," he said. He began flipping back and forth through the pages until he found the one he was looking for. "We were talking about David Gilbert's fondness for eucalyptus honey."

"Of course," I said. I took another bite of my toast and washed it down with a sip of tea. "Claire told me once that when the boy first tasted our eucalyptus honey, his eyes lit up like they were full of fireflies. That's how she put it: Full of fireflies. That's when she decided, right on the spot — Claire was always such an impetuous girl — to make sure that David Gilbert had all the honey he could ever eat in a month of Sundays. I remember thinking that there are no fireflies in California. I meant to ask her where she'd come up with such an exotic image, but Claire was already running on about how she could watch David Gilbert like that forever."

The detective looked up from his note-book but said nothing. He nodded silently for me to continue.

"You know, she used to sing to her bees," I said.

He raised his eyebrows slightly, and so I recounted how every morning, regular as clockwork, Claire used to stop at every hive and sing an old Scottish tune her grand-mother taught her when she was a little girl.

"What was the name of it?" I mused aloud. Detective Grayson shrugged.

"You know the one," I urged. "It started: *'By yon bonnie banks and by yon bonnie braes, / Where the sun shines bright on Loch Lomond.'* Yes, that was it. 'Loch Lomond.' Her father's people were German, but her mother's family was of Scottish descent.

Claire said she learned the song when her family visited her grandparents in Saint Louis one summer when she was just a little girl. She had such a lovely voice when she was younger — Claire, I mean. Clear and delicate as crystal. I'm sorry you never had the chance to know her as I did."

"And how would that have been, Mr. Honig?"

"How would what have been?" I asked.

"How did you know Miss Straussman?"

"As a friend, Detective. A very dear friend."

"And what about David Gilbert?" the detective pressed. "What was he to you?"

"Nothing at all," I said sadly. More sadly, in truth, than I would have imagined possible.

Still, I suppose in light of the detective's apparent line of questioning what came next was inevitable.

"Okay, what was he to her, then?" the detective said, looking up from his notebook to stare straight into my eyes. "David Gilbert to Claire, I mean. Her Detroit relations seem to think he was a nephew or orphan cousin from somewhere down South. They weren't real clear about it. The one thing they were sure of was that David

Gilbert grew up here in the Straussman house."

I nodded my assent.

"That's what's been puzzling me, Mr. Honig. How come you knew all about this young man who lived right next door to you for God knows how many years and yet you never bothered to mention word one about him until now? If I didn't know any better, I'd think you were trying to hide something. Heck, somebody less trusting than I might even think you were attempting to impede a murder investigation."

The detective set his pen down and looked me straight in the eyes. "So what's your take on David Gilbert?"

What I thought was what I had thought about many times over the years, but I had never spoken a word of it to anyone before. Except to Claire, and only that one disastrous time. At this particular moment, however, try as I might, I could see no way around the detective's question but to answer it as truthfully as I could.

"David Gilbert was Claire's son," I replied.

And the detective uttered a low rumble of assent as he took up his pen again and underlined something he had previously written down.

NINETEEN

HOLLOW TREE THEORY: Wild bees live in hollow trees. When wildflowers bloom, bees produce honey. When the space in the hollow is filled, wild bees begin to swarm.

I cocked my head as inconspicuously as I dared, but I was unable to make out even the gist of Detective Grayson's scrawl from my reversed vantage.

"Now, why do you suppose I'm not surprised to learn from you that Claire Straussman was David Gilbert's mother?" he said, not bothering to look up as he wrote furiously in his notebook. I assumed the question was rhetorical and waited for him to make his own reply.

"Well, let me tell you, Mr. Honig," the detective said, setting his pen down and looking up at last, "it doesn't surprise me, because when I'd just about run out of leads

238

I decided to play a hunch."

As I sat across the table from this rumpled, worn-out man, it occurred to me that while doggedness was the bread and butter of Detective Grayson's day-to-day talent, it was his willingness to play hunches that sparked his occasional brilliance. The detective took another one of his great bear sighs as if deciding whether to devour me whole or continue to toy with me.

"I have this old buddy in the D.A.'s office back in Detroit," he said, "and he owes me a favor. So I got him to pull the birth records for babies with the last name of Straussman who were born in Wayne County within a year or two of the start of World War Two. That's about the time Claire went off to live with her cousin in Detroit, as I recall."

"I believe that's what you said," I said, reliving again the anguish I felt at her departure as if it were yesterday and wishing it was yesterday all over again just to say what I should have said then. I wondered at that moment whether there were fireflies in Detroit.

"So, Mr. Honig," the detective said, drawing me back to the point at hand, "I'm sure I don't have to tell you that my buddy didn't find any Straussmans named David Gilbert."

Of course I was not surprised, though I was hesitant to say so aloud. I nodded for the detective to continue.

"Then I remembered something Margaret Lennox's daughter said about the Straussmans having some family down South, in Alabama maybe. So I started calling in a few more favors — and it took a while — but one of my wife's cousins is a social worker in Birmingham and she came up with adoption papers for a baby boy, first name David, middle name Gilbert. Born May 10, 1945. Adoptive parents Marvella and Phillip Straussman. The names of the birth parents were left blank, and the adoption records were sealed. That's how most adoptions were done in those days, but then you probably know all about that."

I drained the last of the tea from my cup as I took a moment to grasp the full implication of Detective Grayson's insinuation. He was right of course, in that I was certain of far more than I had already told him. I knew as well as he did that David Gilbert hadn't been born on that first trip to Detroit, as the detective had initially assumed, but several years later when Claire and Hilda and their mother had gone off together to

Alabama, ostensibly to tend to an orphaned cousin who had gotten herself in trouble with the wrong sort of man — a man who'd filled her heart full of promises he had no intention of keeping — leaving the poor girl penniless and with child, or so Mrs. Straussman had uncharacteristically volunteered to my mother upon their return four months later with a month-old baby in tow.

"It was the only Christian thing to do," my mother had agreed when she ran into Mrs. Straussman outside of church the Sunday after the baby arrived, along with a trunkful of luggage. "The poor girl has no husband, no prospects, and no way of taking care of the child, after all."

My mother later confessed to my father that she was as surprised by the sight of Mrs. Straussman, hobbled as she was by her growing litany of infirmities, leaning on her cane next to the family's automobile, a long-nosed Buick Special, parked at the curb in front of the church with Claire's father sitting silently in the driver's seat. My mother said she was even more dumfounded, however, by Mrs. Straussman's ensuing revelation and the fact that she chose to reveal it to her, of all people, considering their chilly history. I recalled how my mother told my father that she somehow managed to find the words to commend the woman for her Christian charity. Even then, I suspected that my mother was no more fooled by Mrs. Straussman's story than I was, though she never said so in public, and she never knew, as I did with empirical certainty, the child's true parentage.

I stared for a moment more into my empty teacup, choosing my words as carefully as any I ever had.

"Detective, if I understand your intimation, you are laboring under the mistaken impression that I am David Gilbert's father," I said, reaching for the teapot to refill my cup. "Please, let me assure you nothing could be further from the truth."

"So what exactly is the truth, Mr. Honig?" the detective pressed.

"The truth is often quite different from the facts," I replied. "Which do you prefer?"

"I prefer my truth to be based on facts," he said, clearly implying in the tilt of his head that an element of distrust had once again crept into his interpretation of anything I might say.

"The fact is, Detective Grayson, Claire had a brief, sordid encounter with a man," I said after some consideration. I saw the detective raise one of his unruly eyebrows.

"The truth, however, is that she never truly loved the man, nor, I suspect, the son who came of that unfortunate union, and I will regret to my dying day that in all the years I knew this harsh truth I never once uttered a single word of comfort to ease the pain."

With deliberate slowness, it seemed to me, the detective clicked the tip of his ballpoint pen and then flipped the cover closed on his notebook and placed both in his jacket pocket.

"Whose pain are we talking about now, Mr. Honig," he said, "theirs or yours?"

TWENTY

QUEEN EXCLUDER: A device made of wire, wood, or zinc with openings that are large enough to allow worker bees to freely pass between the upper and lower hive components but confine the larger queen and drones to the brood chamber.

Even in retrospect, there is no way now to measure the relative depth of pain suffered by any and all who were touched by the tragic life and death of Claire Straussman, including Claire herself. I am only more certain than ever that Goethe knew whereof he spoke when he wrote that nothing is more damaging to a new truth than an old error.

Shortly after our visit, Detective Grayson was able to locate the boy through his military records. Of course he was hardly a boy by this time. He was still in the military, however, and he had been serving in the

Middle East when Claire and Hilda were killed, an alibi that was easily corroborated by his superiors. In fact, he was serving overseas when the detective reached him by telephone and informed him of Claire's and Hilda's tragic deaths. Though he was hardly overcome by grief, David Gilbert did express some small regret over the manner of their demise.

"I always figured they'd just dry up and blow away some day," he had said, according to Detective Grayson. In the course of their brief conversation, David Gilbert also told the detective that he and his wife had split up six years earlier and that she had taken their daughter back to Texas to be near their extended family.

"Apparently the split was pretty nasty," the detective told me when I inquired after David Gilbert's wife and daughter. "The wife had a restraining order put out on him before she and the girl moved back to Texas."

"I am sorry to hear that," I said. Evidently David Gilbert had become no less reticent in expressing his anger than his forebears had been. I had somehow hoped that his early exit from the family fold might have spared him this curse. But it appeared this was the least of his problems.

"Does this mean he no longer speaks to his wife or child?" I inquired. The thought of living out most of my adult life estranged from those nearest and dearest to me saddened me in ways I couldn't begin to express.

"You could say that," the detective replied. "David Gilbert told me his wife died in a car accident a little over two years after the divorce."

"But what happened to the child?"

"Well, according to him, his daughter's grandparents took custody of the girl and brought her back to Mexico to live with them."

I couldn't help wondering aloud whether such an unconventional guardianship would have been sanctioned by the courts.

"Surely David Gilbert must have contested this situation," I said.

"Well, Mr. Honig, even he admitted there were problems in the home long before the breakup."

I don't know why Detective Grayson's tone softened, but I was grateful that he took the time to explain to me that while David Gilbert clearly hadn't been pleased with the custody arrangement, there was little he felt he could do about it. Because he was stationed out of the country at the time, and based on some particularly damaging testimony regarding a domestic disturbance call that had come out during the divorce proceedings, the grandparents were granted full and permanent custody of the girl after her mother's death.

"Like I said, it was a pretty messy situation all round," Detective Grayson said.

I was reminded of the last time that I'd seen them all together: David Gilbert, his wife, and their young daughter. Despite the contentious circumstances of their visit with Claire and Hilda, the three of them had seemed happy enough. In fact, they had shown all the signs of loving mates and doting parents. It was Claire who had drawn David Gilbert's considerable ire — and justifiably so, I might add — as in the heat of her own anger she had been most insulting to them.

What had struck me then was that David Gilbert had exhibited a physical restraint rare among the Straussman clan in the face of all he'd endured that day. Indeed, the more Claire railed against him, the calmer he'd become, although in hindsight I suppose that what I took for composure may have been much closer to the sear of an ember that burns from within, more likely to flare up unexpectedly than to die out altogether.

However, David Gilbert eventually inquired about whether any formal burial arrangements had been made for Claire and Hilda, and Detective Grayson had informed him they would have been disposed of rather unceremoniously by the state once the collection of evidence and other such investigative formalities had been completed, had I not offered to pay for a decent Christian burial for the two of them. Though he was under no legal obligation to do so, David Gilbert insisted on reimbursing me for the modest costs I had incurred. That is, in fact, how I came to learn of his whereabouts, as Detective Grayson had been kind enough to contact me to relay his offer. When I tried to decline, the detective assured me that David Gilbert had both the financial wherewithal, and the ethical inclination to "set things straight," as he put it, and so eventually I relented.

David Gilbert did not, however, ask me or Detective Grayson where Claire and Hilda had been laid to rest. I assume he never went to visit them either, as I know for certain that I have never seen any flowers placed on their graves other than those that I have brought from my own garden.

TWENTY-ONE

AFTERSWARM: A small swarm, usually led by a virgin queen, which may leave the hive after the prime swarm has departed.

Claire's and Hilda's murders likely would have remained unsolved until this day had it not been for the chance discovery of Claire's diary among an odd cache of keepsakes found in the possession of a pair of young burglary suspects nearly a year after the bees had led me to the Straussman sisters' lifeless bodies.

I had not thought Claire to be the sentimental type and so I was surprised to learn that any personal items such as diaries and vacation souvenirs existed in the first place, just as I was in the dark about the secret cubbyhole in which the Straussmans had kept their valuables.

The evidentiary connection between these items, a routine inventory of stolen goods, and the Straussmans' untimely deaths might not have been made at all had it not been for an offhand remark made by a fellow officer to Detective Grayson regarding a puzzling loose end to an otherwise straightforward string of burglary cases to which he had been assigned. The officer mentioned that he had recovered a rather large trove of stolen goods in a public storage unit situated near a celebrated amusement park in our area. The officer had been able to trace nearly everything he'd found in the unit back to a rash of unsolved burglaries that had taken place over the previous several months and this in turn had led to the arrest of a young man and woman living in a crime-ridden apartment complex adjacent to the parking lot on the park's east side. Most of the contraband Detective Grayson's colleague had recovered from the storage unit was typical of such burglaries: television sets, stereo equipment, computers, video recorders, cameras, handguns, jewelry, and other easily salable items.

What had puzzled Detective Grayson's colleague was a dusty military-issue strongbox dating back to World War II. Even odder was that it held nothing more valuable than a mason jar filled with old pennies and nickels, a dried-up leather bolo tie with tarnished silver clasp and tips, a faded autograph book, and a diary written by a woman named Clarinda J. Straussman. The officer said the various ink and pencil inscriptions were so faded in both books as to be barely legible.

Detective Grayson, who was by this time less than six months from retiring, asked his colleague if he might examine the anomalous strongbox's contents. The officer responded by fetching it directly from the evidence storage locker and depositing box and all on the detective's desk later that same day.

I learned all of this late one afternoon in August of 1993 when much to my surprise I opened my front door and found Detective Grayson standing on my porch. His eyes looked grayer in the dying afternoon light than I'd recalled them being.

"Detective Grayson," I stammered through the crack in the door. I had become much more cautious in my habits over the previous year since my neighbors had been murdered in their own home. "I thought surely you'd retired by now."

"No, not quite," he replied in his usual brusque manner. "May I come in?"

"Of course," I said, swinging my door wide open. Remembering my manners, I offered him a cup of tea, but he declined, saying he was in a bit of a hurry. He told me that there might be a new development in the Straussman murder case. He said it had something to do with the arrest of a pair of burglary suspects the previous evening and he asked if I might be able to accompany him to the police station, where he had some recovered property that he wanted me to take a look at.

"Right now?"

"If you don't mind."

"Let me just get my sweater," I said. "The evening chill affects my old bones more and more these days."

He invited me to ride with him in the front seat of his unmarked police car as we drove the mile or so through what was left of the old part of town to the newly renovated police station, which now abutted the city's main library.

"It's funny how things work out sometimes," Detective Grayson observed rather mirthlessly, reminding me then and there of the true definition of irony as I sensed that there was nothing humorous in what the good detective wished to show me. At least, that is what I thought as he escorted me through the station's security door and led me down a long hallway that opened into a warren of cubicles, which I assumed were the police detectives' new quarters judging from the aroma of fresh paint emanating from the barren beige walls. Barren, that is, save for the line of portraits of previous police chiefs hung in chronological order of service.

Detective Grayson's cubicle, one of six in a cluster in the east corner of the room, was dominated by a large gunmetal desk and a matching institutionally functional gray metal bookcase bolted to the beige padded wall opposite the desk in case of earthquake. I noticed that the shelves were half filled with books on penal codes and other official-looking law enforcement codices.

Detective Grayson settled himself into a rolling chair upon entering his realm and directed me with a stiff sweep of his arm to a stationary wooden chair next to his desk.

"Make yourself comfortable," he said, and as I scooted the straight-backed chair closer to him he pointed to a dull metal box on his desk. It was slightly taller than a shoe box and painted a muddy greenish-brown common to military equipment. I noticed on closer inspection that it had a handle that flattened into its top by two loose metal rings and a watertight side latch. Die-stamped into the metal beneath the latch was AMMO. BOX CAL .50 M2, and on the side ACME U.S.

"Ever see this ammo box before?" the detective inquired. Puzzled, I shook my head. He slid the box nearer to him as if to examine it closer.

"Looks to be World War Two vintage. Still in pretty good shape," he persisted. "Might even be worth something to a collector."

"I've never seen it before, Detective," I said. "I am quite sure of it."

He responded with what seemed to me an indifferent shrug as though he rather expected my response despite his prodding. The detective then released the latch, lifted the lid, and reached into the strongbox. I noticed that GOV'T REJECT was stamped on the underside of the lid in faded black ink. Keeping his eyes on me, the detective pulled out a worn leather-bound book.

"Do you recognize this, Mr. Honig?" he asked as he placed the book on the desk in front of me.

Picking it up, I turned it over several times before leafing gingerly through the yellowed pages, trying not to look too closely at what was written on any one page. I shook my head and handed the book back to the detective.

"Do you recognize it?" the detective repeated.

"No," I said honestly. "I've never seen this before."

"Are you sure? Could you look at it again?"

The detective picked the book back up and fanned the pages slowly under my nose. The musty scent of aged leather and paper — and something else . . . lavender, or jasmine perhaps — assaulted my senses as a word here and there tugged at the edge of my vision. I closed my eyes. It was clear these were the confessions of someone's very private and innermost thoughts. The detective stopped on a page midway through the diary.

"Mr. Honig," he said, and my eyes opened, almost against my will, and fixed on a familiar name midway down the page: Hilda.

Hilda told me today that she wished it were her leg instead of Mother's that had to be cut off. When I asked her why she would want to do such a thing for Mother, she said it wasn't Mother that she wanted to do it for . . .

I felt ill. Sick to my soul. I shook my head.

"Please, Mr. Honig," Detective Grayson said, handing the book back to me. "Please. This is important."

I closed the diary and opened it again, this time to another random entry, penned, according to the date at the head of the page, on June 14, 1934. It was only a paragraph long, and even now I can remember what it said, if not exactly word for word then certainly close enough to the gist and tone of it to render an accurate evocation.

Albert said the strangest thing the other night. He said my name should have been Diana because I reminded him of the moon. I asked him if he'd ever listened to Debussy's "Clair de Lune" and he said he wasn't allowed to listen to secular music. But then he said a funny thing. He asked me if I ever wondered about what went on inside the Harmony Ballroom. I said of course I did. And do you know what that silly goose did? He looked at me as if I was some sort of floozy. And then he said he just shut his window when the music got too loud. I told him he couldn't shut the world out forever, but Lord knows he's giving it the old college try.

Silently recalling the full conversation as if it were yesterday, I could hear in my head the lilt of the playful taunt she had issued. "Don't be such a silly goose, Albert. Be a gander." And then she had laughed, lightly and without malice, amused by the cleverness of her wordplay. I sighed deeply, and thankfully Detective Grayson allowed me the privacy of my memories.

"I thought so," Detective Grayson said simply, anticipating the answer to his implied question.

"Yes, it's Claire's," I confirmed, closing the diary and setting it down on the desk next to the strongbox.

"What about this?" he asked me next, placing a smaller string-bound booklet in my hands. I opened it to the first page and read:

My Memories of My Visit to Detroit, Michigan. June 24, 1942, to November 30, 1942. To Keep my friends / Is my delight / So in this book / I pray you'll write.

I leafed through the pages and read a sampling of entries, penned in an array of different hands and inks. Most were short rhyming couplets that were easily committed to memory. Impersonal little ditties, really. The sort I assume young people used to sign high school yearbooks with. Someone named Gerald A., for instance, had written:

Roses are red / Violets are blue / Your voice is entrancing / And that goes for all of you.

I found myself growing uncomfortable, irritated even, by the recorded implication of intimacy in this unknown Gerald's short rhyme. But I kept my voice steady as I read softly aloud from the following page:

When you are old / And drinking tea / Lay down your cup / And think of me ~ *Blanche*

Other entries, however cleverly worded, seemed to be based on more specific experiences. Soccer games, fish fries, late-night parties down by an unnamed river. There were several messages of this type scattered throughout the booklet. Many were written by the same person: Heddy Sweet.

Her last entry read: *I'm in love with a few / I've been in love with many / But compared to the love for you / It wasn't worth a penny. Yours till the doorsteps . . .* ~ *Heddy*

I had never heard of Heddy Sweet.

Nor could I positively identify any of the other signatures, although I suspected that the final entry signed by "Your Cousin Margie" was written by the same Margaret Louise Lennox who I had met years earlier at the Straussmans' home on the day of Mr. Straussman's funeral. I said as much to the detective.

"Clearly this booklet was a keepsake from Claire's extended visit to Detroit that we spoke of previously," I said, fingering the faded script on the page. There was an eerie prescience to Claire's cousin's words that brought a twinge to my throat all these many years after the fact:

Though now you are free / From sorrow and care / There is many a hardship / In this world so beware.

"Yes, I do believe this is Claire's as well," I said, closing the book gently and returning it to the detective.

"Could you swear to it?" he pressed, and when I appeared taken aback at the prospect of swearing he added: "In a court of law, I mean. We need you to be absolutely sure."

"I'm as sure as I can be about items that until this very moment I had no idea existed," I said. I told him I could confirm with reasonable certainty only that the handwriting on the title page of the autograph book matched my recollection of Claire's script and that the dates inscribed therein corresponded with her previously unexplained absence. I told him also that the diary appeared to have been penned by Claire's hand and, in my brief examination of its contents, some of the entries reflected my recollections of common events and conversations we'd shared.

"Okay, Mr. Honig," the detective said, laying the autograph book next to the diary on his desk. He reached once again into the strongbox and withdrew a black, tightly braided strip of leather tipped on both ends by tarnished silver aglets and gathered in the middle by a silver sunburst backed by silver flanges through which the leather strip was looped.

I'm not sure I was able to completely mask the sharp intake of breath that escaped. I cleared my throat and ascribed my cough to the dust from the old books. The detective narrowed his eyes, and I acknowledged that I'd seen this distinctive western-style tie only once.

"How so?" the detective said, his voice sharpening in much the same way it had the last time he'd upbraided me for my reticence.

"I saw Claire one evening in the company of a man wearing this tie."

"How long ago?"

"Oh, fifty years ago at least."

"Did you know the man?"

"I did not."

The detective tilted his head slightly and raised his eyebrows.

"I assure you I only saw him once, and from afar."

"One of Miss Straussman's gentlemen callers, I take it?"

I nodded, and the detective relaxed his brow as he set the tie next to the books and withdrew a coin-filled mason jar from the munitions box. I picked this up and turned it over in my hands several times. I told Detective Grayson that the jar appeared to be the same sort of container Claire and Hilda generally used to bottle their honey, although I allowed that these were common enough among beekeepers as to be individually indistinguishable.

Although the detective remained close-lipped for the most part, I had long since begun to suspect the nature of the situation and was eager to do all I could to be of assistance.

"Okay, then," Detective Grayson said, "I need you to do one last thing for me."

"Anything," I said. I was then ushered into a small anteroom with a large glass window that looked directly into another, slightly larger room into which six sullen-looking young men, each carrying a numbered placard, were led single file.

"Any of these young men look familiar to you? Take your time, Mr. Honig."

Brown-skinned, with close-cropped hair and insolent half grins, they all wore baggy calf-length dungarees, knee-high white socks, and either crisply pressed white T-shirts or short-sleeved plaid cotton sports shirts, also meticulously ironed so that the creases on the sleeves seemed sharp enough to cut through flesh.

"No, I'm sorry," I said, "I don't recognize any of them."

One of the scantily clad young women in the next queue did look vaguely familiar, however.

"Okay, Mr. Honig, that's very good," Detective Grayson said slowly as if to mask the resonance of urgency in his voice. "Which one?"

"Number two," I said after some hesitation.

Detective Grayson pushed a button on the wall and leaned toward the speaker next to it.

"Number two, step forward."

The young woman squinted her eyes and took one small step closer to the mirrored glass. I took a reflexive step back.

"Don't worry. She can't see you through this," Detective Grayson said, nodding at the glass and slowing his words to a cadence I imagined he might use to prompt a six-year-old through a recitation of the alphabet. "Now, can you say for sure whether you saw this girl with either of the Straussman sisters or maybe even anywhere in the vicinity of their house?"

"I cannot say that I have a definitive recollection of her," I replied. "It is just a feeling, really, that I might have seen her somewhere before."

"Think hard, Mr. Honig."

Which of course I had been trying to do all along, but this merely increased my agitation as the more I stared through the glass at the row of young women standing before my hidden eyes, the more they all began to look like so many of the dark new faces that had begun to populate my neighborhood, with their cinnamon-tinted hair. Their meticulously shaved and painted eyebrows and unnaturally lined and painted lips. Their garish tattoos. I do not wish to sound insensitive, but it is so difficult adjusting to the ways of these young people today.

"Mr. Honig."

"I'm sorry," I said, taking mental note again of the inordinate number of times I had uttered this very phrase to the detective. My sincere regret did not mitigate the fact that I could not do more to assist him. "I really cannot say for certain that I've seen her before."

The detective thanked me. He assured me I had helped more than I thought. Silently, we walked back to the station's security door, which he held open as he shook my hand and told me he would let me know if and when any further assistance on my part would be required. He called to a uniformed young officer behind the front desk.

"Could you please drive Mr. Honig home?" It was clear from his tone of voice this was an order and not a request.

"Whether I am needed or not, I hope you will do me the courtesy of keeping me apprised of the progress of these proceedings," I said as the young man followed me through the door.

"Sure thing, Mr. Honig," Detective Grayson said, stepping back from the door to let it swing shut. "I'll keep you posted."

TWENTY-TWO

BALLING: Worker bees form a small suf-
focating cluster around an unacceptable
queen, pulling at her legs and wings in an
attempt to kill her.

I subsequently learned that the young
woman who had seemed so familiar at the
police lineup had been linked by other
physical and circumstantial evidence to the
crime, the most damning of which were
several partial fingerprints found on the
duct tape that had covered Claire's mouth.
On the advice of the public defender that
had been assigned to her case, she agreed
to reveal how she came to be in possession
of Claire's most intimate property and was
persuaded to testify in court against her
male accomplice in hopes of receiving some
measure of leniency from the court. The
young woman, whose name was Christina
Perez, alluded to a sad history of emotional

abuse and neglect in her childhood and admitted to Detective Grayson that since running away from her family several years previous she had fallen in with a bad crowd. She confessed that both she and her male companion, Mr. Garcia, were dependent on drugs and that they were not above breaking into houses in search of money and convertible contraband to pay for their illicit habits.

I learned some of Miss Perez's history from Detective Grayson, who proved true to his word about keeping me informed about the case. I learned a bit more from Mr. Billings, the earnest young prosecuting attorney who met with me in preparation for my court appearance. Most of what I learned, however, came from the young woman's own testimony at her companion's trial, which took place a scant three months after the arrests.

I should explain that while my own time on the witness stand was relatively short, I felt obliged to attend the trial in its entirety out of respect for Claire and Hilda Straussman, who had been reduced to our neighborhood's impersonal sobriquet — the Bee Ladies — as they were almost exclusively referred to in the two or three brief newspaper accounts that covered the arrest of

266

the suspects and the subsequent murder trial. Sadly, there was little discernable actual public interest in them, judging by the empty seats in the courtroom and the speed by which the trial proceeded.

Jury selection took most of the first day, with opening statements commencing the following morning. After an early lunch break, the first witness for the prosecution was called. This was Officer James Potts, who detailed the circumstances of the initial discovery of the metal strongbox containing Claire Straussman's diary in the storage locker that he and his partner had searched in connection with a series of home burglaries he had been investigating.

As a witness, I was forbidden to observe any of the trial proceedings prior to my own testimony and so I waited outside the courtroom with Detective Grayson, who was scheduled to testify after Officer Potts. While we waited, Detective Grayson explained to me that as the primary officer assigned to investigate the burglary case, it was up to Officer Potts to explain how he had been made aware of the metal strongbox and the contents within and to establish how he had come to conclude the box and its contents belonged to Claire Straussman.

"Then it'll be my turn, Mr. Honig," he

said. "I'll explain how I made the connection between the evidence in his case and the Straussmans' case, and then that's where you come in."

The detective tried to calm my nerves, which I feared were getting the best of me as we sat on the cushioned benches outside the courtroom. "Billings is going to ask you to identify the stuff in the box, just like I did before, and he's going to ask you about finding the bodies. Are you going to be all right with that, Mr. Honig?"

Both he and Mr. Billings had gone over this several times already. I nodded my assent as the door to the courtroom swung out and the bailiff called the detective's name.

"Just remember to keep your answers short and to the point," he said, clapping me gently on the shoulder. "You'll do fine."

Twenty minutes later, the door swung open again and my own name was called. Despite Detective Grayson's kind words of encouragement, I felt my knees grow weak as I followed the bailiff into the courtroom, which was smaller and much tawdrier than I imagined it would be. Not at all like the grand, richly paneled galleries with columns and floor-to-ceiling windows such as the ones in the movies I had watched as a boy. I

268

noticed one of the fluorescent bulbs above the prosecutor's table flickered sporadically, threatening to go out completely at any moment. I found myself holding tightly to the railing separating the gallery from the court proper as I made my way unsteadily across the scuffed linoleum floor to the witness stand, where the bailiff came forward to assist me to my seat. I smoothed down the gaps between the buttons in my cardigan sweater as much from nervousness as vanity. And then, as instructed, I placed my hand on the Holy Bible and swore to "tell the truth, the whole truth, and nothing but the truth, so help me God."

I was asked next to state my name and occupation for the record, which elicited raised eyebrows from several of the younger jurors. They appeared surprised to hear that such a job title as beekeeper existed yet in their world. I started to explain that I had been a beekeeper my entire life, as my father had before me, and that a good living was still to be had selling honey through specialty stores, farmers' markets, mail-order accounts, and personal acquaintances, but Mr. Billings, the young prosecutor, rose quickly from his table and assured the court that mine was an honorable profession, to which the judge agreed. Making reference to notes on his yellow legal pad, Mr. Billings then posed his first question:

"Can you state for the record your connection to the deceased?"

The judge saw the need to direct me to speak into the microphone as I attempted to explain what was, in fact, a rather long and complicated and some might go so far as to deem turbulent relationship. That my friendship with Claire had been forged and then broken over long years of shared intimacies and a common love of bees, however, was of little relevance to the proceedings. Mr. Billings attempted, through constant interruption, to convey to the jury that I had lived next door to the Straussmans for all of my life and so had had ample opportunity to gain a passing familiarity with Claire's handwriting style. That my knowledge of her distinctive script had been gleaned from school compositions she'd shared with me and grocery lists we'd followed when we were younger was likewise deemed superfluous, a point to which the defense attorney concurred by rousing himself long enough to "stipulate" that the books found in the ammunition box belonged to "the deceased."

But even this truncated explanation of how I should be able to identify each of the items took somewhat longer than Deputy District Attorney Billings had anticipated. At the judge's discretion, the proceedings were adjourned just after four in the afternoon.

And so I spent a restless night, sitting up in my mother's old rocker, regretting what I had been forced to leave unsaid that day and dreading even more what I would be asked to reveal about Claire in the morning. I had meant to change out of my good clothes when I got home, but somehow the hours just slipped away as I watched a singular shaft of moonlight creep through my bedroom window, across the floor, and up onto my lap, where I noticed with detached interest that in the cold, reflected light of the moon my hands seemed nearly skeletal as they gripped my pant legs every bit as tightly as they had clung to the courtroom railing earlier that day. "How had it come to this?" I wondered aloud, and I found myself arguing with a tall wisp of a shadow that stood just beyond the reach of the moonlight.

"It wasn't my fault," I insisted to the shadow that rippled like waves of heat off asphalt. And I heard the trees rustle outside, and the leaves seemed to whisper, "It wasn't hers."

TWENTY-THREE

COURSING OR LINING A BEE: The method by which honey hunters observe the foraging patterns of wild bees to follow them back to their hives in order to harvest the honey within.

"You did good yesterday," Mr. Billings assured me when he saw me pacing the hallway as I waited for the courtroom doors to open the following morning. I may not be schooled in the vagaries of the law, but even I caught the false note in the young prosecutor's tone.

"Short and sweet," Mr. Billings whispered as he entered the courtroom. "Short and sweet."

"Mr. Honig," the bailiff called as he swung the courtroom door open at nine a.m. sharp. I took a deep breath and promised myself I would do better, though I feared that in the glare of the public eye my mind might flicker once again like the courtroom's faulty overhead fluorescent bulb.

Thankfully, I began my testimony by simply confirming that Claire and Hilda had indeed stored the proceeds from their honey sales in mason jars like the evidentiary one found in the ammunition box. This seemed to satisfy young Mr. Billings, and he hastened to move on to the last item that had been found in the box.

"Do you recognize this bolo tie, Mr. Honig?" he said, holding up what he called Exhibit 5.

I said I did. I was asked if the tie belonged to Miss Straussman and I replied that, to my knowledge, it did not. Mr. Billings then asked me if I had ever seen it in Miss Straussman's possession. I admitted after a moment's hesitation that I had.

"Can you explain?"

Picking my words carefully, I told the court that I had seen Claire in possession of this leather tie late one evening while in the company of a gentleman whose name I did not know.

"But what became of the tie after that evening, I cannot say," I quickly added. The prosecuting attorney seemed both startled and pleased by the brevity of my reply. After a moment's pause, he smiled broadly.

"Well, it's quite obvious where it ended up," he said. Turning dramatically toward the jury, he pointed to the metal box on the evidence table. "It ended up right here with the rest of Miss Straussman's personal possessions."

Mr. Billings paused again to rifle though his yellow legal pad. He knitted his brow with a look of concern that I sensed was as much for the jury's benefit as it was for mine.

"Now, Mr. Honig," he said, "I know this may be difficult, but I'd like to take you back to the day you discovered your neighbors' bodies."

Mr. Billings had been quite adamant during our preparatory session that I not distract the jury from the point of my testimony by mentioning the sound of the swarming bees that had first drawn me to my neighbors' home. His next question, it seemed to me, was designed to lead me past the humming wires into the Straussmans' house proper.

"What made you think something might be wrong when you knocked on your neighbors' door that day?" His back to the jury, the young prosecutor locked eyes with me and leaned slightly forward.

"I heard their radio playing very loudly," I

replied just as we'd rehearsed.

"And this was unusual?"

"Yes. I thought at first they might have gone somewhere and left it on, except their car was still in the garage."

"And this concerned you?"

"The radio was so loud, I thought perhaps they couldn't hear me knocking," I said. I stared down at my hands, which reminded me of bird talons as they clenched the railing in front of me. "That's when I checked the door and found it wasn't locked."

I was about to explain that I wasn't in the habit of barging into my neighbors' house uninvited, especially considering our current rift, but the prosecutor cut me short.

"And so you went inside?"

"Yes," I said. My voice must have faltered here as the judge asked me once again to speak up so the jury could hear.

"Yes," I repeated, leaning into the microphone. "I was worried."

"And what did you find, Mr. Honig?" Again Mr. Billings angled forward, willing me with his eyes to skip past the abandoned tea service to describe my discovery of the bodies in the parlor. I closed my eyes and took a deep breath, but my lungs felt as if they were deflating rather than filling with air.

"Where were the Straussmans?" he prodded gently. "Can you describe what you saw?"

"They were lying on the parlor rug," I said, my voice sounding unnaturally flat. "Their hands and feet were bound with duct tape. There was more duct tape across their mouths. I saw a scrap of red bandanna protruding from beneath the tape across Claire's mouth."

"And what did you do next, Mr. Honig? Did you try to resuscitate them?"

I shook my head slowly. "I could see they had been dead for quite some time. I went back to the kitchen and called the police."

"And how long before they arrived?"

"No more than ten minutes," I said. "We live just down the street from the station house."

Mr. Billings smiled and nodded to me as if I were a small child who'd just recited his multiplication tables successfully for the first time.

"Thank you, Mr. Honig," he said. Turning to the judge, he announced that he had no further questions, and mercifully, the defendant's attorney chose not to belabor my ordeal with any further questions of his own. Stepping down from the witness stand, I shuffled to the back of the courtroom, where I was about to take a seat in the gallery when I felt Detective Grayson's thick hand grasp me by the shoulder. I hadn't noticed him rise from his seat near the door.

"You don't have to stay for this," he said, leaning in so that only I might hear. "It might be kinda rough for you to hear."

"I know," I said. I wasn't sure I could explain, even to myself, why I felt the need to be there. Perhaps it was because there was no one else beside me who did. For the first time since I'd known him, I deliberately lied to Detective Grayson. "I'll be fine."

I eased myself into a chair by the aisle, Detective Grayson retook his seat directly behind mine, and we waited for the prosecutor to call his next witness, a representative from the coroner's office. He was a young man of Middle Eastern descent, and his task was to establish, in clinical detail, the manner and time of death of the Straussman sisters. It was during his graphic testimony that I first learned that Hilda had most likely died before Claire and that she had choked to death on her own regurgitated breakfast probably, according to the coroner's estimation, within minutes after being bound and gagged and abandoned by her attackers.

"What about the younger Miss Straussman?" the prosecutor inquired. The coroner shook his head sadly before he replied, "She took much longer to die."

At this point, the prosecutor produced what he called a postmortem color enlargement of Claire Straussman lying on a steel table. I was unprepared, to say the least, to see Claire pictured practically naked in the photograph save for a small green sheet draped across her torso. I turned my head away, and it was at least a minute or more before I could bear to look again at the photograph, which Mr. Billings had by this time placed on a wooden easel next to the witness stand.

Claire's eyes were closed, and her taut, finely lined face had taken on the pallid sheen of Hades' paramour. Through the haze of rekindled grief, I heard the prosecutor ask the coroner how he had made the determination as to the order of death between the two sisters.

"Notice these abrasions on the victim's right knee and elbow," he replied. Using a collapsible metal pointer that he had extracted from his suit pocket, he extended it with a ceremonious series of metallic clicks and leaned across the rail. He pointed to what looked like large rug burns on the sides of Claire's right arm and leg. "Here and here."

He leaned forward again and pointed to additional angry red lines encircling Claire's wrists and ankles.

"Notice these ligature marks here and here," he said. He then pointed to the right side of her face, just below her permanently closed lid. "And these bruises on her right cheekbone. We thought at first someone had struck her, but combined with these bruises on her right shoulder and thigh here and here, and these bruises and scrapes on her right elbow and knee, we think she inflicted the damage herself."

"Could you explain?" Mr. Billings prompted.

"Given the severity of the abrasions — notice how the skin is torn and broken around her wrists and the skin on her elbow's been rubbed raw — we believe this indicates the victim struggled for quite some time, and quite ferociously at that, especially for a woman her age."

As I suspected, Claire's indomitable spirit had not been easily extinguished, despite her self-imposed isolation. Hilda had always seemed to me far the more passive of the two sisters.

Mr. Billings proceeded to confirm this suspicion when he next introduced another postmortem photograph, this one of Hilda Straussman, her larger, more amorphous torso just barely contained beneath the standard green autopsy sheet. He asked the coroner to compare the condition of the body in this photograph to the previous one.

"Notice that there is only faint bruising on her ankles and wrists," the coroner said, drawing the pointer back and forth across first Hilda's ankles and then her wrists. "And unlike the previous victim, there are no marks at all on this victim's arms or legs or face."

He punctuated this statement with a series of quick taps on each of the indicated body parts. He reminded the jurors that Hilda had been found with regurgitated food and stomach acid in her mouth and lungs. Again noting the lack of self-inflicted damage to Hilda's body, he concluded that she had obviously struggled very little, if at all, before succumbing to asphyxiation. "She may even have been unconscious at the time, though there is no direct evidence of that."

Mr. Billings then switched back to the photograph of Claire and pointed manually to the distinct bruising on the right side of her face.

"You testified that you originally assumed

this bruising was the result of her being struck. But you also said you no longer think this is the case."

"Yes, sir."

"Would you mind demonstrating how you think this bruising occurred?"

The young coroner looked to the judge, who nodded his assent, before stepping out of the witness box and into the narrow swath of unobstructed space between the judge's bench and the prosecutor's table. Kneeling on the scuffed flooring, he clasped his hands tightly behind his back and awkwardly lowered himself onto his side. Then squeezing his ankles together, he kicked his legs out like a fishtail and raised himself onto his right elbow in almost the same motion, throwing himself forward and smacking his right cheek on the floor. The sound was painfully audible even from where I sat in the back of the courtroom.

The jurors started as one. A few looked uneasily at one another as the coroner raised himself up, preparing to throw himself at the floor again.

"I think we've seen enough," the judge said. The coroner stood up then with a relieved look on his face, brushed his pants off, and again took his seat on the witness stand. At Mr. Billings's urging, he then explicated in clinical detail how Claire had likely attempted to half crawl, half fling herself across the parlor floor, as we had all just witnessed, in a vain attempt to reach her sister who, the young coroner theorized, was choking to death.

The coroner explained that the harder Claire had struggled, the more heavily she would have had to breathe, and it was this repeated heavy gasping for air that most likely had drawn the cloth that had been roughly stuffed inside her mouth ever farther down into her windpipe, where it had ultimately lodged. I could feel my own breath become as labored as I imagined Claire's must have been in the moments before she died.

"Burst blood vessels, or reticulation, in the eyes, and this blue tint to her lips confirms asphyxiation as the cause of death," the coroner said. He shook his head, seemingly moved by his own conclusion. "If she'd have just lain still, she might have survived for quite some time."

Mr. Garcia's attorney's slumped shoulders and ill-fitting suit made him appear from behind every bit as indifferent to his client's defense as his drooping eyelids had seemed when I'd stared at him from the witness stand. Once again, he offered no rebuttal questions to mitigate the horror frozen on the faces of several jurors, and so the judge dismissed the coroner and the prosecutor called his final witness.

"Miss Christina Perez."

Dressed in a modest light blue dress and beige leather pumps, the young lady entered the courtroom, smoothed an errant strand of dark brown hair back into the thick ponytail from which it had escaped, and walked slowly down the center aisle to the witness stand. I barely suppressed a gasp as I was struck by the transformation that had taken place in her since the last time our eyes had seemed to meet through the mirrored glass of the police station's observation room. Gone was the brassy cinnamon-tinted hair and exaggerated eyebrow and lip paint she had worn. This day she seemed smaller, and if not precisely innocent, then certainly much less defiant.

Her testimony lasted through the rest of the morning and on into the afternoon. Miss Perez's former companion, Armando Garcia, did not testify on his own behalf. Indeed, there was only one witness for the defense and he was a medical expert specializing in drug dependency. When his turn came at the end of the day, Mr. Garcia's public defender, whose attention continued to drift from time to time during Miss Perez's recounting of the events of the crime, presented mental incapacity as the only defense for Mr. Garcia's actions. It was a questionable tactic, in my opinion, that was based on the hired doctor's contention that the effects of the young man's purported drug intoxication somehow mitigated his actions at the time the crime was committed.

Looking back now, I am reminded of the words of the Roman philosopher Marcus Aurelius, who observed: "As virtue and vice consist in action, and not in the impressions of the senses, so it is not what they feel, but what they do, that makes mankind happy or miserable." Blaming the greater crime on the deleterious effects of an illegal substance would not have been the defensive strategy I would have chosen had I been charged with plotting the young man's defense.

Miss Perez had claimed on the witness stand that she was not a violent person but that she could not in all good conscience say the same of her companion. While this might be considered damaging testimony on the face of it, she also claimed to love this young man and to believe he was a good person at heart — that it was the drugs he took that made him unpredictable and violent. She swore that neither of them had gone to the Straussman house intending to harm anyone.

"If I'd even thought Armando would have gone crazy like that, I swear to God I never would have brung him with me in the first place," she claimed most sincerely it seemed to me as I sat in the courtroom listening to her testimony. It both saddened and surprised me to learn that the germ of the idea to break into the Straussmans' house came from this young woman and not from her young man, who appeared, at least on the surface, the more hardened criminal of the two.

She explained how, living in one of the small, deteriorating Spanish-style bungalows that dotted our neighborhood at that time, she had often seen the two Bee Ladies working for hours in their small vegetable garden or around and about the handful of beehives that were located to the rear of their property. She said she noticed that they usually spent the entire morning working out of doors and that they seldom finished their chores before midafternoon. More significant, she observed the Bee Ladies selling honey and candles from their front porch every Thursday afternoon, and she noticed that they never left the house the following day. It was Mr. Garcia, she said, who speculated that the proceeds of the Bee Ladies' sales were likely kept at the house and not deposited in a bank account.

"And so this is why you decided to rob them?" Mr. Billings prodded.

"Yes," the young woman said softly, casting her eyes downward. I followed her eyes to her hands, which were coppery smooth and clasped as if in prayer. "Armando said it would be easy. They're like all the old people round here. They live alone, they have money, and they always do the same thing at the same time."

As I sat in the courtroom listening to this young woman's account of the events leading up to Claire's and Hilda's deaths, I found myself unwillingly impressed by the minute level of observation she had accorded to the Straussman sisters' daily habits in preparation for her craven act.

"Then the skinny old lady got stung, and she came back to the house to put something on it," Miss Perez told Mr. Billings, attempting to explain how it was that despite their careful planning Claire had diverged from her routine just as she and Mr. Garcia were attempting to pry the Straussmans' back door open.

"Elsewise, none of this other stuff would

have happened," she said. This other stuff being, of course, Claire's and Hilda's brutal murders.

This was Claire who had died. In my head and in my heart I understood this. But as I listened to Miss Perez continue her story, I found myself almost feeling sorry for her for all she'd gone through because of Mr. Garcia. He seemed a very frightening man, and she seemed so small, so fragile. In her physical delicacy, and the confident manner in which she articulated herself, she reminded me of Claire. But that was as far as the resemblance went. I found it hard to imagine Claire being cowed by any man.

"Go on," Mr. Billings urged.

Miss Perez explained that when they were surprised by Claire's sudden approach, she had yanked Mr. Garcia's arm back from the door and told him to put the credit card back in his pocket.

"The old lady was holding her hand like it hurt," Miss Perez testified, "so I asked her if she was okay."

"And what did Miss Straussman say?"

"She said something like, 'Of course I'm okay, it's just a bee sting,' " Miss Perez replied. "She seemed kinda mad. She said she just needed to put something on it and was looking at us like she was trying to figure out what we were doing on her back porch, so I made up this story about how it was my mom's birthday and that she loved handmade things. I said I'd seen her and the other lady selling honey and stuff on their porch the night before and I was hoping they still had some stuff left."

"What happened next?"

"I told her that we'd knocked on their front door but nobody answered, so we came round back to see if anybody was home," Miss Perez testified.

"And what about Mr. Garcia?" Mr. Billings prodded. She said he went along with her story at first.

According to Miss Perez's account, Claire's initial suspicion had ultimately been allayed by the young couple's apparent interest in her wares. Claire told them she needed to put some bluing on the bee sting she'd just suffered but that if they cared to wait in the kitchen she'd take care of the sting and then go fetch a sampling of honey and candles from which they could choose a gift.

Miss Perez said that the other Bee Lady, who had grown concerned by the first one's extended absence, arrived just as they sat down at the kitchen table.

"The skinny Bee Lady explained what was

going on and the big Bee Lady said she'd go get the stuff. Everything was still going fine except they were old, you know? And really slow. I could see Armando starting to get . . ."

"Impatient?" Mr. Billings prodded.

"Yeah," Miss Perez agreed. "All of a sudden, he just snapped."

"How so?"

"Armando could just go off for no reason," she said. Mr. Garcia, for the first time in the trial, straightened up in his chair, and Miss Perez took a deep, shuddering breath. Of course in retrospect her story seems quite contrived, ludicrous even, but as she sat there on the witness stand, her thick dark hair tied up in a girlish ponytail and her hands folded sweetly on her lap, the young woman exuded a surprising blend of sincerity and vulnerability that I am sure worked to her advantage with both the judge and jury. I believe this reaction could be attributed above all to her eyes, which were so large and unexpectedly turquoise that they positively overwhelmed her coppery face. As much as I tried to resist, I could not help feeling growing surges of sympathy for her.

"So what happened next?" Mr. Billings softly urged. Miss Perez explained that it was hard to tell what had set Mr. Garcia off that morning, but she said that he was always especially unpredictable when he combined alcohol and narcotics, which apparently he had done before leaving their bungalow. She said she only found out afterward that his supply of drugs had run low and that he had been both more intoxicated and more desperate for money than she'd realized at the time. Whatever the cause, Mr. Garcia apparently soon grew tired of Miss Perez's patient game of cat and mouse. Pulling from beneath his shirt a gun that she swore on the witness stand she hadn't known he possessed, Mr. Garcia ordered the two women inside the parlor.

"You know, Armando acts crazy sometimes, but I don't think he meant to kill the old ladies," Miss Perez said. "He was always threatening to kill me, you know? But he just slapped me round sometimes. He never even used his fists."

Miss Perez said that it was the big Bee Lady who agreed to show him how to work the catch on the false door in the sunroom wall where they kept all their valuables. Afterward Mr. Garcia had marched Hilda back into the parlor and tied her up with some duct tape he'd found on a shelf in their pantry and then he'd ordered Miss

Perez to do the same with the skinny Bee Lady. This was after Miss Perez said she'd stuffed all the jars of coins they found in the cubbyhole into several canvas shopping bags they found in the pantry along with the duct tape. They also took a metal strongbox they found behind the jars. She said the last thing Mr. Garcia did was to take off the bandanna he was wearing on his head and hand it to her.

Following Mr. Garcia's orders, Miss Perez explained how she'd torn it in two and stuffed a strip in each woman's mouth and then covered both of their mouths with more duct tape. A few stray hairs found on the strips were what eventually tied Mr. Garcia forensically to the murders.

Miss Perez testified that she honestly believed Mr. Garcia when he told her not to worry. That the two ladies would work themselves loose in a little while and by that time he and she would be long gone. She said Mr. Garcia had family in Rosarito that they decided to go stay with "just until things died down."

Unfortunately, it appeared the pair misjudged Claire's and Hilda's physical condition as badly as they had the women's meager savings. Both women had died before they were able to free themselves from their bonds. And the pair's larcenous efforts had netted them precisely two hundred and seventy-three dollars in small bills and coins in all the jars they found stashed in the cubbyhole and the strongbox. Miss Perez said that she and Mr. Garcia had gone to his cousin's house in Rosarito directly after the robbery and that they didn't even know the Bee Ladies had died until they returned to California several weeks later. But by that time it seemed the police had stopped poking around the neighborhood and so they figured they were in the clear, she said.

I suppose I should have felt satisfied. On the strength of Miss Perez's testimony, Mr. Garcia was convicted of two counts each of first-degree murder, aggravated assault, and armed robbery. He received a mandatory sentence of twenty-five years to life. For her cooperation in his prosecution, Miss Perez had already plead guilty to the lesser crimes of manslaughter and robbery and had received a maximum term of twelve years in prison. But when I heard the guilty verdict, my heart sank even lower than I thought it already could. In the eyes of the law, justice had been done, but all I could think as I trudged out of the courtroom was that the dearest friends I had had in my life had died for less than three hundred dollars, a box of diaries, and a few worthless baubles.

■ ■ ■ ■

WINTERKILL

■ ■ ■ ■

TWENTY-FOUR

CHILLED BROOD: Immature bees that have died from cold or lack of proper care.

In the innocence of my youth, I believed in the absolute nature of truth, and, like Aristotle, I saw philosophy as the science that considers truth. But under the burden of mounting years and the bitter experience of Claire's untimely death, I began to wonder if perhaps the learned French essayist Michel de Montaigne was closer to the mark in his supposition that philosophy was doubt. This much I now know: Though my revelation to Detective Grayson as to David Gilbert's origins had dredged up many painful memories, I had taken some small comfort in the fact that the information I had provided had led at least indirectly to the eventual conviction of the Straussman sisters' murderers. I had assumed that this legal determination would ultimately bring me peace over, if not full absolution from, the part I had played in the whole sordid affair. But I was wrong. While my loyal honeybees continued to provide me with a measure of joy and companionship, my evenings grew progressively colder and darker, and I found myself turning ever more inward to a place where even my beloved books, though they helped me pass the time, provided little in the way of true solace. Truth, I was forced to conclude, is an elusive science at best, and philosophy is the cold comfort we take in our doubt.

Such were my thoughts on a cool summer evening nearly a dozen years after the so-called book had been closed, for all intents and purposes, on Claire's and Hilda's tragic deaths. I was sitting on my front porch swing rereading an unexpected letter I'd received just that afternoon from Detective Grayson.

I remembered the tired smile that had crept across the good detective's face as he gripped my hand warmly at the conclusion of the formal sentencing hearing for the murderers.

"Well, Mr. Honig," he'd said by way of farewell, "I bet you feel a whole lot better now that this case is finally closed."

Case closed. Within the limits of his professional vernacular, they were, I suppose, the two most precise and comforting words he could use to put to rest what must surely have been the very last in a distressingly long and twisted line of inquiries into the darkest reaches of human psychology. I wondered that he had managed to retain even a shred of his own humanity in the process.

"Yes, of course," I'd replied without conviction as we stood facing each other beneath the harsh fluorescent fixtures that lit the interminable hallway outside the courtroom where the final judgment on the case had just been rendered.

The desolation of that long-ago moment resurfaced with palpable intensity as I fingered the edge of the detective's unanticipated missive. It was the first such communication I'd received from him since he'd left the police force at the end of 1993, only a few weeks after the Straussman case had officially concluded.

Dear Mr. Honig,

How are you doing? Well, I hope. Me and the wife are doing fine ourselves. We bought a little spread just outside Coeur d'Alene, Idaho, just like I said we would and we've been living up here for the last ten years. Bet you never thought you'd be hearing from me again!! But here's the funny thing. I've taken up beekeeping. Who would've thunk it? Ha-ha! No, really. I met a beekeeper at the local farmers' market a while back and we got to talking. About you, in fact, and one thing led to another, and a couple years ago he helped me set up a beehive in my backyard. I've got three hives now, and counting.

I gotta tell you, Mr. Honig, beekeeping's really a kick. Even the wife says she's seen a change in me. She says she's never seen me so relaxed.

So here's why I'm writing. One of my hives isn't producing like it used to. I think it might have a parasite infection. I'm pretty sure it's not ants causing the problem. I've been using your old pie tin trick since I set up my first hive. My buddy up here thought the problem I'm having might be due to Tracheal Mites. He showed me this menthol trick, but maybe the weather was too cold for the crystals to vaporize. At any rate, the hive didn't improve. So then we checked for Varroa Mites. We tried using an ether roll on a jar of bees, but we couldn't find any mites on the glass, so we were pretty sure it wasn't that.

So what do you think? Any suggestions at all would be greatly appreciated.

Sincerely,
Raymond Grayson

What I thought first of all, after all these years, was he'd finally seen fit to use his first name with me. That pleased me no end, as did his inclusion of a photograph of himself standing in front of one of his beehives. He had lost a great deal of weight since I'd last seen him as though he had regained a semblance of his youthful vigor. His hair was a close-cropped silver, and his face, though lined from the sun, had lost its soft jowls. He was smiling.

The letter came in the early part of August 2005, nearly a dozen years after Claire's and Hilda's murderers had been sent to jail and nearly two years since my new neighbors began planting rows of crosses in their front lawn. In spite of, or perhaps because of, all that had passed between us, I suppose I should not have been surprised to discover that Detective Grayson had eventually followed my advice and taken up beekeeping as an avocation. What surprised me more was the casual ease with which he had apparently put the solemn weight of his former vocation behind him.

I finished reading the letter for the third time as the ocean chill began rolling in with the evening shadows. I remember savoring the luminous quality of the twilight as I carefully refolded the pages of the missive and slipped it back into its envelope. I thought for a while as to how to respond to his inquiry. There were a few more tests I thought he might try before ruling out varroa mites entirely. I may have closed my eyes for a moment — I can't be sure. I am sure of so little these days. When I lifted my eyes from the envelope clutched in my lap, the graying sky was smeared with streaks of gold and blue and orange, and Claire's older brother, Harry Junior, was standing quietly at the foot of the steps in front of me.

I'd only seen that one photograph of him: the one where he was formally dressed in his short pants and button-down shirt and was sitting like a rosy cherub on the arm of the davenport in his parents' front room, but I was sure it was him. Even without his apple-plump cheeks there to hide the finely chiseled features of the man he might have become, and his baby blond ringlets shorn and faded to dusky brown, there remained yet about him the unmistakable essence of the child that once was in the far-away gaze of his father's steely blue eyes. If there was evil there, I couldn't find it. Only sadness. So much sadness.

I stared at him, fearful that if I looked away he'd melt back into the gathering mist, and he stared right back at me, standing stock-still and silent, his left hand gripping the stair railing and his right foot poised on the bottom step. I knew he was waiting for me to say or do something — to invite him up on the porch, perhaps, or to go to where he stood on the stairs and offer him my hand. As I hesitated, I watched the evening shadows spread like the pitch of avocado honey across the wooden planks beneath the swing on which I sat.

"Where are our crosses?" he said, his voice softened by the down of disuse. I knew what he meant right away: his cross, his mother's cross, his father's, Claire's, and Hilda's. They were all dead, and none but the tears of Ra had been shed for any of them. And now in the very same neighborhood where each and every one of them had lived and died, a garish memorial was being assembled for all to see, to commemorate the passing of strangers whose roots to the land ran no deeper than the patchwork of tidy rose beds and Bermuda grass lawns that had taken the place of the almond, orange, and eucalyptus groves which were already old before Harry and I were born.

"I have no say over the names on the crosses," I heard myself say.

"You have no say over anything," Harry said to me. And as he spoke, small dark feathers spurted in downy puffs from his mouth into the cold night air, and with each puff the sound of his voice grew stronger and coarser, and the feathers sprouted wings and the wings began to beat furiously and buzz and hum and hover about Harry's head in a great Cimmerian swarm.

"We're not as dead as you think," he said, his voice rising above the din. "And that's your fault, too."

TWENTY-FIVE

HEAVING UP THE HIVE: A traditional practice sometimes performed in addition to "telling the bees," it requires that both hive and coffin be lifted at the same moment as the funeral party prepares to leave the house.

Alexander the Great was said to have been buried in a coffin filled with honey. This was in accordance with the oldest beliefs of the ancient Greeks and Romans, who like the Egyptians and the Babylonians before them ascribed certain divine properties to the industrious honeybee and the golden ambrosia she produced. The ancients believed that once earthly existence passed, a human soul remained near men, living underground. That is why a soul could not rest until its human remains were buried in the soil and the rites of sepulture observed. No less than Virgil concluded his account of the funeral of Polydorus with these words: "We enclose the soul in the grave."

The ancients believed such rituals were necessary to confine the soul to its subterranean abode. So, too, it was necessary to call the soul of the deceased three times by the name with which it had been born and to wish it a happy life underground.

"Fare thee well," Ovid recorded, "*Sit tibi terra levis.* May the earth rest lightly upon thee."

To fail to perform these rituals properly was to risk the soul's unhappy return to the earth above.

Though my good Christian father was, as far as I know, devoutly ignorant of the seed of these pagan rites and beliefs, he did hold to a similar custom, one that many old beekeepers I know still observe upon the death of a friend or family member. They call this ritual telling the bees.

My father learned the practice from his own father, who as a boy had performed the rite when a loved one died just as his father had before him. I was six years old when my turn came to perform this traditional rite of passage for our neighbor Mrs. Lupitas, who until her departure from this earth at the ripe age of ninety-two had come by our house once a month without fail to purchase honey from my parents' stock. It had been Mrs. Lupitas who had first welcomed my parents to their new home with a basket of fresh-baked bread and garden vegetables, and in the absence of any other nearby blood relatives, my sister and I had come to think of her as a surrogate grandmother.

On the morning of her funeral, my father called me to his side and handed me the ring of keys that he always carried in the right front pocket of his dungarees.

"Albert, I'm afraid dear Mrs. Lupitas has breathed her last," he said, glancing at the gold watch he had removed from his pocket along with his keys. "It's time to go tell the bees."

With that simple pronouncement, my father proceeded to explain to me that after a death in the family it was customary for the youngest member of the household to visit the hives and tell the bees of the death. And while acknowledging that Mrs. Lupitas was not a true blood relative, he said she had shown our family and our bees genuine affection over the years. Anything we could do to ease her passage into heaven seemed a small favor in return for all her many kindnesses.

To perform the ceremony properly, my

father instructed that I was to go to each and every hive in our family compound and to rattle the keys he had given me as I tapped on the hive and whispered three times:

Little brownies, little brownies, your mistress is dead.

Little brownies, little brownies, your mistress is dead.

Little brownies, little brownies, your mistress is dead.

Then I was to tie a piece of funeral crepe, which my father also produced, to each of our hives. And finally, he said, I was to bring sweets to the hives for the bees to feed upon and to invite the bees to her funeral.

"On a number of occasions in my memory," he added with a mysterious wink, "the bees have seen fit to attend."

"What should I tell them?" I remember asking my father.

"Whatever you think will best ease that dear lady's passage to the Promised Land," he replied.

Laden thus with keys, black crepe, a basket of sugar cookies my mother had prepared for the occasion, and what I believed to be the full weight of Mrs. Lupitas's salvation resting upon my young shoulders, I was left alone to perform the ritual as my father had instructed.

That morning was gray and damp, and our honeybees had been slow to rise to face the chill of the day. Loath to disturb them, I stopped at the first hive I came to and, setting my bundles of funeral crepe and cookies upon it, I shook my father's keys softly and began to whisper the words of the chant he had just taught me. "Little brownies, little brownies," I said, "your mistress is dead."

I thought I heard a stirring inside the hive as I repeated my lines a little louder the second time and louder still the third. By then there was no mistaking that the hum inside the hive had grown in force, and I felt compelled to add that Mrs. Lupitas was a very old woman and that I was sure she would be happier communing with Jesus in heaven than she had been living all alone in her big house with no one to talk to but her old dog Tavish. The words just tumbled out. And then so did the bees, tumbling out in a big black swarm and up into the air, where they gathered in a swirling mass fifty feet above my head. Not knowing what else to say, I took a ribbon of black crepe and wrapped it around the top of the hive and then I placed one of my mother's sugar cookies on the landing board. Finally, with only a single glance overhead, I carried my bundles to the next hive.

I believe it may have been something about the rhythmic jangling of the keys that drove the bees to quit their hives that morning, or perhaps it was the high-pitched rasp of my small voice, because, as truly as I live and breathe, something stirred the bees that day. One by one, I stopped in front of each of our sixteen hives, and from each, as I began to shake my father's keys and repeat the words he'd taught me, a cloud of bees poured forth to join the growing cloud overhead. Soon, the roar of the bees had overwhelmed the sound of my small voice, and I found myself shaking the keys with both hands as I danced in a feverish circle beneath the swarming bees and shouted my childish prayers for Mrs. Lupitas's safe passage to heaven.

"Little brownies, little brownies," I sang out to each hive in turn, and above each in turn the heavens turned dark with bees, "your mistress is dead."

When I returned from my funerary duties later that morning, I was drenched with sweat. My father, who was sitting on the front porch sipping a cool glass of lemonade, dug his bandanna out from his pocket and handed it to me. I wiped my face and hands as clean as I could manage and handed it back to him.

"Have you done as you were told?" he inquired, replacing the muddied bandanna in his pocket as I clambered up onto the porch swing to sit next to him. I nodded, and though I wanted to tell him what had happened and to ask him if anything as wondrous had ever happened to him, I could see from the distant look on his face that he preferred to keep his own counsel. We sat together like that for a spell, rocking back and forth in the late-morning breeze. Then, setting his empty glass down on the wicker table next to the swing, my father asked me if I would sit with him for a while longer.

I settled back in the swing and placed my folded hands upon my lap.

"Bees do not thrive in a quarrelsome family," he said. "They dislike bad language. And they should never, ever be bought or sold for money.

"Bees should be given without compensation, but if such compensation is essential, barter or trade is greatly preferable to cold cash. And you must always be sure to tell the bees when they have changed hands," he said.

My father then told me of a woman who

had come to his father shortly after moving to the farm next door to theirs many, many years ago. She complained to him of the incessant swarming of the bees that had come part and parcel with the place she and her husband had recently purchased. My father said my grandfather asked his new neighbor whether she had bothered to tell the bees they had a new mistress. The puzzled woman averred that she had not, and so my grandfather accompanied her back to her farm and proceeded to visit each of her hives.

"She watched silently as my father walked up and down in front of the hives, talking quietly and calmly all the while, and when he was done the bees settled down and gave her no more trouble," my father explained.

My father then fell into a private reverie that was only broken when a large black crow that had been pecking at seeds in the yard abruptly took to the air in a flurry of flapping wings and dust.

"Mark my words, young Albert," my father said after the bird disappeared from view, "among those who know them well, bees are understood to be quiet and sober beings that disapprove of lying, cheating, and wanton women."

My father then rose from the swing and,

out of respect for Mrs. Lupitas, he adjourned to his room for the remainder of the morning. My mother and sister, meanwhile, were busy in the kitchen, preparing the afternoon meal, and I was left alone to ponder my father's words.

Many years later, I would sit on that same porch swing with my mother as she taught me how to sew.

"Draw the stitch forward, now back by half, then forward by half again," she would remind me as we sat together, her sewing basket nestled between us.

"This loop stitch will not win you any contests at a sewing bee," she pronounced just the week before she died, "but it will hold."

But what if there is nothing of substance left to hold?

Only a handful of hardy workers took to the skies the dark day it fell upon me to tell the bees of my dear mother's sudden passing. The rest seemed content enough to pick and crawl about the stale offering of leftover scones I dutifully set in front of each hive I visited on my mournful funereal rounds.

Thirteen years later, when my father followed my mother to the grave, I had nothing sweeter than a packet of stale graham crackers to offer the bees, and so the morning after his passing I dipped just as many crackers in honey as it would take to lay one out in front of each of our twenty hives that day. The bees seemed satisfied enough, I suppose, sensing somehow it was all I had to give. And as had been the case with my mother's rites, few if any of our bees rose to greet me when I came to tell them of my father's demise. I did detect a deep, soft hum that emanated from within each of the hives that resembled, as much as anything, a funeral dirge, so low and melodic in its own way, bringing me a certain measure of comfort in my hour of bereavement.

TWENTY-SIX

SKEP: An old-fashioned, fixed-frame hive made from woven coils of straw or grass that cannot be opened for inspection or honey harvesting without destroying the colony within. It is illegal to use in many countries, including the United States.

A row of condominiums the color of sand and dirty clouds stands now on the spot where the Straussman sisters lived and died.

It didn't happen all at once. There were probate orders and newspaper postings and planning commission hearings and all manner of official documents filed and appealed by a well-meaning neighborhood committee that had saved several other historic homes from demolition through their civic efforts before the Straussmans' meager estate was finally settled and the bulldozers arrived to plow under the house that had stood on that spot for close to a century.

I considered attending the final city council hearing when the fate of the house was sealed, but since I could not swear to the exact date when it was built, nor could I testify to any particular contribution the family had made to the civic or philanthropic development of the city, I chose to hold my peace.

And, truth be told, the Straussman house had little to recommend it save an old man's bittersweet memories.

Memory is a strange thing. It does not always come bidden on command. It seldom travels in a straight line. I know with empirical certainty that it has been nearly twenty years since Claire and Hilda have passed from this life, and almost fifteen since their family's home was razed to make way for my new crop of neighbors, all nestled cozy as you please into their stacks of homes that look each one just like the one in front of it, and behind it, up and below and on either side of it.

And yet early in the evening when the gray mist has just begun to roll in from the ocean, if I turn my head quickly to the left, I swear I can still see Claire, though just for an instant, standing on her back porch, hands on her narrow hips, wordlessly signaling for me to meet her out in the grove, and it's 1936 all over again.

"Do you know what day it is?" Claire says to me.

"June twentieth?" I stammer.

It was an uncharacteristically warm evening in late June. Claire knew that I knew she would be turning sweet sixteen in just three days. I had already set aside a jar of prized eucalyptus honey for her in honor of this special occasion, and I'd found a scrap of cloth in my mother's sewing basket and a bit of string out in the honey shed in which to wrap it.

"What do you think it's like inside?"

"Inside what?"

"Why, the Harmony, you silly goose!" Claire laughed, slapping my arm lightly. "The music is so inviting, don't you think?"

"It does seem loud," I agreed. I attempted to compare the spacious domelike design of the Harmony Park Ballroom to the interior architecture of a primitive skep. She argued that it looked more like a marvelous shipwreck washed ashore on Treasure Island.

"A boat? Here?"

"Yes, a boat, silly. Overturned and stuck in the sand," she said, crinkling her eyes as if to show me how to see what was clearly not there. "Use your imagination, Albert."

I squinted my eyes.

I must have looked very comical because Claire collapsed in a gale of laughter that was suddenly echoed by more laughter bursting through the open door of the dance hall.

It was unusual for the Harmony's doors to remain open, but the weather was unseasonably warm and humid that long-ago June night. From our vantage along the eastern border of my family's orange grove, we could observe flashes of color and movement as lively pairs of dancers whirled and glided past the ballroom's side door, which had been propped open with a concrete block.

"Will you look, just look at those dresses?" Claire's eyes followed the madly spinning figure of a dark-haired woman clad in a formfitting red dress slit scandalously up the trail of her thigh. We watched as the woman spun and spun in a giddy circle in front of the open doorway, her arms extended out from her sides and her hair flying wildly about her head until, dizzy and out of breath, she fell into the arms of another woman, dressed in a low-cut black sheath, who stood laughing and clapping at the edge of the crowd that had gathered to urge the dancing woman on. After a brief pause, and much to the disappointment of the crowd, the dancing woman whispered something into the ear of the black sheath-clad woman, and then the two of them walked slowly, arm in arm, out the side door of the ballroom and onto a small cement landing, where they stood for a moment, the woman in the red dress laughing and breathing heavily as the woman in black fanned her companion's flush face with her open hands.

"Just look at those dresses," Claire said again, her own hand fluttering for an instant in front of her face, and I admit I was at a loss as how to respond. Claire seemed to me a different person altogether that night. For as long as I'd known her, she had shown a propensity for wearing the simplest of styles and materials: light cotton smocks and blouses in the summer, dark woolen trousers or skirts and bulky sweaters when the weather turned cool.

I had always viewed Claire as a practical girl, levelheaded and not overly concerned with the modes of the day. There is no denying that she had developed into a slender but shapely young woman with fine, well-defined features just like her father's, and thick, dark wavy hair much like her mother's, or at least as her mother's had appeared in the old sepia-toned photographs that crowded the family's mantle. Unlike Hilda, who seemed to have inherited the worst of both her parents' features, I am sure Claire could have turned a head or two at that time had she chosen to follow fashion's whimsy, but she had never shown the slightest inclination to do so. All that would come later: the frills and flounces and flocks of earnest young suitors.

"Have you ever felt real satin?" Claire asked me that night, looking hard into my eyes as if searching for something she knew she would not find.

"Of course not," I had stammered. My mother, bless her heart, was not the type to go in for fancy clothes or fripperies, and she had never dressed herself or my sister in anything so impractical or ostentatious as satin or silk.

"What a shame, Albert," Claire said. She smiled shyly and took my hand and patted it. Then she turned it over to stroke the palm softly, drawing tiny circles on it with her fingertips. "You don't know what you're missing."

Something in her manner troubled me. "And you do?" I said, pulling my hand from hers.

"I certainly do," she replied, matching my gesture with a petulant toss of her hair, which I only noticed at that moment had been loosed from its customary ponytail to tumble in soft curls about her shoulders. Claire closed her eyes and opened them again, the barest hint of that shy smile returning to her lips.

"My mother used to belong to a lodge," she said. "The Daughters of Scotia. We're part Scottish, you know, on my Grandmother Galt's side."

Only a week before, Claire had been in her attic, storing away the family's winter clothes for the season. There, she had come across an old steamer trunk that contained the bulk of her mother's former apparel culled from her more slender years. Tucked between the stylish suits and dresses of that bygone era were several white satin lodge gowns wrapped in mothballs and tissue paper. Claire told me her mother had stopped attending the monthly meetings of her Scottish lodge sisters during the mourning period after Harry Junior's sudden death and she had never seen fit to return. In fact, her mother had grown increasingly housebound after young Harry's untimely demise, shunning all manner of social and civic gatherings, school assemblies, and even church services.

"My mother never seemed to get over the

loss of Harry," Claire said. "My father either."

I could only nod sympathetically and wonder at the absolute transformation that grief had worked over time on the minds and bodies of the once handsome young couple of which irrefutable evidence remained only in the Straussmans' faded family portraits.

Claire confessed to me that she took one of her mother's white silk lodge dresses out of its tissue paper and had held it up in front of her. It was sleeveless, elegant in its simplicity, with a slightly scooped neckline and a high, close-fitting bodice. The skirt was straight and long, she said, with a flare at the bottom.

Claire leaned close and whispered to me that, all alone in the attic that balmy afternoon, she had undressed herself completely and, pardon me, but she said she had stood stark naked in front of a dusty full-length mirror that leaned against one of the rafters and that she had slipped her mother's dress over her head and let it fall like ice water over her exposed skin.

"I had to wiggle a little to fit into it," Claire told me, an odd smile playing briefly on her lips. "I know it's hard for people to believe it now, but my mother was really quite slender and beautiful when she was young."

Not knowing how to respond, I forced a wan smile.

"When Father returned home last Friday, I caught him staring at Mother when she wasn't looking," Claire whispered. She told me that she couldn't help but wonder if her father was trying to rekindle in his mind, if not his heart, the image of that beautiful young girl he had married.

"They met on a train," Claire said. "Did you know that?"

I shook my head.

"Of course you didn't," she said, tossing her hair once again in that most disconcerting manner. "Father was a conductor on the Saint Louis–to–Chicago train line back then."

Claire explained how her mother had chanced to visit her Aunt Maud in Detroit the summer following her seventeenth birthday and that her father had remarked, while punching her ticket, that he, too, had relatives in that same city, and from this common familial geography the spark of romance had been ignited.

"Believe it or not, my father proposed to my mother for the first time just outside of Bloomington, and again at the station in Joliet," Claire told me. "Of course she turned him down both times. After she switched trains in Chicago, they both thought that would be the end of that."

But as fate would have it, Claire said, her parents met again on the return trip, and somewhere south of Springfield her mother agreed to allow Mr. Straussman to come calling on her once she returned to her parents' home in St. Louis.

"My father says that I remind him of Mother when they first met," Claire told me, her voice deadened curiously no doubt by the length of the tale. "He used to say the same thing about Hilda."

I found it difficult to reconcile my image of the moribund Mrs. Straussman with the daring young girl who'd traveled unaccompanied to Detroit and back so many years before. And I was likewise skeptical of Mr. Straussman's sentimentality, given the remoteness of all interaction that I had witnessed between him and his family on the rare occasions I had come in close contact with him. There had always been a distinct austerity to all his words and gestures that could not be ascribed entirely to his — or any — line of work. So, too, did I notice that a certain chill seemed to fall across Claire whenever she spoke of her mother and father as if the shadow that had long ago engulfed the parents had begun to overtake the child.

"Can I tell you a secret, Albert?" Claire whispered, and she again leaned close to my ear. I could feel her breath, warm and moist on my neck, as she spoke. "I didn't put my mother's lodge dress back in the trunk. I have it hidden in my room at this very moment."

I pulled back to stare at her face. Her funny smile was back again, bolder than ever, and full of something like mischief, only darker. This was not the same innocent young girl with whom I'd spent so many hours tending our honeybees and gathering the sweet harvest of their unselfish labors. I found the transformation unsettling.

"Would you like to see it sometime? The gown, I mean," she said. "I'll even let you touch it if you promise not to get it dirty."

I declined her invitation with all due respect. I believe I conveyed as best I could my desire to return to my house earlier than was my custom, telling Claire that I wished to complete my reading of Plato's *Symposium* that evening before I retired. I then detailed my systematic plan for reading what I considered to be the fundamental pillars of Western thought.

"After Plato, I plan to tackle Aristotle, Horace, and of course Saint Augustine," I said.

"You know, I read quite a bit myself," Claire said rather defensively to my ear. "But I read for pleasure."

I asked her what type of books gave her pleasure. "Books about romance and adventure," she said. "Have you ever read any D. H. Lawrence? Or Elizabeth Bowen, or Ford Maddox Ford, or Hemingway or Fitzgerald?"

"You mean fiction?" I said.

"I mean flesh-and-blood stories about what happens outside your head, Albert. Stories that touch your heart."

With that, she placed her hand squarely on my chest, which felt as though it were entombed in lead beneath her magnetic touch.

"Your heart is pounding, Albert," she said. But, thankfully, that is all she said. When I offered no response, she slowly let her hand drop to her side. I took advantage of her welcome silence to bid her good night, though, in truth, the night suddenly felt anything but good.

Claire made no further mention of her mother's dress the next time I saw her. Our evening rendezvous grew increasingly sporadic over the next few months, which I suppose was as much my fault as hers. As I became ever more engrossed in my studies, which would progress through the early Christian theologians and on into the Age of Enlightenment by summer's end, I generally retired to my room directly after supper to pore over the pages of my books rather than to my back porch to contemplate the passage of stars across the heavens as had been my previous custom.

It was Kant, I believe, who said that objective reality is knowable only through the mind that seeks its knowledge and that anything beyond the realm of one's own experience is unknowable. Which is to say, I could not know what Claire was going through during this turbulent time because I was not privy to what was beyond the realm of my own understanding. Nonetheless, I sensed something slipping away that summer, though I did not realize exactly how far it had slipped until, glancing out my window one evening in late August, I thought I saw a figure in white racing through our orchard. Some time later, and to my everlasting regret, I would follow that pale ghost. But not then. Not that night.

TWENTY-SEVEN

THE PROBOSCIS: A complex apparatus that includes the maxillae, labia, and glossa, or tongue, which together form a strawlike tube that draws up nectar, honey, and water, or, in reverse, transfers food from bee to bee.

One of the more puzzling aspects of the worker bee's behavior is her seeming ability to adapt to a succession of diverse responsibilities over the course of her lifetime without obvious training or prior knowledge of the tasks. Even more intriguing is the fact that she undertakes these progressively more complex tasks, as British apiarist Herbert Mace noted, having descended from parents who have never performed the tasks expected of her as neither have the requisite organs or intelligence expected of their daughter. How then, without proper guidance or example, does the worker learn to fulfill her role when the father is a mere depositor of sperm and the queen mother nothing more than the indifferent layer of the fertilized egg?

There are those who theorize that it is through genetic transference, while others look to the worker's food supply for some unidentified secretion or dietary element that is passed along to trigger the instincts and organ growth necessary for her to know how and when to perform the tasks she does. The irony is that in the course of her lifetime she may perform every task necessary for the survival of the hive save one: She cannot produce viable, full-functioning offspring. That task alone is reserved for the queen.

Just as the worker bee fulfills many roles during her lifetime, so, too, a man or woman may develop many roles and levels of human interaction depending upon his or her particular stage in life. I say this only because while the warm bond of friendship that Claire and I had forged in our early adolescence had begun to fray a bit around the edges during the summer of 1936, the common regard for our cherished bees continued to hold strong, and Claire continued to work in our family's apiary during the day, though, as I said, our customary evening rendezvous became ever more infrequent as we left our childish years behind.

As I think back now, I think I might have been less kind than I should have been.

It was during this period of diminishing camaraderie that Claire began to offer up in conversation occasional tidbits of arcane information about the care and habits of honeybees of which even my father was forced to admit he had been unaware.

I recall, for example, an instance when she and I took up what had developed over the summer into an intractable debate as to the merits of alfalfa honey over jasmine. We were helping my father uncap and load a brace of foundation frames into our honey extractor, and as usual I had taken the side of jasmine while Claire stuck stubbornly to her preference for alfalfa.

"It is so utterly common," I insisted as I had a thousand times before. "There is nothing in its color or flavor that is of special worth."

"Of course there's nothing special about alfalfa honey," she said. "It's not the honey but what the bee has to do to extract the honey from the flower that is so fascinating."

Claire described in surprisingly intricate

detail how this wily flower was designed so that if a bee were to sip its nectar directly from the blossom as is customary with other blossoms, it would shut on the bee's tongue, and she would be hard-pressed to free herself. Claire explained that after several such awkward snares, the honeybee learns to approach the blossom from the side to sip the nectar without tripping the blossom. This, Claire said, proved that the honeybee was infinitely more intelligent than most creatures in the animal kingdom.

"And how is that?" my father prodded.

"Well, Mr. Honig, she can measure and interpret information and she is able to learn from her mistakes. I think this makes her nearly human in her ability to reason," Claire said, and with an unseemly glint in her eyes added, "Of course the drone shows no such signs of intelligent life."

Surprised by her sudden erudition on the subject of bee science and the passion with which it was imparted, my father asked, "Wherever did you come up with such a thing?"

"There are some things philosophers can't teach you," she replied, directing her gaze at me instead of my father, who seemed oblivious to her barb.

I could not help wondering what had happened to the shy young girl who had flitted so obsequiously about the kitchen, serving tea and refreshments to her mother and me, at our first meeting only four years earlier. Over a single summer's span, Claire had added a level of haughtiness that could, with very little imagination, be construed as false pride, or so it seemed to me at the time. And, regretfully, I responded in kind, wishing to show my father, I suppose, that I was as learned in apian anatomy as our young neighbor suddenly appeared to be.

"Speaking of bees' tongues, why do you suppose it is that while the queen bee is larger and stronger, and her wings are by far more powerful than her offspring's, her tongue is only half as long as that of a worker bee?" I said, directing my query at Claire. When she did not respond right away, I offered that since the queen's services are not required for gathering pollen or nectar, there is no need for her to have an overly developed organ for this specialized function, while the worker bees must.

"Or just maybe discretion is the operating imperative here," Claire added with another sly wink aimed at my father as if he could appreciate her wit more than I. "A true queen, after all, would never kiss and tell."

"Tell what?" I demanded. Claire seemed

startled by the vehemence of my tone, as, in truth, was I.

"Never mind," she said.

But I did mind. I can't say why, but I did.

I would like to state for the record that while I certainly disagreed then — and still do — with Aristotle's belief that woman is but an inferior man, I wholeheartedly support his contention that all human actions have behind them one or more of these seven causes: chance, nature, compulsion, habit, reason, passion, and desire.

Certainly in Claire's case I would postulate that six out of the seven causes were mustered into action with the most dire of consequences — if not that fateful summer, then soon enough afterward.

TWENTY-EIGHT

DRONE CONGREGATION AREA: Where sexually mature drones from many colonies gather to mate with virgin queens. When a queen approaches, several drones copulate with her on the fly and eviscerate themselves in the process. It is not clear why drones choose a particular area to congregate, only that they will gather there year after year whether a queen is present or not.

Saint Augustine, in the passion of his youth, had been sorely tempted by the lure of the flesh, and by his own admission on many occasions he found his self-restraint wanting. But Augustine repented his former ways. God made man a rational animal, composed of body and soul, he realized. God permitted man to sin, he then wrote, but not with impunity. And God pursued man with His mercy. He let man share a life of generation in common with the trees and a life of the senses with the beasts of the fields, but He made the singular distinction that man shares a life of intelligence only with angels.

When I was young and blinded by the fire of my affection, I believed that Claire was that rare blend of beauty and intelligence that could elevate her to the realm of the spirit. But a change came over her after her visit to Detroit. I say Detroit now, of course, because Detective Grayson was clever enough to discover the truth of Claire's whereabouts posthumously, but at the time of her return midway through her twenty-second year I only knew that she had gone away my dearest friend and had come back profoundly more worldly. When on the rare occasions we found ourselves alone, we rarely spoke as we once had, as only young innocents can.

It was shortly after Claire's return that a steady stream of suitors began to come calling, though I observed that no particular young man came often enough to be called steady.

It became easy to discern when Claire was expecting a new beau. She would emerge from her front door in a fashionable dress with matching shoes and handbag, her hair piled up on her head and her lips and fingernails painted red. And before long she would begin to pace a wide figure eight back and forth across the porch until one young man or another pulled up in front of her house in his spit-and-polish roadster. She hardly gave any of these suitors time to turn the motor off before she bounded lightly down the porch stairs, then waited for him to come around to her side of the car to open the passenger door for her. As always, Claire commanded a certain level of respect even from these casual acquaintances.

I noticed only one young man who for a time frequented Claire's company more than the rest. But even he ceased his attentions shortly after making the unexpected acquaintance of the formidable Mrs. Straussman.

It was early December, and I was sitting on my front porch, enjoying the cool ocean breeze, when I saw Claire come out her front door. I nodded my head in greeting as Claire happened to turn her head, but before she could respond Mrs. Straussman came around the side of the house at the very moment Claire's gentleman caller pulled up in his roadster and bleated his horn to announce his arrival. As I believe I've mentioned before, Mrs. Straussman had lost her lower left leg to diabetes when Claire was still in her teens, but she'd since been fitted with an artificial limb that when used in conjunction with her sturdy badger cane provided her with some measure of mobility. I had grown to admire Mrs. Straussman's ability to move around with seeming aplomb despite her looming bulk, so I cannot say who was more surprised by the sudden tumble she took right in front of the porch, me or the startled young man who had just dashed around the front of his car to open the door for Claire. Needless to say, the young man's courtly intentions were quickly diverted from Claire to her mother as he rushed to the fallen woman's side and began fanning her face with a silk kerchief he pulled from the breast pocket of his suit. At least, I assume it was silk, judging by his otherwise dandified appearance.

Claire, meanwhile, continued to stand by the car door as if she expected her young man to simply abandon Mrs. Straussman, who lay prostrate on the ground. That's when the young man looked up in desperation and spotted me sitting on my front porch.

"You, there," he shouted, a bit rudely perhaps but understandable given the extreme circumstances. "Come give me a hand."

Of course I obliged, and with no small effort the young man and I eventually helped Mrs. Straussman up onto the porch and into her customary rattan rocker. Once she was comfortably seated, the young man dashed back to retrieve the cane abandoned in the grass.

"I'll be all right, now," Mrs. Straussman said. The young man handed the cane to her, and I must admit that despite her fall, she looked as hale as she ever did, though a bit winded, perhaps, and just a little flush in her ample cheeks. "It's the sugar, you know."

"Sugar?"

"Diabetes, lad. It makes me a wee bit light-headed from time to time."

Claire, meanwhile, hadn't budged from her station by the car, and I could see that this had caused her beau considerable consternation.

"Run along now, young man. Don't you worry about me," Mrs. Straussman said, sighing heavily as she caressed the handle of her cane. "I'll be just fine."

And of course she was, although the same could not be said of the couple whose evening she had so precipitously interrupted. While I couldn't catch their words exactly, it was clear from their tone that a disagreement had sprung up between Claire and her gentleman caller over her apparent indifference to her mother's infirmity, and soon enough he climbed back into the car and drove away, leaving Claire standing alone at the edge of the roadway.

"Don't you say a word," she said as she strode past me into her house, and I was left alone on the porch with Mrs. Straussman for a moment longer until she said once again that she was quite all right.

"Go on home, now," she said, straightening the folds of her heavy black dress. "Clarinda can take care of me."

I stopped briefly on my own front porch to wave good night. I never saw that particular young man again, and after a time most of the others gradually stopped coming around as well.

My desire to follow Claire never waned. But neither did my sacred obligation to my home, my family, and of course my bees. Claire and I were different in that regard. She felt burdened by filial duty to home and hearth throughout most of her troubled years on this earth; in her heart of hearts she always desired to be somewhere — anywhere — else. And sadly, as I so often told her in the waning years of our friendship, with her eyes locked on the distant horizon, she seemed sadly unprepared to appreciate the simple bounty that lay before her. At least, that was how I saw it. Claire was just as apt to point out to me that I was blinded to the possibilities of mystery and adventure by my own habit of keeping my nose so to the grindstone. Which is all true enough, I suppose, but as Claire would also no doubt say were she able to speak today, it's all just so much water under the bridge.

On the rare occasions Claire deigned to visit with my father and I as we worked together in our apiary, she no longer dove right in with a helping hand like she used to, more often than not quickly retiring to the kitchen, where she spent an inordinate amount of time assisting my mother in the preparation of meals or some other such household chore. I don't know what they talked about — or even if they talked at all — as my mother adhered to strict rules of female confidentiality regarding anything said between the two of them. And Claire hardly ever spoke directly to me other than to say hello or good-bye or ask about my health or the well-being of our family's bees.

Still, I worried about her, and I tried as best I could to watch and protect over her without arousing her considerable ire.

Despite her later accusations to the contrary, I never spied on Claire intentionally. Even when I saw her slip out of her house at night, I did not follow her into the grove as I once had. It was only by chance that I stumbled upon her private affairs that one and only time so very long ago.

TWENTY-NINE

THE QUEEN'S BURDEN: The life span of a queen is four to five years, compared to the six to seven weeks of her daughters. Her color is more golden. Her sting is more curved. The facets of her eyes, however, are fewer by several thousand, and though her brain is smaller her ovaries are enormous.

It was an unusually steamy night, even for August, when the nightly ocean breeze generally finds a way to work its magic on all but the most obdurate daytime heat even this far inland, and as I recall the music was reverberating off the walls of my room and people were shouting and laughing as they always did on Saturday nights at the Harmony Ballroom. Between the noise and the heat, it was next to impossible to sleep, and so even though it was well past midnight I decided I might as well get dressed and take a walk out to our number fifteen hive to retrieve the smoker can and gloves I'd carelessly left behind earlier that day. I didn't want my father to discover my mistake. He was, I must admit, a bit of a stickler for order.

"A place for everything and everything in its place," my father always said.

I was still sitting on my back porch steps, lacing up my shoes, when I saw a white blur dash through the trees beyond my mother's garden. It was none of my affair, I told myself, as I wove slowly through the orderly rows of orange trees that converged into darkness beneath the dim illumination of the rising moon. The night air was thick with the aroma of ripe oranges, and I had to duck to avoid being struck by low-hanging clusters of fruit. I was bent over in just such an evasive maneuver, in fact, when I was startled out of my own reveries by the sharp braying sound of a man's laugh followed by a flurry of low whispers coming from somewhere nearby. I hesitated a moment, but then I realized one of the two voices was Claire's, clear as the silver moonlight that shone through the trees.

"*Hola* yourself, kiddo," she said, and I looked up just in time to see a lean, hard-looking man in a dark long-sleeved shirt with embroidered white trim and a woven leather tie with silver tips that matched the pointed toes of his black leather boots that tipped out from beneath the cuffs of his dark trousers. Claire threw her slender arms around the man's neck, and the moonlight reflecting off her dazzling white gown cast both figures in an otherworldly glow that drew my unwilling eyes to them like a moth to a flame.

Transfixed for the moment, I watched with revulsion as the dark-clad man loosened the leather band from around his neck and lifted it slowly over his head as he unbuttoned his shirt with his other hand. Then he slipped the tie around Claire's neck and pulled her closer to him. With her lips nearly brushing his, she whispered something else I could not hear and I turned to go. But as I did, a twig snapped sharply under my foot, and I froze when both their heads turned in the direction of the sound. Partially concealed by the trunk of a tree and the darkness all around me, I remained for the moment undetected. To move, I realized, would be to risk giving myself away. And so reluctantly I stayed, and I saw more in the next few moments than I could erase in a lifetime.

I cannot say if it was the first — or even

the only — time Claire met this man in the grove. I only can say that he was not one of her "regular" callers, who for the most part had already fallen by the wayside by this time. I will venture, however, that there was a swagger and self-assuredness to this man's movements that the previous callow young men had lacked. This man seemed older — nearly old enough, in fact, to be her father. But where her father was reed thin, milk pale, and distant in bearing, this man, though still lean, was more robust, swarthy even, and given to bursts of raucous laughter where no good reason for mirth existed that I could detect.

Little that might be construed as tenderness or even true affection seemed to pass between the two of them either before or after their unholy coupling. Whereas the man expressed his lust in a chorus of grunts and guttural moans, Claire bore her defilement in relative silence, with only an occasional whimper emitting from her lips as the force of the man's excitement drove him to the edge, it seemed to me, of abandoning all senses. Repelled by what I saw yet unable to turn away, I welcomed the sharp sting of tears that diffused my vision until the act was finished and the man collapsed onto the perfect white mounds of Claire's exposed breasts even as a small sigh of relief escaped unbidden from my own trembling lips.

And then it was over.

With very little conversation between them, they presently drew themselves apart. I held close to the tree trunk as Claire, cool as ice, slid her dress back down over her head, slipped her shoes on, and scurried past me into the night. I waited a few more moments to allow the man time to pull up his pants, buckle his belt, smooth his hair, and saunter back toward the Harmony Ballroom. Then I hastily retrieved my smoker can and gloves and finally, under the cover of darkness, I returned home to my bed and an uneasy sleep.

Four months later, Claire, Hilda, and their mother went off to Alabama to take care of a poor unmarried relation. And six months after that, they brought David Gilbert home. Dark and brazen, he grew up calling the elder Straussmans Pappa and Nana Straussman. The younger women he referred to as Aunt Claire and Aunt Hilda, more out of deference to the gap in years than anything else, I believe, as their relationship was always portrayed to outsiders as that of distant cousins.

David Gilbert was raised as a shame baby,

but the true shame was conveniently deflected from Mrs. Straussman's willful daughter onto the illusory Suzanna Gilbert. Despite the family's machinations to the contrary, I believe there were many in the neighborhood that suspected David Gilbert's true origins, though none came forward to confront the Straussmans or the child directly to my knowledge.

I am not one to judge.

I believe the Straussmans did what they thought they must do, given the indelicate circumstances and prevailing social strictures of the day. And of course in hindsight, given the chance to do it over again, I do not think I would have allowed myself to be insinuated into this untenable situation as I seemed to have set all manner of tragic events in motion despite my best intentions. In truth, I had sought only to bring presumptive mother and son closer together, but to my everlasting regret all my well-intended words tore asunder what few familial bonds they had stubbornly clung to, inauthentic as they may have been.

THIRTY

THE LANGSTROTH HIVE: Patented in 1851 by Reverend Lorenzo Lorraine Langstroth, it has become the standard in modern hive design. Incorporating the concept of bee space, this boxlike, stackable structure contains removable frames to which bees attach their wax honeycombs.

My new neighbors construct strange memorial displays on their lawn because they have chosen to believe that truth lies within the pulse of electromagnetic signals. They record names and dates on tiny crosses as if these simple inscriptions are the sole measure of a person's life and death. But life is not a simple arithmetic equation. Life is algorithmic in its complications. The flap of a drab moth's wing may have as many consequences — if not more — than the flutter of her infinitely more ethereal cousin's. Have my neighbors, through their tawdry memorial displays, convinced me that the power lines that now strangle the sky above my home are responsible for all the deaths in our little community? I think not.

But have I noticed that my hives that lie directly beneath the transformers from which the power lines emanate consistently produce less honey than the others? Perhaps.

Don't get me wrong. I understand that there is a difference between causation and correlation, and that it often takes time to discern the difference. Yet I believe it is no small coincidence that so many of the world's most accomplished thinkers have arrived at great truths by studying the complicated laws, labors, and physical discourse of the honeybee.

Such truths are not easily won. The esteemed poet Virgil concluded after much serious thought that bees collected their embryos like dewdrops from leaves and sweet plants. The Roman scholar Varo thought that bees collected wax not from the labors of their sisters but from the excrement of flowers, and Pliny the Elder wrote that echoes could kill bees.

To his credit, Aristotle was the first ancient to study bees scientifically, and he was the first to discard the long-held belief that bees were the products of autogenesis, spontaneously born from the carcasses of dead oxen. He persisted, however, in the mistaken belief that the hive was a patriarchal society, a notion with political correspondence in humankind that persisted into the seventeenth century when an English beekeeper named Butler reported that the "Kingbee" was really a queen because he had seen her deposit eggs. It took the Dutch savant Swammerdam to confirm this observation and to overthrow once and for all the rule of kingship in the hive with his invention of the microscope, which he used to examine the internal organs of dissected bees.

Within the grand scope of human learning, the very idea that a queen bee is born and raised for the sole purpose of populating the hive is a fairly modern concept. So, too, is the recognition that drones are born for the singular task of fertilizing the queen's eggs and hence spend the greater bulk of their short lives eating and carousing and making a general nuisance of themselves in exchange for that one purposeful moment on earth when they will be called upon by death-defying instinct and biochemical attraction to pursue their virgin queen high into the dazzling afternoon sky to mate with

Her Royal Highness on the fly.

The German poet Wilhelm Busch referred to drones as "lazy, stupid, fat, and greedy." But considering the unhappy fate of those brazen few strong enough and determined enough to fulfill their carnal destiny in one simultaneous instant of ecstasy and disembowelment — and that their remaining brothers, their collective purpose served, will be cast out of the hive by their unsympathetic sisters and left to freeze to death or to starve as soon as the winter chill arrives — such judgment seems overly harsh to me.

Claire was well schooled in these basic facts of bee behavior, but like Busch and my cross-bearing neighbors today she often failed to grasp the underlying truth behind the facts.

And so Claire made mistakes. Not so much out of ignorance as arrogance. False pride. Vanity. Call it what you will, but I never heard her once admit that she was wrong. About anything or anyone. And, sadly, I observed the direst of consequences in this regard the day I witnessed firsthand the sort of familial damage to David Gilbert's fragile psyche that I had only imagined having been heaped upon her. In Claire's defense I must say that I understood then as I still do now the source of her considerable wrath. Through David Gilbert's carelessness and neglect, he had caused the needless death of thousands upon thousands of precious bees — bees that Claire had lovingly acquired and scrupulously attended to for no other reason than to indulge her most genuine but sadly unacknowledged affection for the boy. To come unexpectedly upon the terrible devastation of her hives that awful afternoon must have been a cruel blow that no doubt pushed her over the brink of reason into the lower realm of unbridled emotion.

It was the raw fury of her cry that caused me to drop what I was doing without a second thought to my own bees' welfare and race immediately to her side that awful day.

While I was not privy to his demeanor within the four walls of their abode, it seemed that while David Gilbert was considerably darker in outward appearance he was correspondingly more light-hearted and generally less gloomy in spirit than I remember any of his elders to have been save Claire herself — or at least the Claire I remembered in the flower of her youth. David Gilbert had that same spark when he was young. On many a morning, I had watched him scurry cheerily off in the company of two or three equally carefree young fellows who made a habit of stopping off and whistling for him in front of his house on their way to school. And just as often I would observe this same group of youngsters take their insouciant leave from him each afternoon at the very same spot.

In this regard, I suppose, some things never change. While the elder Mrs. Straussman, as she grew ever larger and less mobile, was less apt to accost the neighborhood children who chanced to pass by her house, by the time David Gilbert reached school age the mere mention of her name held the same dark sense of foreboding among this new generation of children as it had with mine. I never saw a single one of his young friends venture onto the Straussmans' front lawn, let alone breach the inner sanctum of that cursed house. That particular feat of youthful valor remains mine alone to claim.

But that is neither here nor there. On the particular afternoon of David Gilbert's unintentional transgression, his school chums had already bid their good-byes and he had gone into the house when Claire called for him to join her in the backyard. This I saw with my own eyes, as I was sitting on my back porch doing my clumsy best to mend a small tear in the elbow of my sweater, and from what I was able to gather from the shouting and recriminations that came later it was during this conversation that Claire had mentioned to David Gilbert that the oil in their hive pans had grown dangerously overrun with leaves and debris and she asked him to walk to the store to buy several new cans of motor oil with which to replace the contaminated supply. He promised that he would, and, in fact, he was well on his way to fulfilling his promise when he happened upon a pair of his schoolmates on the road to the store. The boys were hurrying to the Straussman house to ask if he could come out to play a game of baseball with them as one of their regular teammates had been injured the day before. David Gilbert said he informed them of the errand he had to run first, but his young friends insisted that the game was about to start. They begged him to come along at once.

And so David Gilbert put off his trip to the store until after the ball game. To his credit, he had scurried back to fill the hive pans with water before running off with his friends to the ballpark, assuming these makeshift moats would keep any marauding ants away from the hives just as well as oil, at least until the game was over.

To be fair, they were never really David

Gilbert's bees, despite Claire's best intentions. It had been Hilda, and not he, who Claire had enlisted from the start to care for the hives she'd acquired as a present for his fifth birthday. In fact, I was surprised that David Gilbert had been asked to put the oil in the pans that day. It was only later that I learned that Hilda had taken to bed the day before with a light-headedness that was subsequently diagnosed as the onset of diabetes, the same illness that had so debilitated her mother.

In retrospect, I think perhaps that it wasn't so much David Gilbert's understandable mistake that angered Claire as much as it was his growing indifference to the things that mattered to her.

Hilda may not have understood Claire's passions, but she always indulged them. I recalled the moment a handful of years earlier when, despite her fear of bees, Hilda had agreed to help Claire perform the ritual transferring of ownership of our colony of bees to them.

"Our bees are sensitive creatures who crave order in their lives. When that order is disrupted, we find that something sweet will soothe their agitation," I'd told Claire the day after my father and I had given her one of our hives so that she might start an apiary of her own. I gave Claire one of my mother's leftover scones, which she'd wrapped in a tea towel.

"Order, schmorder," Claire had sniffed as she'd reached back and clutched Hilda's hand, who appeared reluctant to stand so close to the new hive.

As much for Hilda's benefit as anything, I expounded on the orderly progression of labor in the hive that was in the purest sense a natural affirmation of the Hegelian system of order within the universe, explaining in precise detail the stages and purpose of each bee, from worker to drone to queen.

"For God's sake, Albert, don't you think I know your so-called Hegelian hierarchy of the bees by heart by now?" Claire said. "But just because you say it's so doesn't mean it's true."

Indeed, she proceeded to inform me in a somewhat opprobrious manner that there had recently emerged a new school of thought that allowed for more specificity and individuality of labor within the hive, which some scientists believed was due, she said, to the genetic diversity implicit in the multiple partners a queen bee instinctively takes in the course of her nuptial flight.

"All of which proves what?" I prodded only after she at last deigned to conclude her exegesis on bee colony propagation.

"It proves," she replied, "that even within your precious ordered society diversity is needed."

"Within reason, of course," I agreed.

"Reason be damned!" she exclaimed. "It's what every hive needs. It's what we all need. New blood. New experiences. Otherwise, we just wither away and . . ."

"And what?" I pressed. There had to be a point to her speculative digression.

"I don't know," she said. "I just think that order can't be the end all and be all of existence. It seems to me the universe has a way of upsetting everything just when you think you have it all figured out."

"Do you mean me particularly or humanity as a whole?"

"Oh, for God's sake, Albert . . ."

Though I did not approve of the irreverence of her language, I was convinced of the passion behind Claire's conviction. I waited for her to clarify her notion, but she had no more to say, and the silence seemed to set like amber around her.

"In the best of all worlds," I conceded, "the introduction of new blood may strengthen a declining hive, but it has been my experience that just as often it destroys it."

"That's what I love about you, Albert," Claire said, shattering her stony silence with a sudden sharp laugh. She dropped Hilda's hand and took my mine in hers. They felt as smooth and cool as I imagined her mother's satin gown felt to her so very long ago. "You're so safe and secure in your own little world, you almost make me feel safe there, too."

"So what about the bees?" Hilda interjected out of the blue — or so it seemed after having been all but ignored for the better part of the morning. In my own defense, I can say only that Hilda had always appeared content to remain in her sister's shadow.

"That's what I'm about to explain," I said, feeling my cheeks redden as I slipped my hands from Claire's before turning purposely to face Hilda. "Thanks to our rapping on their hive last evening, these bees know that something is out of order in their world. That is why you must welcome them to their new home this morning by letting them know they have a new mistress now."

And, even as I spoke, a few field bees had already begun to poke through the grass at the entrance of their hive. I instructed Claire to unwrap the scone I had handed her earlier and to break off a few small chunks and place them on and around the grass thatching. Then I handed Claire my father's key ring, which he'd given me that morning for just this purpose, and I told Claire to shake the keys at the hive as she repeated the following phrase three times:

"Little brownies, little brownies, your mistress is here."

Hilda issued a skeptical little snort, which seemed contagious — at least to her sister.

"Are you sure?" Claire said.

"It will only take a moment," I urged. I believe that if Hilda had not been there, or if my father had been there instead, Claire might not have hesitated at all. "Please, Claire. If for nothing else, for my father's peace of mind."

"For your father, then," Claire said. Taking a deep breath, she stepped toward the hive, jangled the keys softly, leaned her face in close to the hive, and began to whisper so softly I almost couldn't hear her words, but clearly it wasn't to me she was speaking. As I've often said, Claire had a transcendent gift for the language of bees, and this occasion was no exception as almost as soon as she had uttered the first words of the phrase I'd just taught her bees began issuing from the hive in groups of twos and threes, many brushing her lips as they flew by. By the time she'd said it a second time, a cloud of bees had surrounded her, and before she could move an inch they had covered most of her head like a living crown. Out of the corner of my eye I saw Hilda open her mouth as if to scream, but an urgent look from me thankfully stayed her voice.

"Stay still as you can, Claire," I said in my most soothing tone.

But Claire showed no sign of fear. In fact, she broke into a broad smile, and her voice was strong and clear as she intoned for the third and final time: "Little brownies, little brownies, your mistress is here."

Hilda, meanwhile, had raised her hand to her mouth as if to stifle any sound that might escape, and I noticed that a few bees had broken away from Claire to circle the space above Hilda's head. And then, as if satisfied that Hilda posed no threat, the bees circled back around to Claire to rejoin their sisters, who clustered now upon Claire's head and arms and upper torso. Finally, when it looked as though Hilda would burst from stoppered horror, the bees began to depart in a slow stream toward the Straussmans' blossoming almond grove to the west of the clearing.

"I'm fine," Claire assured Hilda, who had

begun tugging at the collar and sleeves of her sister's summer blouse convinced she would find a sea of welts on the exposed skin of Claire's neck and arms. Even I had to admit I had been worried.

"See? No stings," Claire declared as she turned her arms over and back again. "They just wanted to get to know me."

All these years later, I still wonder if her bees were the only ones who ever truly knew Claire. I do know that as hard as I tried, I always seemed to come up short in her eyes. I suppose it also goes without saying that despite Claire's oblique encouragement, very little new blood was introduced into my immediate family — or hers, for that matter — and what did flow served to disrupt rather than strengthen either.

From the very beginning, David Gilbert never stood a chance.

When David Gilbert returned home from his ball game, elated by a game-winning clout that had crowned him hero for the day, he found Claire, beside herself with anger and despair, bent over thousands of drowned bees floating in the water-filled hive pans.

"One thing!" Claire had wailed as I crossed the break in the hedgerow. Her voice seemed unnaturally shrill in the absence of the customary background hum of her hives. "All I asked you to do was one simple thing."

"I swear, Aunt Claire, I was going to take care of it right after the game," David Gilbert said sullenly.

"One thing," she repeated. "And for what? A game?"

"It's not just a game," he countered, a brash note of defiance shading his words. "It's baseball. The Big Train got his start here. Right here. Do you even know who Walter Johnson is?"

"One of your silly ballplayers?"

"Your bees are what's silly, that's what!"

"My bees?" she said, her voice rising like white-hot ash.

"I hate them," he said. Though she raised her hand to the boy, to her credit Claire did not strike him.

"I hate you," she said instead.

And I watched David Gilbert's eyes flitter and his jaw set as Claire drew a quick, sharp breath as if she could somehow call back the only three words that I ever saw her regret.

Judgment, as my father would say, is the province of the Lord, and so I would not for the life of me condemn Claire outright. I will say, however, that had I been faced with a similar disaster, I can only pray that I might have acted with more Christian restraint than Claire was able to muster toward the boy that day. As it was, my well-intentioned attempt to intervene on his behalf was met with nearly the same level of fury that his original transgression had provoked.

"Boys will be boys, Claire," I said as delicately as I could, though I must admit I possessed no particular affinity for typical boyhood pursuits such as our national pastime. Clearly David Gilbert had not intended to harm the bees, I tried to tell her, but to no avail.

"You stay out of this, you pompous old busybody," Claire said to me. And then she turned to the boy and grasped his thin shoulders and called into question his intelligence and his trustworthiness. For a moment I feared she would shake the very life out of him. Instead, she simply sighed.

"What were you thinking?" she said at last, her voice sounding more weary than angry. "What were you thinking?"

"Nothing, Aunt Claire," he said sullenly as Claire released her grip on him. "Nothing at all."

Which I believe was true enough, as I do not believe there was any conscious intention on David Gilbert's part to blatantly disobey Claire's command. But as is so often the case when a child does not understand the reason behind a particular dictum, he may not foresee the harm in skirting around it. To his way of thinking, he had merely done the next best thing by filling the trays with water instead of oil.

"The bees are drawn to the water, David Gilbert," I explained as calmly as I could once I was sure Claire's anger had truly abated. Clearly this was a point of bee nature that Claire had neglected to impart to him. "They fly into the pans for a drink, but they can't stay afloat for more than a moment before their wings are soaked and, unable to fly away, they soon drown. Bees don't like the smell of motor oil. They try never to land in oil."

"I'm sorry," David Gilbert had said, his eyes downcast and his hands jammed deep into the front pockets of his dungarees. "I didn't know."

I turned to Claire, expecting her to acknowledge the boy's apology, which appeared sincere enough to me, but the silence was broken only by the buzz of a solitary field bee that flitted nervously above her hive mates' watery grave. David Gilbert looked from me to Claire and back to me again, and then he turned and walked slowly into the house. Thinking to console the boy, I took a single step forward.

"I told you to stay out of this," Claire said to me, and then before striding purposely into the house and slamming the door behind her she said, "One thing! One thing! That's all I've ever asked."

It was Cicero, I believe, who observed that no snares are ever so insidious as those lurking as dutiful devotion or labeled as family affection. You can escape from an open foe, but when deceit lurks in the bosom of a family it can pounce upon you before you have spied it or recognized it for what it is. I believe Claire cared for David Gilbert in the only way she knew. What I didn't yet see was that the family ties that bound her to this desolate little boy were already stretched as fine as spider's silk.

THIRTY-ONE

WORKER BEE: The sexually undeveloped female who under normal circumstances performs all the necessary chores to maintain the hive save one: producing offspring.

How does a friendship unravel? One thread at a time, I suspect. Claire and I continued to wave to each other across our yards. From time to time we found reason to chat about the goings-on around us as neighbors, but once I'd made the mistake of intervening on young David Gilbert's behalf the fabric of our conversations grew ever more threadbare.

"Did you hear they're tearing down the old Pickwick Hotel?" I remember Claire saying to me one day when we met on the street. I was walking home from the public library. I'm not sure where she was going. I may have forgotten to ask. I know it must have been sometime in 1975. This was during the first big redevelopment phase of the old downtown. Nearly all the old buildings — the Fox Theater, the Office Barbershop, the SQR, Rexall Drugs, Hurst's Diamonds — were all being razed to make way for a gleaming glass-fronted city hall complex and new central business district.

David Gilbert had graduated from high school ten years or so earlier and had long since left the family fold.

"I can't believe they want to tear it down," she said. "It's a real shame."

"I suppose so," I agreed.

I had no intimate knowledge of the Pickwick Hotel — or any other hotel, for that matter — having never spent a night in any room but my own. I had come to admire the Pickwick's distinctive architecture, however. Its Spanish-style bell tower had been, for much of my childhood, the tallest, most distinctive structure in sight. I believe there is something about the perceived permanence of long-standing edifices that reminds us of our younger, better selves, while at the same time they play on our desire for mythic immortality, for at least as long as they stand. Though I've never been to Notre-Dame, I imagine this is the reason why more than half a millennium after its completion even those who do not believe in God find themselves awestruck standing beneath its soaring Gothic arches.

Not that the Pickwick could hold a candle to the architectural significance of Notre-Dame, but I believe there was still something of the tragic landmark of memory and desire that drew David Gilbert back to his childhood home on the unfortunate day in 1981 that marked the absolute end of my friendship with Claire. He'd returned home after nearly twenty years away, hoping, I think, to forge anew his familial bonds by seeking any scrap of information about the mysterious Suzanna Gilbert, around whom he had constructed a most tragic mythology of genealogical redemption. Having begun a family of his own, he said he wanted to start it out on firmer footing than he himself had known as a child. He told Claire and Hilda, in the vernacular of the day, that he wanted to "get in touch with his roots" and to show his family that despite everything that had gone before he had turned out okay.

Who is to say what ill wind blew me into the midst of this brewing storm? I hadn't even realized Claire had company that day until I arrived at her doorstep. Having been cloistered inside my honey shed all morning extracting a new crop of jasmine honey from my numbers seven and eight hives, I hadn't noticed the unfamiliar vehicle parked out on the street in front of the Straussman house. It was only by happenstance that I decided to stop over at lunchtime to bring Claire a jar of the honey and to tell her about a new foundation frame manufacturer that I had found advertised in my monthly supply catalog.

As I told Detective Grayson the day he asked me point-blank about the nature of the relationship between Claire and David Gilbert, things seemed distant, a bit awkward, yet calm enough when I first arrived at the Straussman house that afternoon. David Gilbert, his wife, and daughter were sitting in the parlor with Claire and Hilda. Hilda was pouring steaming black tea into the gold china cups they saved for company, passing one to David Gilbert, and one to his wife, while he recounted for Claire and Hilda the story of how he'd met his wife through her brother, who was a "buddy," as he put it, from Texas, where their military unit had been stationed.

In exchange for my gift of honey, I was politely invited to join this unexpected family reunion for tea and cookies, and while I declined the offer of tea I graciously accepted a small plate of shortbread cookies, which Hilda handed to me without comment.

I settled into the Straussmans' parlor divan, which despite its age had retained its velveteen nap nearly unblemished. David Gilbert explained to the small gathering exactly how he and his wife had met. He related that she had traveled with her parents from Mexico to attend his military base's annual Memorial Day celebration and parade and that she had caught his eye when she'd waved at her brother, who was marching next to him in the parade.

"The rest," David Gilbert said, nodding to his wife, who nodded demurely, "is history."

"So I see," Claire responded, smiling not at all unkindly at David Gilbert and his newly announced family but clearly still measuring the situation.

"She was by far the prettiest girl there," he recalled proudly, nodding, it seemed to me, more deferentially to his wife thereafter. I noticed that his wife whispered occasionally to him in Spanish when he seemed to embellish a point beyond her idea of the simple truth as he narrated the ensuing details of their brief courtship. His wife seemed to understand the English language well enough, from my observation, but she appeared less confident with the spoken word, unlike her dashing young helicopter pilot who had always been far more loquacious than any other Straussman I knew save Claire.

Courtship history accounted for, David Gilbert next announced that he and his family had just been reassigned to our local Marine outpost, which had been converted after World War II from a staging base for dirigibles to one for military helicopters. His new base, which he'd been assigned to the previous spring, was only a scant few miles from the childhood home he'd fled without so much as a proper good-bye as soon as he had come of legal age. He told Claire that with the passage of time had come forgiveness. He told her — most earnestly, it seemed to me — that he'd truly come to regret his callous abandonment of the only family he'd ever known and he hoped that he and they could patch up their differences and try to become friends. Rather ceremoniously, David Gilbert then presented Claire with a framed photograph of himself posed in front of a Marine helicopter as a small token, he said, of his sincerity.

"Let's let bygones be bygones," he said. Claire somewhat awkwardly took the photograph after a moment's hesitation and placed it on the mantle next to the photographs of her deceased parents.

Predictably, the little girl had grown bored by this extended conversation. Long before the photograph exchange I noticed that she had begun to fiddle with the porcelain knickknacks on the mahogany end table next to the divan where I sat. So did Hilda. Just as it appeared inevitable that the delicate figurines would be damaged by the child's play, I was relieved to see Hilda approach her directly and ask if she would like to know a secret. What little girl could resist?

"Yes, ma'am."

Taking Hilda's thick hand in hers, she permitted the older woman to lead her from the parlor and into the adjoining sun-porch. It was, to my eye, much more cheerful, and as they would say today, more "child-friendly," being less formally furnished with durable wicker furniture, handmade throw rugs, and various species of potted plant. Thankfully, the child and her temporary guardian were still exploring the unexpected mysteries of this agreeably spartan room by the time the conversation in the parlor veered sharply away from reconciliation.

"I don't want to cause my mother any problems," David Gilbert was saying when

I turned my attention back to the conversation at hand. "I can understand what it must have been like for her in those days. All alone with no one to turn to but you and your family. Believe me, Aunt Claire, I'm grateful for all your past kindness. And Aunt Hilda, too."

"You're more than welcome," Claire said with an unmistakable air of finality that seemed to signal that, at least for her, the subject had been politely but decisively concluded.

"But, Aunt Claire," David Gilbert said, clearly recognizing Claire's unspoken intent but unwilling to let the matter drop, "I just want to know where I came from."

"This is where you came from," Claire insisted. Fine lines converged at the corners of her eyes as she spoke.

"You know what I mean, Aunt Claire," David Gilbert said evenly, his frustration reciprocating in the childish set of his tawny jawline.

"I know there's no good reason for you to go dredging up the past now," Claire rejoined. "What's done is done."

"Look, I don't want to cause my mother any problems," he repeated, his voice taking on an extra layer of urgency that made me recall the reckless indiscretions of his youth.

"I'm not angry with her or anything like that. I just want to know who I am. I want my daughter to know who she is. Why is that so hard for you to understand?"

Strangely, at that moment I found it hard to understand my own ambivalence toward David Gilbert's wish to establish for his still innocent daughter a viable link to her matriarchal past. I could not help wondering whether the old saw that genetic traits skip a generation was true or not. Meanwhile, the tenor of the conversation was becoming ever less cordial, and I began to wish I hadn't retained such casual access to Claire's home or her affairs. To say I grew uneasy by the accusations that were cast that afternoon would be an understatement of the most ineffable magnitude. I could no more imagine what it must have felt like to be accused of rank ingratitude for all the bountiful blessings of my own birth and upbringing than I would deign to call my dear mother cold and unfeeling no matter what the provocation. As Wittgenstein so rightly noted: "Whereof one cannot speak, thereof one must remain silent."

And so I strove mightily to hold my tongue. I truly believed it wasn't my place to interfere. I set down the plate of short-bread cookies Hilda had passed to me earlier and stood to make my exit as gracefully as possible, but Claire would have none of it. She turned to me and demanded that I support her charade, which grew more and more indefensible with each passing moment.

"Tell him, Albert," Claire demanded.

"Tell him what?" I replied, appalled already by the task I feared she'd set before me. I remember quite pointedly that she once told me she knew better than to ask me to lie for her, but sadly she was unable to keep her own counsel.

"Tell him his mother's probably forgotten all about him by now," Claire said. "Tell him it's best to let sleeping dogs lie."

To lie. It is a verb with so many meanings. To recline. To be buried in a specific place. To have sexual intercourse with. To speak an untruth.

"Like you?" I snapped before I knew what I was saying.

"And just what do you mean by that?" she said in that haughty tone of voice I had always found so unbecoming.

"What I mean is, which do you propose that I start with — the sleeping dogs? Or the lies?"

I lamented the rashness of my words as soon as they had escaped from my lips. With

God as my witness, I never intended to say what I did, but regrettably I said it nonetheless.

David Gilbert, who had remained silent during this short exchange, turned his back on Claire and directed his next question to me. "You know more about my mother than you're letting on, don't you, Mr. Honig?"

"I suppose I do," I replied. His eyes narrowed, and I sensed he was processing the thoughts he'd not yet dared to articulate. "And I suspect you do, too."

"What's that supposed to mean?" he said, oddly mirroring Claire's demanding tone, and regrettably, still in the heat of the moment, I remained less circumspect than I perhaps should have.

"You must have heard the rumors when you were younger," I responded. I saw Claire's eyes dart quickly from me to David Gilbert and back to me again. I saw also in that instant that she knew I suspected her secret and her eyes commanded me, and then silently begged me, to say no more. But it was already too late.

Sophocles wrote that a lie never lives to be old. But, just as surely, its death is seldom applauded by those who would live the lie. Understandably, Claire tried for a moment more to deny the truth by discrediting the truth teller.

"He doesn't know what he's talking about, David," she said, smoothing an errant wisp of graying curl from her eye. "He's just a ridiculous old man who has nothing better to do than listen to the idle gossip of anyone who's ever bought a jar of his precious honey."

"Please, Aunt Claire, don't . . ." David Gilbert said quietly, his voice faltering just a bit.

But she would not relent. "I made a promise to your mother . . .

"For God's sakes, Albert," she said, turning to me. "How could you? How could you even begin to give credence to those vicious old tales? I thought we were friends."

"I only say what I say because we are friends, Claire," I said. "You know I speak the truth."

"You wouldn't know the truth if it bit you on the nose, you pious old fraud," she retorted. It was odd how that one remark could so put into perspective the passing of the years. Yes, I was getting older. But so had she. I could see it then in the pale blue-veined hands that she waved in front of my face for emphasis. Those same sweet hands had once seemed so supple and smooth when they had reached for mine so long ago. But then, she had always reached for more than she could possibly hold.

"Claire, I saw you," I said as gently as I knew how, wishing I had the strength to grasp those hands. To silence their wild fluttering dance with a calming gesture. Of friendship. Of faith. Of loving concern. "I saw you with that man — you know who I mean — in the orange grove just outside the Harmony Ballroom. You were together, and I saw what you did."

I believe that, in time, Claire might have forgiven me for attempting to debunk the lie of David Gilbert's parentage. Knowing his persistent nature, it was sure to come out sooner or later, if not from me then from someone else. What she could never forgive me for was revealing the source of my knowledge. It destroyed her, I think, to know I had witnessed the terrible shame of her lie. She was silent for a very long time as I watched a palpable chill overtake her features.

"You were spying on me?" she said finally.

"It's not what you think, Claire," I said.

"You were spying on me," she repeated, her tone no longer assuming the question.

"Claire, I didn't mean to . . ."

"You didn't mean to — what?"

"I didn't mean to watch you . . ."

"My God, Albert."

Before I could begin to clarify the convergence of circumstances that led to my unintentional discovery of her indiscretion, it was already too late. Her hands were clenched in tiny bird fists.

"What kind of a degenerate louse would watch?"

"I didn't watch, I simply saw." I tried to explain the distinction, but she would not listen to reason. Indeed, as reason gave over to emotion, Claire began to harangue me with all manner of insults that of course I dismissed, knowing they had been spawned as much from her own guilt as my incidental disclosure.

"Just tell me this, Albert," she said, "did you enjoy it?"

The question was on the very face of it absurd, and I did not hesitate to tell her so.

"Enjoyment was anything but on my mind," I said.

"Oh no, Albert, you enjoyed it," she insisted despite my protestation that I could not imagine how anyone could take pleasure from another's fall from grace, especially someone as dear to me as she herself had been. But Claire was beyond adamant.

"You know it's true. In fact, I think you enjoyed it so much you went back again looking for more. That's what I think."

I assured her that any visits, day or night, that I made to the grove, then or after, were purely utilitarian in purpose. But of course Claire simply continued to impugn my motives as a way of justifying her own indelicate actions. Through all of this, David Gilbert and his wife maintained a dismayed silence. The seed of the original discussion seemed to have gotten lost in Claire's emotional digression.

"Please, Claire, what's done is done," I said, making a first and final appeal to her long-dormant maternal instinct. "Whatever you did or I saw is beside the point. You've been given a second chance to make things right with David Gilbert. To give him what you couldn't give before. You can both start over again . . ."

"How dare you, Albert," she said, lowering her voice to a hot whisper. "How dare you presume to know what's best for me or anyone else with a drop of human blood still flowing in his veins."

"Please, Claire," I urged, "this could be a blessing in disguise. It can't have been easy for you to live with a lie like this for all these years."

"How would you know what I've had to live with?" she hissed without giving me the opportunity to answer. "You have no right to judge me. None of you do."

She began to rage at me in earnest as David Gilbert, clearly reeling from the unexpected revelation, made a futile attempt to put the conversation back on track.

"Is what he said true?" he asked.

"Of course not," Claire snapped.

David Gilbert pressed the indelicate issue further than even I cared to see it pressed. "Who was he?"

"It doesn't matter," Claire said curtly. "He's dead."

"But how? How did he die?"

"Unexpectedly," she replied, softening her tone for an instant. "For no good reason."

"Tell me about him," David persisted. "Please."

"Why?"

"It changes who I am," he insisted.

"Your father's dead," she repeated coolly. "Nothing Albert or I can say will change that."

Perhaps it was impolitic, but I attempted to intercede one last time on David Gilbert's behalf.

"But, Claire," I said, "can't you see this isn't about me or you?"

"The hell it isn't," she said quietly — so quietly, in fact, that I'm not sure anyone but me heard her.

"This means a lot to me," David Gilbert said.

"To you?" she retorted, her anger rising again to full volume. "For God's sake, can't any of you understand that nothing good can come of this?"

"Please . . . *Mother,*" David Gilbert practically begged, addressing Claire by this endearing sobriquet for the first — and likely the only — time in his life. He was rewarded with the startled stare of a wounded deer.

"Do not call me that!"

"Please, I just want . . ." David Gilbert began, but he was not permitted the courtesy of finishing his request.

"You want what? What if I can't give you what you want?" Claire said, presumably to David Gilbert though her eyes remained locked on mine. And then to his wife she turned and said, "Tell him. Tell him he should be thankful for the family he has. Tell him to stop chasing after ghosts."

While, as I said, I did not put much stock in Claire's outburst as I am certain it arose more from shame than anger, David Gilbert was not nearly as forgiving. Crushed by her denials, he stormed out of the room and returned a few moments later with his little girl and Hilda trailing swiftly behind him. Unaware of all that had transpired, the child ran straight to her mother, her tiny fists crammed full of silver coins.

"*¡Mira mira!*" the little girl crowed as her mother smiled nervously and put her finger to her lips.

"Look at the honey money!" the little girl squealed.

"Tini!" the mother said sharply. "Shhhh!"

If only Claire had heeded her command as well as the child did. Blessedly, only a few more words were spoken in anger, and then it was all over.

Cursing God under her breath, Claire looked to Hilda, to me, to David Gilbert, the child, the child's mother, and back to Hilda.

It was as if thirty years had melted away in an instant. David Gilbert's face grew as sullen and hard as the last time we'd heard her curse as he wordlessly gathered up his family's belongings and shepherded his wife and little daughter out the front door and into their station wagon while Claire stared at them from the front porch.

"Goddamn it," she whispered again as David Gilbert pulled the car away from the curb.

THIRTY-TWO

THE EGG: It has been written that to the human eye, the *Apis mellifera* egg resembles a cross between a tiny bit of sausage and a poppy seed. All female honeybees start out as fertilized eggs undifferentiated in purpose or hierarchal rank. All males, or drones, come from unfertilized eggs.

There is a particularly malignant aberration of the general rule of bee nature that is known as the laying worker. Though not common, neither is it unheard of to find a normally sterile female who fancies herself a queen and in the full manifestation of the charade can hoodwink an entire colony into participating in this tragically melancholy form of self-delusion.

While the process is not completely understood, apiarists believe that the normally functioning queen produces, in addition to the millions of eggs she deposits in prepared cells throughout her long life, a special pheromone known as queen substance, which during the height of her fertility prevents rival queens from developing and at the same time inhibits the underdeveloped ovaries of her naturally chaste daughters from producing eggs. In the normal cycle of the hive, it is the gradual reduction of this queen substance that is part of the natural aging process which triggers the raising of a new queen to take the old one's place. But if that cycle is disrupted and a reigning queen in her prime suddenly ceases to function before another can be produced, an upstart worker will occasionally step in to fill the void.

As I said, the laying worker is not the norm. Ordinarily, if a queen dies unexpectedly and there are yet fresh eggs in the hive, the deceased queen's entourage begins at once to feed a select few larvae as soon as they hatch from their cells the royal jelly that will transform one of these anointed few into a new queen to take the old one's place. If there are no fresh eggs ready to replace the old queen when she ceases to function, however, a beekeeper may have to intervene with the introduction of a new queen from outside the colony. This is crucial, for if the hive is unable to produce a new queen and the beekeeper is negligent in his caretaking duties, the hive becomes vulnerable to the insinuation of a fraudulent queen, which, to my way of thinking, is the most pitiable of all situations. For if there is no true queen, there can be no new brood produced to replace the workers, who will all expire in due time. In such moments of crisis, the will to survive is sometimes so great that one bee — if not several — may begin to exhibit the uncharacteristic behavior of laying eggs. And while their intentions are certainly noble, the results are most often disastrous.

Unlike a bona fide queen, who adheres to the orderly, circular egg-laying pattern of purposeful groupings designed to facilitate the eggs' care, the laying worker is both physically and temperamentally unsuited to the task of reproduction and she deposits her eggs haphazardly, some high on the edge of a cell, or two or three in a pile, according to no particular sequence or strategy, as she wanders willy-nilly about the hive in an amateurish mimicry of her prematurely deceased liege. And even more damning to the laying worker and the hive, she has not had the benefit of the traditional nuptial rites of passage and can lay only unfertilized eggs, which in turn can produce only drones — and undersized drones at that. Without fertilization, no more worker bees can be born to replace their rapidly aging sisters. The circle is broken, the order of the hive abrogated, and, for all the best intentions in the world, the colony dies.

But it does so slowly and insidiously. To the human eye, the laying worker looks no different than her sisters, and so even after her existence has been detected through the telltale increase of random drone cells she is next to impossible for the beekeeper to root out of the hive. Once a laying worker has sufficiently established her royal command, even the introduction of a proper fertile queen is rarely successful, as the charlatan's loyal entourage, with suicidal zeal, will surround and suffocate the rightful queen to protect the false sovereign.

Without a proper queen, the doomed hive falls into what can only be described as a state of deep despair. As fewer and fewer new drones are hatched and no new workers mature and sally forth to forage for the nectar and pollen that is the lifeblood of the hive, those who are left to grow old and die, alone and unmourned, take to standing about the entrance of the hive and staring lethargically out at the world they no longer care to partake of on any significant level. They are, for all intents and purposes, dead long before their wings stop beating.

THIRTY-THREE

ELECTRICITY: Bees do not operate efficiently near electrical currents and so should not be placed underneath high-tension wires. While honeybees may survive, their numbers will not increase and their honey production will go down.

Perhaps it was the shock of the discovery — the absolute and unflagging shock and horror of seeing Claire's lifeless body so cruelly defiled and discarded — and the niggling parade of questions and intrusions into the most intimate details of my personal life and Claire's following in the wake of her death that sealed my lips for so long. Or it may have been nothing more than the forgetfulness of an old man. But after all was said and done, after the tragic manner of Claire's and Hilda's deaths had been explored and analyzed and exposed to the indiscriminate eye of public scrutiny the truth of the matter was, I had somehow never gotten around to telling the bees. And what is perhaps even more inexcusable is that for far too many years before, I had told the bees nothing else about Claire.

Nothing at all. At first, I suppose I told myself that my bees could see for themselves that she had stopped coming around, and they could not help but know the reason why. And by that I do not mean her brutal murder, though certainly I should have said something about it, but here I am referring to the eleven years of nullity that came before her death when she went about her business and I went about mine as if nothing had happened between us. Nothing ever. I regret this now, just as I regret the irrevocable words I spoke that severed all friendly intercourse between us, erasing the history of decades of camaraderie and leaving an unforgivable silence in the breach.

As I've said many times, bees are sensitive creatures by design. They know, for example, by the slightest shift in my gait, gesture, or intake of breath, when something is troubling me, and so for this very reason I try to keep my emotions on an even keel when I am in their presence.

I know now that I should have told the bees of her tragic passing the moment I discovered that Claire had died. But I should have told them other things, too. Long ago I should have told them that I, like Claire, had been dead longer than I have been alive. I should have told them that I had died a thousand times since the night I chanced to follow Claire out into the groves and nothing was ever the same again.

But I didn't. I went about my business as if nothing had happened. As if I had not seen with my own eyes what Claire was. What she had become. That was the first unforgivable sin. Not that she had done what she had done but that I had seen what I was never meant to see. And that I had spoken the truth. Rather that I had been torn to pieces by wild dogs than to have broken my silence. That was the second, far greater sin, but I could not help myself. In my heart, I was afraid her heart had already grown as cold as her mother's had before her. I could see it in her eyes when she looked at David Gilbert. As if there was no flow of common blood beating in their veins. I could see the same flitter of hurt pass across his face that used to dart about her eyes when Claire's mother had spoken to her in that chilling way she had of speaking about, around, but never directly to her.

I saw it just as clearly when we were still young and I could not respond in kind to what I perceived to be Claire's rudderless initiation into womanhood. Not that there weren't times in my own clumsy youth when I wasn't sorely tempted to offer her more than simple words of guidance.

That is when I most often found my own guidance in the ancient wisdom of Saint Augustine, who had found peace in the contemplation of the divine after suffering through his own temptations of the flesh. Augustine wrote that there is this fundamental difference between the temporal and the eternal: A temporal thing is loved more before we have it because when we do it does not satisfy the soul.

Though Claire steadfastly refused to see me after our final falling-out when David Gilbert brought his family to visit her in the autumn of 1981, I never stopped caring about her welfare. While David Gilbert had made it quite clear that he wanted no more to do with either her or Hilda after the terrible things Claire had said to him in the heat of her anger — and she made it just as clear that I had become persona non grata in her eyes — I knew she had no one else to look after her but Hilda. And given her fierce reclusiveness, Hilda was scarcely better than no one at all.

One evening, not long after David Gilbert's disastrous visit, I left my own dog-eared copy of Saint Augustine's *Confessions* on the Straussman sisters' doorstep with a personal note to Claire rubber-banded around it, urging her to take comfort in Augustine's words as I once had in my own times of trial.

I found the book back on my own doorstep the following evening. My note was tucked within the book's worn pages, with an addendum penned in Claire's distinctive cursive script:

I liked him better as a pagan, she had written. *He was honest enough to say that while he wanted chastity and continence, he didn't want it right away. You should take a lesson from your precious saint, Albert. At least old Auggie lived a little before he decided to turn all holier than thou.*

I of course felt anything but holy as the silence between us continued unabated through the following decade. I am sure the silence between the Straussman sisters was nearly as absolute, as it was as much a part of Hilda's daily habit as breathing, and even though Claire was certainly a savant at bee communication, I am not sure she ever managed to draw much true verbal communication from her sister. But I could be wrong, since I had seldom been privy to what went on behind closed doors in the Straussman household — and I suppose that is as it should be.

But please do not mistake estrangement for indifference. I continued to run into Claire and Hilda from time to time at the Harmony Park Ballroom. Of course it wasn't called the Harmony by this time. The dance hall had been shut down by the city fathers sometime in the early eighties and reopened as a community marketplace called the Peppertree Faire, where booths were laid out like an old English square, and every Saturday through Tuesday we all set up our wares beneath the ballroom's great yawning hulk. As an established local merchant, I was awarded an enviable table near the front of the building. A few months after the Peppertree opened, Claire and Hilda managed to acquire a table near the back.

It was not a prime spot. I feared the Straussman sisters would soon founder without some assistance and so I began to make a habit of paying several of my regular honey customers on the sly to purchase a dozen or so of the Bee Ladies' beeswax candles that they also sold every Thursday from their front porch. I thought it was the least I could do for them under the circumstances.

I believe the candles were Hilda's handiwork. They had a certain clumsy charm to them that seemed far too ingenuous for Claire to have produced. The jars of bee pollen and royal jelly they sold along with their honey and candles were all affixed with a pen-and-ink *Bee Ladies* label in Claire's familiar cursive script, a quaint sobriquet that the Straussman sisters had apparently adopted without irony. I had not realized how popular ancillary bee products such as those the Straussman sisters sold had become with the public and so was quite surprised to learn during the course of their murder investigation and subsequent trial that they had been able to stash away even a few meager dollars from their labor.

But that is hardly the point. In the lingering aftermath of our estrangement, even the bees in my own keeping seemed to lose a little more heart each year.

I believe it was Maurice Maeterlinck who said that it matters little whether we think of the remarkable nature of bees as a product of instinct or intelligence for either is only another way of revealing our own ignorance in this regard. Maeterlinck believed that what we call instinct is perhaps cosmic in nature, an emanation of the universal soul. It is what Virgil referred to as *mens divina,* divine thought, the divine spirit.

Which I suppose is as close to anything as the root of the ancients' belief that a bee is a corporeal manifestation of the soul on earth and to fail to tell the bees about a soul's departing is to deny that soul its due. Certainly in this modern age there are many people, like my new neighbors, who would scoff at such seemingly superstitious beliefs.

To such self-assured skeptics, I can only echo Montaigne's admonition to beware of absolute certainty. Even the certainty of doubt. "Nothing is so firmly believed as what is least known," he warned.

I believe this is something of the gist of Harry Junior's message, and it is why I suppose he felt compelled to visit me a final time.

He was clearly recognizable, and by this time I greeted him as I would an old friend, as he stood some distance away cloaked like a forlorn sentry in the shade of the remaining eucalyptus stand that borders the north side of my property. As before, he didn't speak at first, preferring to hang back in the shadows, watching as I attempted to introduce a new queen to my number fourteen hive.

I should have realized weeks earlier that the hive had gone queenless, but I'm not as young as I used to be and when the mornings are overly damp it takes my knees a good hour or more to limber up and then I can't always walk, except on the best of days, all the way out to check on my outlying hives as often as I should. Sadly, by the time I got around to noticing something was amiss with my number fourteen it was already too late. The hive was deep in the thrall of a laying worker. I knew in my heart of hearts that it was a terminal situation.

I told Harry I didn't hold out much hope that the new queen would be able to overthrow her lowborn pretender, but for the sake of the hive I had to let her try. Harry moved a little closer then, smiling that sadchild smile of his that melted away as quickly as it was formed.

"The dying are held back from their repose by the love that will not give them up," Harry Junior whispered in a voice like the rustle of eucalyptus leaves in a hot September wind. And yet, the air was still, and I noticed that even the bees in my number fourteen grew quiet when Harry Junior spoke.

"It's out of my hands now," I said.

"You know better," he said, smiling that faint wisp of a smile of his again.

"What would you have me do?" I said.

"You know what the old beekeepers say?" he inquired.

"They say many things," I replied as Harry Junior emerged from the shadows to stand with me beside the hive.

"You *know* what they say," he repeated, placing his hands lightly on my shoulders. So lightly, in fact, that I felt their heat more than their pressure and I could not be sure whether they rested on or hovered slightly above the threads of my worn cotton jacket. "When the bees look out, you look in. To do so too late is to observe the protracted death rattle of a hive so bereft of order and purpose that even the dead are left unattended. And those forlorn few who remain are hardly enough to form a warming cluster."

And as he spoke, as if beguiled by the melancholy rhythm of his words, the bees in my number fourteen began to issue slowly from the hive in a great consuming wave that gradually surrounded and obscured Harry Junior from my sight.

"It's too late," I said.

"You look in," Harry Junior repeated, his

voice both swallowed and amplified by the roar of the swarm.

"But I can't bring her back," I said.

"You can let her go."

THIRTY-FOUR

COLONY COLLAPSE DISORDER: There has not been a satisfactory explanation for the profound loss of beehives that has taken place since 2006. Some apiarists are beginning to believe there is no single cause but rather a perfect storm of pathogens, parasites, pesticides, poor beekeeping practices, and even electromagnetic emanations from cell towers that are to blame.

From my singular perspective, it is perhaps forgivable that I had for so many years viewed the tragedy of Claire's murder as a one-dimensional event: a tragic point in time that began and ended with the horrific image of her lifeless body that, once beheld, instantly and irreparably transformed all my most cherished memories into the seed of my most bitter regrets.

Even after I read in the newspaper about

the poor misguided young woman who had been found dead of a drug overdose in a liquor store parking lot not more than a mile and a half from where the Straussmans' old house once stood, I failed to draw the connective tissue between the individual points.

Instead, I regret to say that I may have smiled slightly to myself, drawing even a modicum of satisfaction from my belief that this unfortunate woman had received her just desserts after all. It seemed to me a sad but fitting end to a senseless tragedy all around.

And even when her name appeared on my neighbors' cross several days later, I was not surprised by their misguided need to place the blame of her death on the malevolence of science.

As a man of both faith and reason, I blamed the end of this young woman's sordid life on her very human inability to control her wanton desires. And to be quite candid, I took great comfort in my mother's oft-stated belief that God works in mysterious ways.

But of course as my dear mother also used to say, "There are none so blind as those who will not see."

I suppose that it took me so long to see

what had been right in front of my nose because I did not want to admit my own complicity in the progression of acts that had unfolded over the years as inexorably as distaff Greek tragedy.

Blind to the convergence of causal events and relationships, I had for so many years missed the most basic yet telling signs that Claire's and Hilda's murders had been anything but a random act even though this had always been the most troubling aspect of their deaths from my point of view.

I recall how at the very beginning of his involvement in the case Detective Grayson had been likewise disturbed by the apparent motivelessness of the Straussman sisters' murder. This of course was before we learned for certain that robbery had been the indirect cause of their deaths.

And so at the beginning of the investigation, which was well before the bungled burglary had been discovered, the good detective had asked repeatedly whether I had noticed anything missing from the house when I found the Bee Ladies' bodies. And over and over again I told him that in all my recollection of the house there had been little of value to recommend it to strangers and, from my limited observation of the Straussman sisters' affairs since our friendly discourse had ceased, a sudden appetite for material possessions would have been a most unlikely change of disposition for either of them. Which is to say that like their parents before them, the Straussman sisters had led an austere life.

In the early days of the investigation I had told the detective more than once, in response to his unremitting inquiries, that the only household treasure to speak of that I could recall in all the years I'd known them had been the golden tea set of which Mrs. Straussman had been so inordinately proud. And that was the very item that had been left in plain view on the kitchen table when I'd discovered Claire's and Hilda's bodies.

"If robbery had been the motive, that tea set should have been taken," I reasoned. "It's rimmed in twenty-two carat gold, after all."

The detective, however, had just as vehemently disagreed, explaining to me in that gruff, impatient manner I eventually grew to find almost endearing that porcelain pieces such as these were far too fragile to easily transport and so would likely have held little appeal to any robber, despite its relative twenty-two carat gold value.

Odd, then, that it was its relative value which finally persuaded me of the true significance of the tea set having been left out on the table that fateful day.

"You must look in," Harry Junior had told me in no uncertain terms the last time I saw him. And as I sat long into the night pondering his words, I found my attention drawn without conscious thought to the incessant humming of the high-tension wires that run past my bedroom window. And as I wondered at my neighbors' folly, God's will, and my own incertitude, I attended more closely to the magnetic dissonance of the power lines. And it was then that the continuous flow of electrical current slowed — almost imperceptibly at first, but after a time I began to perceive a series of rapid, interlocking oscillations from which I could differentiate the algorithmic whir and snap and sputter and buzz of each connection from within the aggregate swarm of electrons pulsing through the lines — and as I listened long and hard to the indistinguishable hum, individual notes became distinguishable, and the single point upon which I had for so many years been so exclusively focused suddenly, without warning, became two, then three, four, a half dozen, a dozen, and infinitely more. The laying worker. The cross-tempered hive. My neighbors' crosses. The crosses in the grove.

The china dolls. The golden china. The silver coins. The silver duct tape. And with each new note, the line took on yet another dimension of painful memory, connected by time and space, that became a symphony of notes weighted by the composite sights and sounds of each tragic movement. Of course Harry Junior had been right all along. I cannot say for certain why or even how I knew it then, but there it was: There had been no marauding strangers. No robber bees. When a hive goes bad, it nearly always does so from within.

I dug the first letter Detective Grayson had written to me out of the drawer of my telephone stand, where I'd kept it along with other important correspondences. We had exchanged three or four more letters in the interim, mostly about beekeeping. It was in that first letter, however, that he had included his telephone number, along with a polite admonition that I "stay in touch."

Nevertheless, I am sure Detective Grayson was surprised to hear my voice when I reached him by phone at his home in Idaho as he had always been the one to initiate all verbal contact between us prior to this point.

"Someone came to visit them that day," I told Detective Grayson straight off after identifying myself and exchanging perfunctory pleasantries as I assumed distant acquaintances such as we were did. "Someone they were happy to see."

"See who, Mr. Honig?" he responded, clearly taken aback by my unexpected call, and with good reason: It had been nearly two decades since we'd last spoken directly. "What are you talking about?"

"I'm sorry, Detective," I replied, "I'm referring to Claire and Hilda Straussman's murderers of course. Those two young robbers weren't telling the whole truth about what happened that morning."

There were more questions and answers and more words, some of them more profane than I care to relate, before Detective Grayson deigned to pay attention to what I should have told him years ago if only I'd realized it then.

"They were invited in."

"Who?"

"Miss Perez and Mr. Garcia."

"That already came out at the trial," he said.

"No, only that they were invited into the kitchen to look at the candles and such."

It was a small distinction but an important one, one that I should have realized at the time.

"The gold tea set was left out on the table," I said. "The Straussmans brought that set out only for company. They never drank from it when they were alone."

"But what difference does that make?" the detective said. "Those two punks admitted they killed the Straussmans. They were tried, convicted, and sentenced to prison. The case is closed, Mr. Honig. Done. *Fini.* Over and out."

"But don't you see?" I said. "They said that Claire and Hilda were outside working with their bees when they first attempted to break into their house. They said it was only by happenstance that they were discovered."

"I still don't get where you're going with this," the detective said. I'd almost forgotten how impatient he could be. I reminded him once again that Miss Perez had testified at the trial that Claire invited her and Mr. Garcia into the kitchen to view the honey and candle samples and that it was at this point, before they'd brought their wares out, that Mr. Garcia grew impatient and demanded they show him where they kept their valuables.

"So?"

"But if Claire and Hilda had gotten up early to work in their apiary only to be interrupted by our young criminals, why were there no candles and honey left on the table? Why was their table set for company?"

"I don't know. Maybe the Perez woman forgot to mention their little tea party. Or maybe they were expecting someone later," the detective speculated.

"I don't believe so. There was tea already poured in the cups and milk was in the pitcher," I reminded him.

"Okay. But the only prints we lifted off the cups were Claire's and Hilda's."

I could tell by the slight shift in the tone of his voice that I had finally piqued his interest.

"What if the tea set was left out from the night before?" Detective Grayson queried.

I firmly dismissed this possibility, reminding him of the family's obsessive tendency toward cleanliness.

"I'm sure someone came to visit them that morning. Someone special enough to bring out the company tea set."

"Well, that puts us back at square one," the detective said. "You yourself said they were practically recluses. So who would've come to see them?"

"Detective," I said, "do you have any idea what happened to David Gilbert's daughter? Tina or Tini, I believe her name was."

"I really don't know. The grandparents

were from somewhere in Mexico — Sonora, I think. I assume she's still there."

There had of course been no real reason to assume otherwise. Once David Gilbert had been dismissed as a suspect, there had been no need for further inquiry into his family. And so the detective, for all of his investigative diligence, had missed the obvious. As had I.

In the cycle of the hive, no single action of any one of the thousands of honeybees who reside within it occurs in isolation, but, cloistered in the solitude of my own grief, I had failed to consider all — or, in truth, even any — of the other people and circumstances leading up to and away from the one overriding moment in which I had remained frozen for so many years like an insentient insect in amber.

"Could you perhaps use whatever investigative connections you have to look into what happened to David Gilbert's daughter?" I asked. "I know you're retired, but you must have some friends on the police force."

"I suppose I do," he said after a moment's pause. "But really, Mr. Honig, what difference would it make? We already know who killed the Straussman sisters."

"But we don't know why," I said.

"Sure we do. It was a stupid mistake by a couple of stupid punks. That's all there is to it."

"Did you know that the Perez girl died last month?" I said.

The detective admitted that he hadn't been aware of it.

"I don't exactly keep tabs on my old cases anymore. Especially ones like this, Mr. Honig. You know, the ones that are *closed*," he emphasized.

"I understand that, Detective, but . . ."

"But what? Look, I wouldn't lose any sleep over her."

"It's not my sleep I'm concerned about," I said. "Or hers."

I told him about the crosses in my neighbors' yard. About the name on the twenty-first cross — Christina Perez — and how I didn't recognize her name at first, but, when I did, it made me think about Claire and Hilda all over again.

"What neighbors? What crosses?"

I patiently described my neighbors' gaudy mock cemetery, their tasteless holiday displays, and their silly signs detailing their strange electromagnetic theories.

"Oh, jeez louise," he exclaimed, more or less. "Not those crazy meth heads on Gain

Street? Mr. Honig, those guys are tweek-
ers."

I wasn't familiar with the term. Detective
Grayson explained to me as best he could
what it meant to be a methamphetamine
addict.

"They're full of conspiracy theories and
all the chemically induced energy in the
world to go hog wild on them," he said. "We
busted those Gain Street crackpots on possession once. Not enough to nail them for a
felony, but . . ."

"Be that as it may," I interrupted, "Christina Perez was the name on the cross."

"Well, hell's bells, Mr. Honig. They were
druggies. She was a druggie. Not to sound
too callous, but I'm not exactly surprised
she OD'd. She admitted she was an addict
at her trial. Jesus F-ing Christ. That was
their whole defense: 'Boohoo. The drugs
made me do it.' Look, Mr. Honig, cats like
that don't usually change their spots."

"I'm sure you are correct. Believe me
when I say that the cause of her death isn't
particularly important to me at this point.
That she was mourned by my neighbors,
crazy as they may be, is what matters. I am
sure Christina Perez was profoundly connected to this place."

There was an audible sigh, followed by a

long pause. In my mind's eye, I imagined him swiping his mouth with his hand and tucking his shirttail into his trousers. "So what is it again you want me to do, Mr. Honig?"

"I would like you to investigate the present whereabouts of David Gilbert's daughter," I said. "I suspect that *Tini* is short for *Christina.*"

THIRTY-FIVE

BEE VENOM: The poisonous matter se-
creted by special glands attached to the
stinger of the honeybee, it is used primarily in defense. Derived from the Latin *vene-
num,* meaning drug, poison, magic potion,
or charm, it is related to the Latin *venus,*
for love or sexual desire.

Hydraulically speaking, a bee's stinger is a
marvelous example of divine engineering,
but as an offensive instrument it is curiously
ill designed. Delicately tapered and polished, it is, under close examination, actu-
ally two separate daggers forming a V shape,
with tiny barblike serrations running along
each dagger. And at the top of the V rests a
small poison sac that supplies the venom
released through tubes running through the
daggers. When driven into the flesh of its
victim, the barbs catch like tiny fish-hooks
and spurt venom into the wound. But as

any experienced beekeeper knows, one never removes a stinger by grasping it directly between thumb and forefinger. To do so merely squeezes the sac and releases more venom into the wound, which makes the sting even more painful but seldom deadly, as, in most cases, the venom is more irritating than lethal to any foe but her own sister.

And in those rare cases where death does result, it is more often an accident of nature — a reaction to other, unforeseen factors rather than by design or with intent. But the worker bee who does unleash her stinger upon a perceived enemy renders herself an irrevocable death sentence — and a needless one at that — because, given enough time and calm surroundings, the stinging bee theoretically should be able to work her stinger free from the wound without damage to herself. But that is seldom, if ever, the outcome. This is because once aroused, even the most placid and intelligent bee abandons all reason, invariably ripping the stinger from her body, rupturing her abdomen, and in the end dying in much the same manner as the hapless drone who mates on the fly.

Contrary to common wisdom, the stinger-less worker bee's death is not necessarily instantaneous. In an effort to determine how long a honeybee could live without her stinger, scientists discovered that within a protected environment — and by that I mean one in which she is separated from her hive mates — a worker could lose her stinger and yet go on about her business for up to five more days, flying about, eating honey, and grooming herself, even with her tattered intestines trailing behind her all the while.

Of course it should be noted that in the relatively short life span of a worker bee, those five days are roughly equivalent to an additional ten years of human life. But if, on the other hand, the stingerless bee is forced to remain with her sisters, she is always attacked and unmercifully driven from the hive, where she soon succumbs to the chilling consequences of isolation. It is this psychic ostracism from her own kind that kills her long before the physical consequences of the wound can run its course.

But this tragic tale is only half told. Like a separate sentient being, the stinger, once detached from the bee, continues to work its way deeper into its victim's flesh even as it keeps pumping venom into the wound. Indeed, the pumping action is so strong that it can penetrate a felt hat or a leather belt or shoe, and continue thusly for up to twenty minutes after it has been detached. But to what end?

I can say this much for certain: The physical wounds we see are often much less virulent than the broken hearts we hide. And the pain we inflict upon others continues to do damage long after we have taken our leave. It matters not whether the hurt is intended or not, the pain is just as sharp, or perhaps even sharper, for all its grave indifference.

By the time I heard from the good detective by telephone for the last time, I hardly needed him to confirm what I had long since deduced. The final thread of the Straussmans' tormented family line had died just as the others had before her, alone and unmourned by her own.

"You were right," Detective Grayson said. David Gilbert's daughter, who had been released from prison in 2005, had died of a drug overdose in a liquor store parking lot not more than a mile from where the Straussmans' home once stood. It had been two months and seventeen days since I'd first seen Christina Perez's mysterious memorial display on my neighbors' front lawn.

"Looks like Christina's father and that crazy woman from Gain Street's father served together in the military. First in Texas and then on that helicopter base not far from where you live," Detective Grayson informed me. "I'm guessing those two girls were pretty tight when they were younger."

I said I wasn't surprised. "Perhaps that's why she came back here."

The paper trail, as the detective called the official records, was there for any to see if only it had occurred to any of us to look. On record was a missing person report that had been filed by Christina's grandparents with both the local Mexican authorities and several police agencies in Southern California, where they feared the girl may have returned to in order to renew old acquaintances she had made while still living on the Tustin Marine Base with her parents during presumably happier times.

The detective also informed me that Christina's father had been unaware of her flight from Mexico, as he had been deployed on a training mission in Saudi Arabia when the girl had disappeared, and friendly contact between him and his deceased wife's family had long since ceased.

Of course had he chosen to attend the trial of the two young people accused of robbing and killing Claire and Hilda, I am sure that he would have recognized his own daughter, despite their years of separation, and her double life would have been exposed. Or David Gilbert may have chosen to remain silent. At the heart of this troubled man, I cannot say for certain in which direction the bad blood would have flowed stronger: toward the woman who had first loved and then denied him or toward the daughter who had similarly renounced him.

It was only in hindsight — and a very long hindsight at that — that there was any real reason to suspect a connection between the preternaturally composed young woman who had sealed the mouths of the Straussman sisters forever with the fatal strips of silver tape and the exuberant little girl who'd been dazzled so many years before by a handful of silver coins.

Time does not heal all wounds.

As Castelvetro once noted, there are two dimensions to tragedy: one accessible to the senses and external and measurable by the clock, the other accessible to the intellect and internal and measurable by the mind.

For all these years, the tragic deaths of the Straussman sisters had been portrayed by everyone involved — from the police investigators to the district attorney's office, the public defender's, the newspaper reporters, and the perpetrators of the crime themselves — as an unfortunate accident of fate.

But then there was the tea set. The company tea set.

I am sure, even now, that the burglary had been planned much as Christina had testified to at the trial. But I no longer believe she chose the Straussmans' house by accident.

A secret cache of coins must have seemed like quite a king's ransom, and, as all childhood memories do, the size of the treasure would have grown with each passing year. Just as bad blood never fails to poison the vessel.

It may have been a chance automobile drive past the Straussman house that stirred Christina's childhood recollection of her one and only visit to her father's estranged family, or she may have been obsessed for years by her memory of their "honey money," but what does it matter? Either way, she deliberately set out to rob her own family.

And that is only the half of the tragedy. I am certain Claire recognized, on some visceral level, this grown-up child and welcomed her into her home, just as I have to believe that Claire had truly come to regret the harsh words she had spoken to drive David Gilbert and his family away from her that awful day. Else why would his picture have been displayed among her family photographs on the mantle? The opportunity to make amends must have dispelled any natural suspicions that Christina's sudden appearance on her doorstep may have aroused.

I can only wonder what might have transformed this simple larceny into something far more heinous. Perhaps it was, as Christina testified, merely her young man's violently impetuous nature that turned the morning's events so murderously awry. Or perhaps it was something much closer to home. Something Claire might have said over an innocent cup of tea that reminded this dolorous young woman of all she'd lost. Or of all she'd never known. There is no telling how deep her wounds ran or how long they'd festered.

This much I am sure of: After the secret treasure had been plundered and Claire and Hilda had been bound and gagged, Christina had to have washed and put away the teacup she'd drunk from. And she had to have known precisely what she was doing and what the consequences would be. Once Claire realized who Christina was and what she wanted, it was already too late.

Indeed, it has been too late for as long as I have held my tongue out of cowardice and spoken half-truths and foolish pride.

Yesterday morning, I lingered longer than perhaps was necessary in my mother's herb garden, weeding, watering, and trimming back spindly growths. I suppose it may seem strange to some that I still call it my mother's garden since she's been dead for more than sixty years. But it was for her that my father cleared the tiny patch of earth which borders our back porch, and it is in her memory that I have maintained its useful verdure. I don't cook with herbs. I hardly cook at all these days as I find my appetite waning with the years. I do, however, enjoy watching my bees flit between the tiny buds that sprout on the basil and oregano this time of year, filling their pollen sacs until they seem far too burdened by their rich bounty for their delicate wings to carry them aloft.

There aren't as many bees now as there used to be. There will be even fewer next year, I imagine, as there are fewer trees and flowers each year to pollinate.

I can only wonder what will happen to this garden when I am gone. Left to their own devices, I would like to imagine that my remaining bees will continue to comb these delicate blossoms for the life-sustaining pollen and nectar that these fragrant plants produce. But I know better, as I am sure that once I have departed my sister's children will have no desire to reclaim the land upon which our dear parents chose to settle and raise a family.

And so.

Eventually I am sure our home, our orchards, our garden, and everything else I hold dear will be gone. And so will my bees. Replaced by more houses and people and gas stations and convenience stores. I don't regret the march of progress, the changing face of the neighborhood — truly I don't. What I do regret is that after I am gone, there will be no one left to remember how the moonlight used to shimmer like silver gossamer beneath the trees and that here on this sweet patch of land there once lived a woman who died unmourned by all save one.

I believe Kierkegaard said it best, when speaking of his beloved Regina: "I was too heavy for her and she was too light for me."

Kierkegaard was not speaking of tangible weight, the measurable differentiation between one heart and another. He was a philosopher. I am a simple beekeeper. One who on this day has paused to consider the marvelous banality of a postal scale that is able to calculate the weight and distance of human correspondence and ascribe an absolute, definitive value to it.

Yesterday afternoon, I received a package in the mail from Detective Grayson. The value of the red-inked postmark, stamped Coeur d'Alene, was five dollars and sixty-eight cents. Inside was a handwritten note that said simply: *I thought you should have this. ~ Raymond*

The note was rubber-banded around an old diary. It was Claire's diary. I cannot say for sure how or why the good detective was able to procure this precious artifact from the police department's evidence storage locker. That is where I was led to believe it would languish forever since there was no next of kin who wished to claim it. When I'd asked what was to become of the diary on the day the Straussman sisters' murder trial concluded, Detective Grayson had urged me simply to forget about it.

I have forgotten so many things over the years.

I don't cook much these days, I find I've lost my appetite. I use my kitchen table as a desk of sorts. It is where I read, when I have the heart to do so, because the light that streams through the window like golden honey over my sink cheers my fading eyes.

The light was still bright when I sat down at my kitchen table and I opened the diary. Its spine cracked, both audibly and visually, from all its long years of disuse. I turned to the first page:

March 7, 1928: That silly goose! What does a girl have to do to get noticed anyhow?

I turned to the next page and the next and the next. I read into the afternoon, and on into the dusk, and on through the night, rising only once to switch on the electric light overhead.

They were intimate pages, stories of a life, some light and delightful, that reminded me yet again why I had first been drawn to Claire. But there were darker pages, too, dark in a way I had only suspected, and there are details that will haunt me to my own lonely grave.

Perhaps Harry had died from pneumonia. Claire seemed to have some doubt when she wrote that her mother revealed the doctor's diagnosis to her shortly after she'd returned from Detroit in one of the few moments of intimacy the two ever shared. Claire had certainly wanted to believe her mother's account. Before penicillin, such deaths were common. It was a simple

424

explanation, but not a satisfying one to Claire, who had herself been the luckless recipient of physical punishment from her father if I read between the lines correctly. What was beyond dispute was that their grief — her mother's and father's — destroyed them all, conflating and diminishing them in all manner of insidious ways.

The loss of her mother's leg and the heft she'd acquired in the progression of her diabetic illness had, much like the public account of Harry Junior's death, explained everything and nothing at all. To Hilda's way of thinking, according to Claire's diary entries, it became the underlying reason, or the continuation of the reason, why her father first turned to her. It was much more complex than that, I am sure, but to a girl who had been, if not every bit as vivacious, as desirable even, as her mother once had been, it was how a sad desperate need to please a father whose heart had hardened from lack of use had gone so wrong. And, in time, Hilda's hope of diminishment became her only hope of salvation. In that incisive, precise way she had of expressing herself from the first day I'd met her, Claire had tried to explain how blowing up and whittling away everything beautiful about herself, and the reflection of what her mother once was, had been the only way Hilda knew how to protect herself.

Claire had been the only one to fight back. It was why she'd gone away and, tragically, why she'd also come back. Claire had returned from Detroit to protect Hilda. This ultimately selfless act had both drawn her to and cost her everything and everyone she had ever tried to love.

I had been sorely wrong about the man with the bolo tie. He had been the escape, not the trap. He had died too soon. A soldier on leave, he had been a hero in the war. And Claire had loved him dearly, his strength, his confidence, his laugh. He had died in an automobile accident not more than a mile from the Harmony Ballroom. The tragedy — the deep sorrow — of her life had been that it was her father who had lived on for another twenty years and, in yet another drunken moment, had taken advantage of his daughter, against her will, when she was weakened with grief. As Harry Junior tried to tell me, when a hive goes bad, look within.

I am certain I must have nodded off a time or two as I read because late-afternoon shadows had already begun to cross the kitchen table when I finally closed the old diary on its last entry, written in Claire's

426

distinctive bold scrawl, just a week before she died.

Thursday, April 30, 1992. That silly old fool. Does he really think we don't know what he's doing? We need the money, but not that much. I told Mrs. Stevenson to buy the candles if she liked them, but not to do us any favors. I don't think she'll be back again. Good riddance, I say.

I sat for a while, I don't know for how long, fingering the rough, brittle spine of the diary. I can only assume the diary had never been scrutinized as carefully by the police investigators when it was first found as it perhaps should have been. Or that even if they had read it carefully, the oblique significance of its many telling details had been missed or misinterpreted by all but the one person in the world who could have understood. But I had refused to read more than a page or two of this diary the first time I'd held it in my hands. I thought I had done enough. I had identified the handwriting on its pages.

The evening shadows had deepened further by the time I rose stiffly to take a clean plate from my cupboard, spoon a few tablespoons of honey onto it, and break apart the heels of a loaf of store-bought bread that had grown stale in a plastic bag sitting atop my old chrome toaster.

I nudged my back door open with my shoulder, which I suspected ached from more than the simple chill of the evening, and I trudged across my porch, down the stairs, and out to my number one hive, the plate of honey and bread in one hand, which shook ever so slightly, and Claire's diary tucked under my other arm.

Most of the field bees had already returned to the hive as I plucked a sticky bit of bread and honey from the plate and set it on the hive's landing board. I reached into the pocket of my old dungarees with my free hand and withdrew my key ring, which I began to jangle softly in front of the hive.

Little brownies, little brownies, your mistress is dead.

I set the plate on top of the hive. I slipped Claire's diary from beneath my arm and set it next to the plate. I jangled the keys again and then set them on the hive.

Little brownies, little brownies, your mistress is dead.

I wiped the honey off my fingers on my trousers, having abandoned my habit of carrying a bandanna in my back pocket some time after Claire and Hilda were buried. I picked up the keys and shook them again.

Then I set them down and picked up the diary.

Little brownies, little brownies, your mistress is dead.

I opened the diary, its leather spine cracking in yet another crooked line. I turned to the first page, cherishing the sweet fragrance of jasmine that wafted gently upward as I began to read softly aloud.

A few errant field bees stood at the entrance to my number one hive. Their wings flapped slowly as if they wished to take to the skies again, to search one last time for something sweet to cherish before nightfall.

ACKNOWLEDGMENTS

Elizabeth George: Friend, mentor, inspiration. I only hope I can give back as much to others as you have given to me.

Deborah Schneider: Your passion has been a beacon.

Marysue Rucci: I spent a year of revisions railing against you and being in such awe of your editor's eye at the same time. You told me over and over that I would only have one shot at my first novel and you wanted it to be the best it could be. Thank you for pushing me so hard. And thank you, Sara, for all you've done since.

Diana Lulek: Thank you for being such a calm, supportive voice when I needed it most.

Nancy Brown: You may have read just about everything I've ever written; thank you, girl.

Suki Fisher: Your novel is next.

Barbara Fryer: You're a wild woman. You

are my inspiration.

April, Tish, Elaine, Chris, Steve, and Reg: You were there just about from the start. Your eyes were key.

Gloria, Grant, Suzan, Sandy, and Jan: You've been in my corner so long, the edges are starting to round.

And finally, to my glorious family: John, Christen, and Sean. Thank you all for your patience and belief in me. Hope you are ready for more rosemary chicken.

ABOUT THE AUTHOR

Peggy Hesketh's writing has appeared in *Calliope* and the *Antietam Review,* and her short story "A Madness of Two" was selected by Elizabeth George for inclusion in her anthology *Two of the Deadliest.* A long-time journalist, Hesketh teaches writing and rhetoric at the University of California, Irvine. *Telling the Bees* is her first novel.

The employees of Thorndike Press hope you have enjoyed this Large Print book. All our Thorndike, Wheeler, and Kennebec Large Print titles are designed for easy reading, and all our books are made to last. Other Thorndike Press Large Print books are available at your library, through selected bookstores, or directly from us.

For information about titles, please call:
(800) 223-1244

or visit our Web site at:
http://gale.cengage.com/thorndike

To share your comments, please write:
Publisher
Thorndike Press
10 Water St., Suite 310
Waterville, ME 04901